Letters in the Fire

Ann McVeigh

Chapter One

The damp stain on the ceiling resembled an outline map of Australia. There was even a smaller additional stain in exactly the same position of Tasmania, but even though she was staring straight at it, the similarity failed to register on Sarah's consciousness. She lay on her back on the unfolded bed-settee with one hand behind her head and the other on her stomach. She finally turned her head towards her prone partner.

'Danny, we're going to have to think about moving out of here and we should really do it soon, while I'm still able for it.'

'Yeah, suppose', Danny mumbled, managing to imbue those few syllables with an underlying 'not this again' theme.

'And Danny, have your documents arrived yet? You know we can't get married without them.'

'Not now love', sighed Danny, turning his back to her.

Sarah returned to staring at the damp stained ceiling. Her other hand moved down on to her stomach. She could feel the swelling and the hardness of the growing embryo. The thought of being a mother both excited and frightened her. She was only nineteen years old and, like most women, looked forward to having children of her own one day. But so soon! Sarah still felt like a child herself although she would never admit that to Danny – nor to anyone else for that matter. In fact, it was the argument she had used when her grandmother had expressed doubts about her moving to London: 'Oh Gran! I'm not a child you know!' Sarah had worked for the same firm of accountants since leaving school four years earlier, and when the firm decided to close their regional office and had offered her the chance to continue to work in the same type of job in London, she had jumped at the chance. She could not believe how quickly her life had changed since that day, almost a year ago now, when she had first stepped off the train and into Danny McAllister's life.

She let her thoughts stray back to the moment of their first meeting. She had just stepped out of Victoria Station and was struggling with the battered old suitcase her grandmother had given her to transport her entire belongings to London. The belongings had not seemed very substantial when spread out on the bed at home in Yorkshire, but after hauling them off the train and down the length of the terminal building, they were gaining weight by the second. She had just set the case down to change hands again when a voice from behind said, 'Here, let me help you with that, love'.

She remembered that initial rush of fear as the warnings about the rogues and vagabonds who preyed on innocent young girls sprang into her mind. She turned quickly to meet the bluest set of blue eyes she had ever seen. Or maybe they just seemed so under the shadow of the long, thick, black eyelashes.

He spoke again: 'Where ye for?' as he swung the suitcase as lightly as a child's toy.

No-one that good looking could be a villain, she thought. And that voice: it was not an accent she was familiar with and it was certainly not a London one.

On such flimsy evidence she decided to trust him with her worldly possessions.

'I'm not going far – just round the next corner actually, I'm moving in to a flat there.'

'Are ye now? Well isn't it lucky for me that I'm going that way too?' It was at that point, when Danny smiled down at her, that Sarah believed she fell in love.

It was not far to the small flat she was renting but in the time it took to reach it they had introduced each other, discovered that hers was a Yorkshire accent and his a Belfast brogue, that each was working in London far from friends and relations and that they both liked coffee. Conveniently enough, there was a new-style espresso bar just two doors from her flat and after Danny had insisted on carrying the suitcase all the way up to the fourth floor, she felt he needed something to revive him. As there was no way of making as much as a cup of tea in her new home until everything was unpacked, unwrapped, washed and sorted, his suggestion that they try out the new coffee bar was eagerly seized upon.

Three cups of espresso later, Sarah bade Danny a reluctant goodnight. She had never known a man who was so easy to talk to, nor one who made her laugh. He had even made her see moving to London as the exciting adventure she had thought it would be when the idea was first mooted. She had anticipated that it would be exciting, different and one big adventure but, as the point of departure had drawn closer, she had begun to feel ever more apprehensive. By the time she had actually arrived in London, she had felt scared, small and inadequate. Victoria Station alone had almost overwhelmed her. Her entire village could, with just a little squeezing, have fitted in to the same area. Danny had lifted her spirits again and she felt ready for anything. Even returning to the tiny little bed-sitting room (as the letting agent had described it) had not dampened her enthusiasm. She knew it was not ideal, situated as it was up four flights of stairs, with a shared cooker and a communal bathroom, but it was near to the station and it was cheap.

The first four hours of her occupation had been spent cleaning every surface, including the gas stove on the landing that she shared with the tenant across the hall. She tried to envisage what her neighbour would be like and hoped they were the sort of person that cleaned up after themselves. Next on her cleaning list was the shared bathroom. The bath was quite old and stained but as clean as it could be, which was a relief to her. It also had a shower, which Sarah was keen to try out, never having had one before. As a child she had bathed in a tin tub hauled in front of the fire on a Saturday night, then, shortly after she had moved in with her grandmother, the Council had installed a new indoor toilet and bath in the house as part of the post-war reconstruction programme, and that was seen as a real luxury. She held the prospect of a shower before her not just as a reward but as a necessity after cleaning her new home. It was hard to imagine that such a small flat would need so much work. By the time she had finished cleaning, unpacking and putting everything away however, and had her first shower, which she enjoyed enormously, she had achieved her aims: firstly, to make the place as clean as possible and secondly, to tire herself out so that sleeping in a strange bed would not present a problem. And sleep she did, and dreamt of Danny.

The next day was Sunday and Sarah had planned to make sure her clothes were ironed and ready to wear for the week ahead. She had hung up the new suit her grandmother had bought her in Halifax as a going away present: 'You'll have no need to look ashamed in front of anybody, Londoners or no'. Sarah thought it a lovely suit, with a tightly fitted moss-green jacket with three-quarter length sleeves and a pencil shirt trimmed with black piping. It made her feel very sophisticated, but she still felt guilty that her granny had had to take out a twenty pound Prudential cheque to pay for it. It would take her the best part of a year to pay it off. Her grandmother, however, had insisted and the bigger part of Sarah was delighted at owning such a posh article of clothing. She planned to wear it with a plain white linen blouse that had, despite the careful folding, become so crumpled as to be un-wearable in its present condition.

She turned on the stove and had just put the iron on the hob when she heard footsteps on the stairs. She had expected it to be her neighbour, whom she had yet to meet, but when she saw Danny climbing the last flight of steps she grinned with delight.

'I was just passing and wondered if you were settling in all right?' he asked. She had assured him she was and that things were just fine.

'In that case, do ye fancy going for a stroll down by the river? I could show you some of the sights of your new home.'

It took Sarah less than half a second to decide between the ironing and a stroll with Danny.

As they walked together down Victoria Street towards Westminster, Sarah felt none of the shyness she normally felt when talking to strangers. Danny had an easy way with him and he did not seem in the least bit pushy, in fact, his manners were those of a perfect gentleman. Although she had only just met him twenty four hours ago, she felt as comfortable with him as with her friends back home.

They walked. They talked. They had several breaks for coffee. It was such a pleasant day she wanted it never to end. But, as the sun started to set, she knew that she had to finish the ironing and getting to her new job in time meant rising at six thirty in the morning. Even though she was normally an early riser, this was a bit earlier than she was used to, and she did want to leave herself plenty of time to get to the office. After all, it would not pay to be late on the first day.

As they drew nearer and nearer to her front door, Sarah kept hoping that Danny would make a date to see her again. Her disappointment when he made no mention of meeting up almost spoiled her day. He had seen her to the door, mumbled something about her being 'safe and sound now', then turned and waved as he bounded down the stairs. She almost cried with frustration. If only women could ask men out! It just did not seem fair to her. She had not slept well that night wondering if she had inadvertently said or done something to upset him. By the time the alarm clock rang she felt washed-out and depressed. Her exciting adventure had turned again into a trial.

Her first day at her new job had been rather daunting. Although she knew the general pattern of the work, there were a few little things they did differently in the London office. The words 'That's not how we do things here, dear' started to grate after the first five times. She had tried to stay cheerful and polite and had chided herself when she found herself thinking 'Bloody Southerners!'. Things were done differently there though. Back home there would have been a bit of banter and teasing of any new start. Here, while they were not exactly stand-offish, they were not falling over themselves to be friendly either. One of the older women had showed her where the tea room was and explained the rules for its use, but she had gone off to meet her own friends and had left Sarah to eat a solitary lunch.

The second day was not much better, nor was the third. There was no-one else of her age employed in the office and she had felt very isolated. People only spoke to her to point out what she had done wrong. Without anyone to talk to at work and no-one to complain to or laugh with at home, she had felt more and more lonely. When the woman in the corner shop had snubbed her when she tried to make conversation, Sarah had gone back to her flat and cried herself to sleep. By the end of the second week, she was seriously considering going home. In fact, she had been sitting down at her small formica dining table, fountain pen in hand, staring at the words 'Dear Granny' on the blue unlined Basildon Bond notepad, and wondering what to put next, when she heard the knock on the door. She had jumped up to open it and, when she saw Danny, the relief of seeing a friendly face was so great that she had thrown her arms around him and kissed him repeatedly.

That was the night she lost her virginity.

Chapter Two

Danny feigned sleep but his mind was racing. He, too, was remembering his first meeting with Sarah. His memory was not quite so rose-tinted. He had finished work a little earlier than usual as it was a Saturday, and was on his way to the Queen's Arms for a well-deserved and much anticipated pint when he had noticed this little slip of a thing struggling with a battered old suitcase half as big as herself. He had hesitated only a moment between the pint and the distressed damsel before taking the suitcase from her and hoping she was not going far. He remembered to this day how her smile had quickly replaced the startled look but to this day, could not decide whether it was the start or the smile that made him feel sorry for her.

They had chatted easily enough as they walked towards her new abode, although she had been rather breathless trying to talk and keep up with him. She was a tiny little thing, only about five foot two or three, compared to his six foot one, and had to take two steps for every one of his. When they had reached her door, she had offered him a drink but it was quickly established that the flat was lacking somewhat in the tea-making essentials. She did not seem the type you would take into a public house so he had suggested a coffee instead at one of those swanky new espresso bars. He had never been in one before but thought Sarah would like it.

He endured three cups of the frothy disgusting brew the staff put in front of them when coffee was ordered. He never drank the stuff so was not sure if that was how coffee was supposed to taste, but Sarah seemed to like it. She was really chatty: in fact, she had done most of the talking, allowing him to give her 'the once-over' as his mates called it. While she told him about losing her parents during an air-raid and how her grandmother, an old-school Baptist, had taken care of her since she was eleven, he studied her flawless fair skin, her tumble of thick black curls and, when she brought the coffee cup to her mouth, the bitten fingernails. He liked that about her: the combination of beauty and vulnerability. However, as he walked her home again, he knew it would not be wise to continue their friendship. Although there was a lot he did like about her, one thing he did not like was her religion. After all, hadn't his mother threatened to disown him if he ever took up with a Protestant?

Danny's mother, Mary Ann McAllister, was a staunch, not to say bigoted, Catholic. Protestants were the root of all evil, according to Mary Ann. They got the best houses, the best jobs, the best wages, and they conspired together to keep the Catholics down. She had fed all her children this diet of prejudice and hatred. Her tales of how her father had had to walk to the shipyard to save the penny tram fare, and had to stand outside the gates waiting to be picked for a day's work, only to be turned away in favour of a Protestant, was almost like a mantra, and served as a dire warning against the untrustworthiness of more than half the population of Ireland. Her children were 'encouraged' to be good Catholics.

She had brought Danny to the chapel when he was seven years old to be trained as an altar boy. This, she thought, would help prepare him for the priesthood. Having a son as a priest was the highest accolade a devoted

Irish Catholic mother could hope for. Unfortunately, Danny showed little inclination for education in general and none at all for Latin, and both he and his schoolmaster were happy to part company once Danny turned fourteen. At that stage his mother, having conferred with the teacher and the priest, reluctantly accepted the inevitable and found him a job with a neighbour's brother. An 'apprenticeship' it was called that mainly involved running to the bookmakers to place bets for the rest of the workforce, running to the shops to buy them their Gallagher's Blues cigarettes or the *Racing Post*, and making the tea over an open fire in a smoke-blackened tin with almost the entire quarter-pound bag of tea leaves tipped in. They liked their tea strong and sweet. At first Danny had found it repulsive, being used to the thin, weak, unsweetened brew his mother served up, but before long, he too, preferred 'a decent cup a tay' as it was called by the workmen. And gradually, almost without noticing, he picked up the rudiments of the job as well. Five years later, he was one of the best journeymen joiners in the trade and never short of work. When the chance of a big contract came up in London, his boss had offered him such a good wage he would have been a fool to refuse it. Although his mother uttered dire warning about perfidious Albion, she also, without any sense of irony, felt totally justified in taking whatever money England had to offer. So off he went to the big smoke, finding lodgings in a house in Kilburn where the landlord did not mind Irish people – 'Long as the rent's paid in time, don't care if they's Mongolians – long as they pays in cash.' The lodgings were not cheap – Danny could have rented an entire house in Belfast for the money he was paying for one shared room – but the rest of the gang lived there as well so he had some company. They were a great bunch for the most part and, as they would say back home, 'the crack was mighty', but come the weekends, the married men all went home to their wives and families, leaving just him and Elvis.

Elvis's real name was Robert Stewart Campbell, not that anyone but his mother called him by it. He had acquired his nickname because of his passion for all things American and for his love of Rock and Roll music as performed by the likes of Elvis Presley. His workmates, with typical building site wit, had christened him Elvis as soon as he started growing his hair in a Presley-like quiff, a quiff that he took every opportunity to comb into submission with a steel-tail comb. Elvis had one of the new transistor radios that he carried everywhere, much to the jeers and teasing of his workmates who, nevertheless, equally enjoyed listening to the music as they worked and were often to be found singing along to 'that modern rubbish'. As his mother lived in Scotland, and was thus too far away to visit every week, Elvis spent most of his weekends in bars where his type of music was played. He and a few of his friends had even set up a band of their own, with a couple of cheap acoustic guitars and a saxophone picked up in a second-hand shop. What Elvis lacked in talent he more than made up for in enthusiasm and would talk to Danny for hours about the finer points of tempo, rhythm and harmony. Danny often went along to hear him and his band play, even though he much preferred jazz and was not keen on smoky bars. Still, anything was preferable to staying in staring at four walls, and he enjoyed having a few jars with 'the lads'.

It was on one of Elvis's rare visits home that Danny, finding himself at a loose end that Sunday, had decided to see if 'thon wee lass', as he thought of Sarah, had settled in to the poky little flat he had escorted her to the day before. He had intended simply to say hello, in the same way he would have dropped in on a new neighbour back home. Admittedly, she was not a neighbour in the sense they would have used in the Belfast streets, where anyone more than a few streets away could be viewed with a jaundiced eye, but he could still remember his first few days in London and how eager he would have been to see a familiar face. At heart, Danny was kind: he genuinely thought calling on Sarah was no more than a friendly thing to do and, as it was such a lovely sunny day, he ended up inviting her for a stroll down to the river.

They had walked for hours, she doing most of the talking, with him teasing her gently now and again and being amused at how serious she took everything he said. She reminded him a little of his youngest sister, Anne-Marie. She was about the same height and build of Sarah, and with the same black hair, so he treated her much as he would have treated Anne-Marie. He had no notion of 'walking out' with her in the traditional Irish sense. She was a cute little thing but, while she was easy to get on with and not too hard on the eye, Danny had reservations. No point in getting involved with a girl who was not Irish Catholic; otherwise he would never be able to bring her home to meet his mother. So while he thought, briefly, that she was his kind of girl, he dismissed the thought and escorted her back to her flat in plenty of time for him to get to the pub just as it opened.

Chapter Three

Two weeks after he had first met Sarah, Danny joined the rest of the lads for a few Friday night drinks in the White Swan or, as his mates referred to it, the Mucky Duck. The bar had seen better days but the owner had tried to revive it by installing a jukebox, setting up a minuscule stage and putting on live music. He reckoned that for every band member playing, several of their friends would turn up to support them and buy large quantities of alcohol, and who knows, one or two of the bands could even prove popular. Elvis's band was one of several playing that night, so Danny joined his friends, who were propping up the bar, ordered his usual pint, and turned to survey the scene.

He was half way through his pint of mild when he noticed the girl in black. She had blonde hair swept up in a high ponytail and was wearing an off-the-shoulder top and very tight-fitting black trousers. Her lips were a vivid red against her pale skin, attenuated even more by the black makeup ringing her eyes. Her appearance was such that Danny's mother would have called her 'fast' and warned her son to stay away from the 'likes of thon'. But with no mother there to sound dire warnings, Danny continued to gaze at her. She eventually noticed him staring, but did not seem annoyed - rather the opposite in fact. She showed signs of being equally as interested in him as she glanced his way several times with a smile on her face. When she leaned over to exchange a few words with her friend, the friend immediately looked round eagerly in Danny's direction, only to be slapped back into pointedly looking the other way. It soon became obvious to his mates what was going on and then the teasing began:

'Ai man, she's giving you the glad eye!'

'More like the glass eye! She must be blind to fancy you, lad!'

'She must be blind the way she's splashed on thon make-up!'

Danny just grinned.

He thought she looked very attractive in an off-beat sort of way. Certainly not what he was used to. But then again, if you excluded his sisters, he had not had that much experience with girls and certainly not girls like her. Back home the only real opportunity to meet girls, not counting after Mass on a Sunday, was at the Plaza on a Saturday night. There, all the girls danced with their friends while the boys lined the wall nearest the bar. Towards the end of the night the MC would announce the last dance and the band would strike up a slow number. It was at that stage that the boys would leap into action and the crossing of the floor began. One lad after another would approach a chosen girl with the immortal words: 'My mate fancies your mate and wants to know if he can walk her home?' There would follow some intense negotiations between the females that could have put the United Nations to shame: 'All right, he can walk her home if your mate with the winkle-pickers walks me home - but no funny business!'

Danny had walked a few girls home, and the final demand was rarely met. Having said that, he was still a virgin as the sort of girls he usually met lost no time in telling him that they were not that kind of girl. In a way, he did not mind; he still had a romantic idea of what real love was and thought it perfectly acceptable that a girl should wait until marriage. After all, what man wanted to marry damaged goods? But he had also learnt quite recently, from Elvis's mates, that there were plenty of girls out there who did not need a wedding ring and who *were* that sort of girl. He continued to appraise the blonde in black, wondering what type she was but making bets with himself that she was the second type.

He was still musing how far she would go when he noticed her making quite a show of getting up from her seat and checking through her handbag. Danny felt a quick dig in his side from Elvis's elbow: 'Get a move on! She's probably leaving. Go on, buy her a drink and ye never know yer luck!' Danny needed little coaxing. He strolled over in what he hoped was a casual manner: 'Do I know you from somewhere?' It was a line that had never failed at home where everyone did indeed know someone who knew someone from somewhere.

'Well if you did, you wouldn't have to ask, would you?'

The retort put Danny off his stride. This was not the expected and normal reply. Back home they would normally tell you who they knew who knew you or the name of your cousin or your auntie – or indeed some member of the extended family. From there the conversation would progress more or less along well-rehearsed, structured lines. Danny could hear his friends sniggering in the background. He cursed himself for leaving the group and approaching the girl because now he was vulnerable. What was worse, he could not think of a smart comeback. He left too long a pause before mumbling something about his cousin Kate and rejoining the lads, his face starting to beam purple.

Although the rest of his friends continued to derive a great deal of amusement from his discomfort, Danny barely heard them. His embarrassment was making him angry and he felt belittled. He was not cosmopolitan enough to recognise that he had not actually been rejected: the girl, Barbara, was simply playing her own game by not making it too easy for him to pick her up. She had been bemused when he blushed, mumbled something and turned away. She grabbed her friend and made for the ladies.

'Do you think he really did think he knew me?' she asked her friend Clare anxiously.

'Don't be daft! But you'd think he could have come up with a better chat-up line than that!'

Clare and Barbara then spent a good ten minutes touching-up their make-up and planning their strategy. By the time they emerged from the ladies, looking fabulous and with a battle-plan at the ready, it was too late. Danny had swallowed the last mouthful of his pint and left. Had he had a full pint to finish, who knows how the night would have ended? As it was, Danny slouched along the road, hands dug deep in his pockets, kicking anything that got in his way. He believed that he had made a fool of himself in front of his friends so had declared that he needed something to eat in order to cover up his hasty departure.

Thankfully, none of the lads had offered to come with him as he knew he would not be able to even pretend to eat a bite - his stomach was in knots. Why do girls do that? he asked himself. He was sure she had fancied him, otherwise he would not have gone over to her. Yet she had come out with some wisecrack that left him looking like a right idiot. He supposed that that's what girls like her were like. He would have been better off taking that nice wee girl from Yorkshire out. She would never have come out with a put down like that. He stopped short, taking stock of his surroundings. Susan, Sarah, Sheila – whatever her name was – lived very close to where he stood. On an impulse, he turned in the direction of her bed-sit.

The feeling that he had been cheated out of a girl's company stayed with Danny and give him the impetus to knock on Sarah's door. The look of joy on her face when she saw him was as nothing compared to the force that nearly knocked him off his feet as she flung herself into his arms. 'Oh Danny! Danny! I thought I'd never see you again! It's so lovely to see you! Come in! Come in!' Danny was relieved that he did not have to think of an excuse for being there, and her obvious pleasure at seeing him started to mollify his bruised ego. He accepted her offer of a coffee and started to relax as she babbled on about her life.

As she chatted, Danny noticed she used every excuse to touch his hand, his shoulder, even his hair. He had no notion that he was the first friendly face Sarah, a normally gregarious, out-going girl, had had an opportunity to talk to for almost a fortnight. She was like a starving creature reaching out for food. Given his experience of life and the night's events, he mistook this need for friendship as a come-on: she, being desperate for company, did not like to refuse his advances in case she was left alone again. After they had made love, Sarah lay contented, believing she had found someone to love her.

Danny had fallen asleep and was dreaming of the blonde-haired girl in black.

Chapter Four

Sarah was worried.

Here she was, six and a half months pregnant and still no sign of a wedding ring. True, she had been almost four months gone before she realised she was pregnant, but surely two and a half months was plenty of time for Danny to send over to Ireland for his birth certificate and baptismal lines and whatever other papers he claimed he needed. She thought getting married simply involved a trip to the nearest Registry Office, where they would pay the fee and book the date. According to Danny, however, as he was not born in England, he had to provide proof that he had not been married before, he was of sound mind and there were no other impediments before he would be able to legally marry. This was taking more time than Sarah would have liked. She was sure people in work were looking at her swollen stomach and even though she was trying to disguise the bump by wearing baggy jumpers, it was only drawing more attention to her. After all, who wore woolly jumpers, baggy or not, the last week of August?

Sarah moved from the filing cabinet to her desk and flicked open her work diary. She counted the days to her due date. When the doctor had announced that she would deliver on or about the fifth of November, she had grimaced to herself and thought it appropriate - because there would be fireworks if her granny found out she was about to become a mother before she was a wife. Her granny had a name for people like that and it was not one to be repeated in polite company. She sighed as she realised that a wedding needed to take place within four weeks or there would be no way to disguise her upcoming motherhood.

Her thoughts were interrupted by her manager, Mr Boyd. 'Miss Trafford, can you come to my office, please?'

Sarah picked up her notepad and pencil and followed him into the wood-panelled room. He sat behind his desk and indicated that she was to sit on the seat in front of it. Sarah sat, poised to take dictation.

'Miss Trafford, and it still is Miss Trafford, isn't it?' he asked, stressing the Miss. Sarah's mouth dropped.

'I'll take that as a yes then, shall I? It has come to our attention that you are, how shall we put it? In a delicate condition?' It was put as a question but one to which no answer was expected or required. 'I am sorry to say that your – condition – places us in a very awkward position. We are a respectable firm and, as such, cannot be seen to in any way condone behaviour which can best be described as breaking the bounds of decency. To allow you to continue to work here in your – condition – would not sit well with our clients. We will, therefore, be asking for your resignation forthwith.'

As the impact and meaning of his words dawned on her, Sarah crumpled. She had hoped to announce that she was getting married, which would have given her an excuse to quit her job without revealing the real reason. Now, she would be leaving in disgrace. Her notebook dropped to the floor as she cradled her face in her hands and cried. Mr Boyd shuffled uneasily in his chair. He was not an unkind man, and he was quite fond of young Sarah in an avuncular way but he was also an elder in his local Methodist church. He could not permit a sinful woman to remain in his employ. And anyway, he consoled himself, it was company policy. Still, coping with a crying young woman was not within his remit and he felt uncomfortable and, unusually, out of his depth. He strode to the door and called for Miss Wilson. When she arrived, they had a short conversation in very hushed tones, before Miss Wilson put her arm round Sarah's shoulder and lead her off to the ladies restroom.

Miss Dorothy Wilson tried to be kind but, if truth were told, she really had no time for girls who got themselves in trouble. In her opinion, they were either silly or wanton or both. She held these convictions with the absolute certainty of one who had never succumbed to temptation, principally because it had never been offered. The term 'dried up old spinster' may have been coined especially for her. Unlike her boss, however, she had handled this sort of situation before when another silly girl in her section had succumbed to the charms of an American sailor several years before. She fetched Sarah a glass of water and lent her a tiny lace handkerchief, patted her on the back a few times and made soothing noises. When Sarah managed to regain some composure, Miss Wilson sat beside her and offered her advice.

'I'll get your things from your desk and tell anyone who asks that you've been taken down with a stomach bug. You stay here until I fetch them. There's a cardboard box in the stationery cupboard. That'll do. I think you'd best get a taxi home, you're in no state to take the tube. And don't worry about your wages. Mr Boyd says he will post everything you're owed out to you, so you won't have to come back into the office ever again.'

She bustled away, leaving Sarah feeling lonely and dejected. If only she could have managed to conceal her, she paused, mentally imitating the accent Mr Boyd had use, 'condition', for a few more weeks. Half an hour later, tear-stained and upset, she left the ladies room, accompanied by Miss Wilson. Although she kept her head down she could feel everyone's eyes following her. She could practically read their minds too. You did not carry a cardboard box with all your private possessions thrown in if you only had a tummy ache. Her face had flamed crimson, the pulse in her forehead had pounded and she wished the ground would swallow her. It was the longest walk of her life. The three mile walk back to her bedsit, by contrast, passed in a flash.

Once home, she sat on the bed, still wondering what to do next. The thought of going home to her grandmother without a wedding ring on her finger terrified her. Facing her grandmother would be bad enough but being the talk of the neighbourhood would be too much to bear. Danny would have to go to Belfast and collect all the documentation he needed. His mother obviously could not be relied upon to find and post the required documents. Danny had asked her just over six weeks ago and still no sign of them. Sarah reasoned to herself that his mother did not appreciate the urgency of the situation, nor did Sarah want her to. If Danny went back home for a few days, he could gather up everything he needed and the wedding could go ahead. Obviously not the wonderful white wedding she had always dreamed of, with a fairytale dress with a long train and a full veil and tiara, her chosen mate standing tall and proud beside her, with all her friends gathered around and her granny dressed up to the nines in her best dress and a fancy hat. Another sigh escaped her. It would probably be just her and Danny with Elvis and his girlfriend, Barbara, as witnesses.

She looked in her purse. There was probably not enough money there for a ticket to Belfast so she rummaged through her underwear drawer until she found her saving book. With Danny helping with the rent, she had been able to save a little, which was just as well, she thought. She glanced at the clock. If she hurried, she could just make the bank in time to make a withdrawal. From there, she went to the station and handed over her savings to, hopefully, buy her future.

Chapter Five

It had been a tough day at the building site. They were two men down and in danger of falling behind in the contract. The foreman, normally a decent bloke, was pushing them hard. The contractor would lose money for every day the job went over the deadline and bonuses for the men would be lost too. They were half an hour late in packing up and Elvis had asked Danny to join him for a pint in the Mucky Duck. He was tempted, but when Elvis advanced the information that Barbara would be joining them later, Danny made his excuses and headed for home.

Danny had never quite got his head around the fact that Elvis had stepped into the breach caused by his early, embarrassed, departure from the pub. Elvis had engaged Barbara in some witty banter and within a week, they were an item. Danny still felt as if razor blades grinded in his stomach whenever he heard the rest of the lads teasing Elvis about his beatnik girlfriend. He could not understand why he felt jealous, if that was what he was feeling: after all, he had Sarah, one of the sweetest little girls you could hope to meet in a month of Sunday walks. Yet, Barbara was the one who occupied his thoughts and dreams.

By the time he got to their bed-sit, Danny was hot, tired, irritable, hungry and thirsty. When he realised there was no dinner cooking on the stove, he paused for a moment, perplexed, before opening the door,.

'Sarah?' he called out tentatively.

He heard a sound from the bed and turned to see what he had originally thought to be the unmade bed un-crumple itself into Sarah's shape.

'Oh Danny!' she cried, falling towards him, 'I'm sorry, I'm sorry! I'm so sorry' she sobbed, burrowing herself into his chest.

Danny was alarmed: 'Sorry about what?' he asked anxiously.

It was some minutes before she could compose herself enough to explain to Danny that her employers had discovered her 'condition' and had terminated her employment. Initially, Danny was relieved it was not anything more serious but that quickly turned to anger at how Sarah had been treated.

'I'll go round there and knock his bloody teeth in, the sanctimonious aul' bastard!' he raged. But Sarah begged him not too. Apart from embarrassing her more, it would do no good.

'No Danny', she decided. 'The only thing to do is for us to get married. No-one will employ me if they know I'm living over the brush with someone and with a baby on the way. At least if we're married, you'll get a tax allowance and maybe a rebate that we can live on until after the baby's born. Then I can get someone to look after it and try for another job under my married name. I can't ask old Mr Boyd for a reference because he would put in something about my "lack of moral fibre" or whatever he called it. Danny darling, we can't put it off any longer.' There was silence for a moment as the full import of the situation started to sink in.

Sarah had several hours advantage on Danny. 'Look! Look!' she commanded, turning to snatch something from the table. 'I've booked you a seat on the Belfast coach. It leaves Victoria at 9.30 tomorrow night and you'll be back in Belfast by lunchtime on Thursday. You can get all your documents on Friday and be back here by Monday. We could be married next weekend!'

Danny's mind was reeling. Married! Oh, they had talked about it once Sarah had discovered, rather belatedly, that she was pregnant and he had agreed that they would have to get married for the baby's sake. But he had not really permitted himself to think about it. Despite Sarah's nagging, he kept putting it off in the unrealistic hope that somehow, if he ignored it, it would all go away. He had not, as he had told Sarah he had, asked his mother to forward the papers he would need: knowing her, she would guess why they were required. Now, though, now that other people knew about it, Sarah's pregnancy became real even though he still had difficulty believing he was actually going to be a father. To a baby! and marriage! Yes, he cared about Sarah, he told himself, and he owed it to her. After all, he was her first, as she was his, and it would be wrong not to make an honest woman of her. But marriage! And a kid! For a moment he rebelled. Sarah was trying to trap him, control his life. He could see his future stretching in front of him and he did not like what he saw. He felt he had to take some kind of control, however flimsy. Instead of dealing with the bigger issue, he chose to focus instead on the details.

'Where'd you get these?' he demanded, plucking the tickets from her hand, not really listening to her explanation.

'Trying to get rid of me, are ya? Well, ye can think again! I'm going nowhere! No! To hell, with it! I am going somewhere – I'm away for a drink!'

With that, he slapped down the tickets and slammed out the door, leaving Sarah falling to her knees, clutching her stomach and crying her heart out.

Chapter Six

Danny bounded down the stairs two at a time. He had no idea where he was going, he just wanted to get as far away as possible and to block out any thoughts of duty or responsibility. Old habits die hard, however, and he soon found himself in front of the Mucky Duck. Making straight for the bar, he ordered a double Irish and a pint of bitter. Getting really drunk seemed like a very good idea. He was still waiting for his drink to arrive when a voice at his side said: 'Thought you weren't going out tonight?'

He turned to face Elvis. He had forgotten that Elvis and Barbara would be in the pub.

'Change of plan' he spat out through clenched teeth. Elvis appeared not to notice Danny's lack of good humour.

'Come and sit with us.', he urged, lifting the pint that had just arrived and heading for the table where Barbara sat waiting. Danny had little choice but to follow him over.

'Are you OK?' asked Barbara looking at him in a quizzical manner as he sat down. 'Fine, fine' he replied, burying his head in his pint, trying to avoid any further questions. Elvis was his closest friend but Danny had not told him that Sarah was pregnant. To do so would have made it real. He toyed with the idea of telling him now but when he glanced at Barbara, something put a stop to his tongue. He told himself that he would rather tell his mate when they were alone because Elvis would understand whereas Barbara would probably get upset and generally act like a female.

It dawned on him that Elvis and Barbara were sitting by themselves as a couple. Usually, they were surrounded by other friends and work colleagues.

'Where's the rest of the lads?' he asked. Elvis gave an exaggerated sigh and nodded towards Barbara. 'They've all gone on to the Red Lion. We're playing a gig there tonight but Clare hasn't showed up yet and Babs didn't want to wait for her in a pub all on her own. Women, eh? But if she doesn't come soon we'll have to go on without her. I can't afford to miss this gig. They're paying us twenty quid! Twenty! How's about that, eh? Fancy coming down to watch? Give us a bit of support like?'

Danny declined and, after a bit of coaxing, Elvis gave up trying to change his mind. 'Tell you what. If you really don't want to go, how's about you stay here with Babs and keep her company 'til Clare shows up? Then I can head on over and make sure everything's set up right.'

A few 'if you don't minds', 'alrights' and 'if you're sures' were exchanged and Elvis finished his pint and headed off. Danny and Barbara sat in awkward silence for a few moments.

'What time did Clare say she was coming?' Danny enquired, wondering how long it would be before he could continue with his get-drunk-quick plans. He felt somehow that it was not right to get drunk while he was babysitting Barbara. She took another sip from the nearly empty half pint glass of lager and lime she was nursing before saying that Clare had been due at seven o'clock. Danny glanced at the pub clock: it was twenty past now. 'Is she normally late?' Barbara looked at him through her kohl-ringed eyes: 'You can go if you want. I can wait outside for her. Give her another ten minutes in case she missed her bus or something.' Danny blushed. He had not meant to give the impression that he wanted to be rid of her, even if it was true. He protested that he was more than happy to keep her company and offered to buy her another drink. Barbara shot him another look that he could not interpret, then shrugged her shoulders and asked for another half of lager and lime.

Danny was not entirely comfortable in Barbara's company: the exchange during their first meeting still rankled with him. So, for Dutch courage, he knocked back a tot of Irish whiskey at the bar before returning to the table with another pint for himself and the drink Barbara had requested. She thanked him, leaning forward to lift her glass. As she did so, her loose-fitting top sagged open and Danny could see the top of her bra. He shifted uneasily in his seat.

'How's Sarah?' she asked. Guiltily, his eyes shot up to her face. She still had that strange look in her eye that he could not decipher.

'She's pregnant'.

Danny was shocked. Had he actually said that out loud? To Barbara of all people? Why had he done that? What was he going to do now? How could he retract it? What would she think of him? A thousand confused thoughts ran through his head before Barbara silenced them all with the words: 'And are you going to keep it?'

Danny stared at her blankly. Keep it? He certainly had not expected that response. He was not sure what he had expected but that hit him for six. It had never occurred to either Danny or Sarah that there was an alternative to having the baby.

'What do you mean, "keep it"? What else can we do?' He immediately felt stupid as soon as the words were out of his mouth. He knew exactly what she meant. He had heard whispers of what happened to certain girls who, having got themselves into trouble, had known how to have it fixed. It had never occurred to him that his situation could be fixed. Respectable people such as himself and Sarah would not do anything like that. But in his head a voice whispered 'There's a way out!'.

'How far gone is she?' Danny stared at Barbara again. 'What do you mean?'

Why was he suddenly acting like a complete idiot? He knew exactly what she meant. He shook his head trying to recollect exactly how far into her pregnancy Sarah was.

'She's almost seven months gone.'

'Oh dear. It's too late then.'

'What do you mean, too late?' Danny felt like a drowning man who had suddenly had a life line yanked away from him.

'Well, anyone I know will only do it up to five and a half months. That's when the child quickens. They say after that it's murder. Why didn't you say something sooner? You must have known. We could have helped you then.'

Danny slumped miserably, rubbing his forehead with his right hand.

'I don't know. I suppose I thought if I didn't do anything it would just go away. It just never occurred to me that we could have – well – you know …'

47

His voice trailed away.

Barbara moved round the table and put her arm around him. He looked so dejected she felt sorry for him.

'Come on, it's not the end of the world. You won't be the first couple to lie to your kids about the year you got married.' She gave another of her looks: 'You are getting married, aren't you?'

Danny sat back with a sigh.

'Sarah wants us to, but …'

'But what?' Barbara prompted.

'Well, if I tell me ma that I'm getting married to an English Protestant she'll flay me live. And if I tell her I have to … I mean, if she knew I'd got a girl into trouble, even a catholic girl, … Well, it doesn't bear thinking about.'

'Come on!' Barbara chided. 'She can't be that bad. She'll probably fly off the handle a bit but in the end, she'll calm down. After all, it will be her grandchild.'

For some reason, Danny did not find that thought comforting.

'And what about your dad?' Barbara continued. 'Won't he be able to talk her round. For some reason men are usually more reasonable in these circumstances, well, with blokes anyway. Different if it's their daughter.'

'Dad died when I was a kid. Mum brought us up on her own. There were six of us, so it wasn't easy for her.'

'Six!' exclaimed Barbara. 'God, you are Irish Catholic aren't you!'

Danny gave her a look: he hadn't expected anti-Irish bigotry from her. She was smiling, however, and he realised she was simply trying to break the sombre mood by teasing him. He grinned ruefully.

'Hmm, yeah. If he hadn't died when he did, there could have been twenty of us, like the family down the street.'

'No! I don't believe you! No-one could have that many kids!'

'Yes, they did! There were four sets of twins and one set of triplets. The rest were ordinary but the Council had to give them two houses to fit them all in.'

'But that means', Barbara counted in her head: 'Sixteen pregnancies! My God! Did she not know what was causing them, or something? She should have talked to my mam after the first four!'

She laughed, but Danny was suddenly sober again. Inadvertently she had reminded him of his situation.

'Does your mam do …' He couldn't put it into words If fact he was not sure if he even knew the right words for the procedure that 'put things right' as he had heard it described.

'Abortions?' Barbara lit a cigarette before she continued, leaving Danny to feel embarrassed and gouache, and also relieved that the bar was almost empty so that no-one could overhear their conversation.

'No, she doesn't do them but she knows a woman that does who's got a really good reputation. She's never had anyone die on her. Well, apart from that one, and she only died because she didn't go home right away.

The girl was afraid her mother would find out she'd had an abortion, so she wandered the streets for hours, finally went to a toilet in the park where she passed out and because no-one knew she was there, she died of the cold. Well, with losing so much blood, and it being January and her without so much as a coat on, I think she basically froze to death.'

Danny listened in horrified fascination. This was not a world he was – or wanted to be – familiar with.

'How do you know all this?' he asked and it suddenly occurred to him that it was, perhaps, by first-hand experience. Barbara seemed to read his thoughts.

'Oh, don't worry. It's never happened to me. Believe it or not, I'm still a virgin. It's just that I'm from the East End. I think we're born knowing things like that.'

Inexplicably, Danny was relieved to know that Barbara was a virgin although he, or rather, his face, did express some surprise.

'I know', sighed Barbara wearily, flicking the ash from her cigarette, 'Elvis likes to suggest in front of his mates that we're at it like rabbits every night.'

'And you don't mind?' asked Danny incredulously.

'It's a bloke thing. Most blokes lie about not being a virgin and most girls lie about being one. I let him tell his mates that we've done it, and he's so grateful, he'll do anything I ask.' She shrugged and flicked her ash again. 'People think because of the way I dress, I must be a slut. Having a boyfriend protects me against the creeps who want to try it on because they think I'm easy. And I like Elvis. He makes me laugh.'

'But don't you .. like … well …'

'Love him?' She stubbed out the cigarette and shook her head. 'He'll do until someone better comes along. In the meantime, we have fun together but it's nothing serious.'

Why, Danny asked himself, am I so happy to hear that?

Chapter Seven

Sarah dragged herself to her feet and moved to the wash basin by the door. In the mirror above the small sink her tear-stained reflection stared back. The mascara she had applied that morning had mostly been rubbed away but there was still a residue around her eyes. She ran the cold water tap and splashed her face. The cool water took the sting away and made her feel slightly better but did nothing for the black circles under her eyes. She decided to take a shower to help clear her head. After feeding a few pennies into the meter to ensure there would be enough warm water, she sat by the unlit gas fire and thought about what to do next. She tried to rationalise the events of the evening.

Sarah was a woman in love, and like any number of women in her situation, she was able to exonerate her man from any blame and accept the fault as her own. After all, she reasoned, she had been very shocked when Mr Boyd had challenged her about her 'condition' but she had had time to get used to the fact, whereas Danny had just had it sprung on him. He was simply confused and angry. He would be fine when he thought about it for a while, just as she had been. He would come back after he'd had a few drinks and they would discuss sensibly what they would do next. He'd be hungry when he comes back she reminded herself and decided to nip to the shops while waiting for the immersion heater to do its job. She bought him a chicken pie that she could heat up when he came home and, as a treat, a couple of cans of beer.

Leaving her purchases on the red formica-topped table, Sarah gathered her soap bag, bath towel and dressing gown. Stepping gingerly into the hallway to make sure no-one was around, she slipped down the hall to the communal bathroom and tapped lightly on the door. She was relieved no-one was using the facilities. After nearly a year of sharing a bathroom with strangers, she still felt very shy about it. She locked and bolted the door and climbed in under the hot running water. As she stood under the steaming stream of water, letting the shampoo suds slip down her swollen body, she continued to reassure herself. Danny just needed some time to himself. It was the shock. He'll be fine and we'll get married and everything will be wonderful. She wondered what to wear for the Registry Office ceremony.

The water started to run cold so she stepped out of the shower, pulled her robe around her, gathered her belongings, and returned to her room. As she made herself a cup of tea, she could hear her neighbour moving around inside his bed-sit. She had been in her flat almost a year and she still had not met him. An occasional glimpse of him on the stair and the sound of the door closing at a quarter past six every morning and seven o'clock every night told her he was there but he never bothered her, and she had never had any reason to bother him. She and Danny had made up an entire fictional life for him and had laughed about it on any number of occasions. She still thought it odd, however, that she had never met someone who lived so close. Back home, she had known everyone in the village and everything about them. Carrying in her cup of tea, however, she was, for the first time, glad that London was so anonymous. She preferred that no-one in the house knew she was pregnant.

Putting the teacup and saucer on the old-fashioned mantle-piece, Sarah decided to make the bed and lie there, rather than turn on the fire. After all, they would have to start watching the pennies from here on. Making herself comfortable, she reached for her tea, turned on the radio, and settled down to wait for Danny.

Danny, meanwhile, was at the bar ordering yet another drink for himself and Barbara. Bringing them back to the table, he remarked that it looked as though Clare would not be turning up at all.

'It's not like her', said Barbara, 'she's normally never late.' 'Well, we can go see Elvis play if you want.' Danny offered.

'I thought you didn't feel like it tonight?' she scoffed.

'Aye, sure that was then: this is now.'

'It's OK. I didn't really want to go anyway. Going anywhere when Elvis is playing is a drag. He and the rest of the lads tend to spend all their time either setting the stuff up, strumming it and going "one, two, one, two" into the microphones, or they're taking it down, loading the van and blaming each other for hitting bum notes. I only ever go if I've got Clare for company. At least we can have a laugh together. Sitting on my own waiting for Elvis to remember I'm there isn't my idea of a good night out. No, actually, I think I'll just head home after these and have an early night.'

'If it's what you want. I'll walk you home when we finish these.'

Barbara and Clare shared a flat in a new purpose-built block. At nine o'clock on a summer's evening it was still light enough to see the modern, angular, brick and glass building, complete with balconies, car parking spaces and allocated garages nearby.

'You live here?' Danny enquired, practically awestruck. 'It's a bit posh, isn't it?'

'Don't be daft! It's just a place to live.' she replied, searching for her keys.

'But how can you afford a place like this in London?' Danny felt that he and Sarah were paying an arm and a leg for one small room with shared facilities. This looked like a mansion in comparison and, he reckoned, it would have a price to match.

'Well, I do share with Clare and that helps with the mortgage.' She paused: 'But mainly I can afford it because my dad put down a hefty deposit for me.'

'Your dad rich, then?' he joked. 'I thought you said you were from the East End. Didn't think there were too many millionaires down that way.'

'Let's just say, he works in insurance. But enough about him.' She beckoned him inside the communal hallway. 'Fancy a coffee?'

He followed her up to the first floor where she unlocked the door into an apartment bigger than any house Danny had lived in during his entire life. Although he worked on the building sites, his work as a joiner was finished long before the homes were, so he had never seen the end product of his labour.

Walking in to the living room, she tossed her handbag onto table and invited him to take a seat. 'Tea, coffee, beer, wine or gin?' she asked.

Danny was flummoxed. 'Beer', he called as she disappeared into the kitchen. He looked around the comparatively spacious living room. Not sure if the modern-looking couch with its spindly legs would actually hold his weight, he sat down very gingerly. It was actually surprisingly comfortable so he leaned back and took in his surroundings. The room was almost twice the size of the bed-sit he shared with Sarah not taking into account the separate kitchen from where Barbara was noisily rattling crockery. Apart from the turquoise couch on which he sat, there was a similar armchair, an odd shaped item he presumed was a coffee table and what looked like a small sideboard on stilts. The walls were painted a soft cream colour and above the fireplace was a painting in various shades of green and blue that looked like it had been painted by a five-year-old. Modern Art, he surmised with a touch of disgust. He preferred his paintings to look like a picture rather than paying good money for something a chimp could do. Still, he admitted to himself grudgingly, it did, somehow, manage to look right in this setting.

He was jolted out of his musings by Barbara calling from the kitchen. 'There's a note here from Clare. Apparently her mother's taken ill. She's had to go home for a few days.'

'No wonder she didn't turn up at the pub.' said Barbara as she returned to the living room and handed him a beer. It was so cold it felt uncomfortable in his hand and he had to set it down on the table. 'How do you manage to keep it so cold at this time of year?' he wondered aloud.

'I just keep it in the fridge', she laughed.

Danny could barely take it all in. Elvis had never mentioned any of this. The posh flat, the expensive furniture, the upmarket artwork – and wine! She had wine in a fridge! This was the most luxurious home Danny had ever set foot in. He suddenly felt uncomfortable.

'I'm not sure if I should be here, really', he muttered halfway to standing up.

'Relax', Barbara ordered, pressing him back down with a soft hand on his shoulder. She moved to the fireplace and with a click flicked on the electric fire that immediately sent a warm glow around the room.

'It's starting to get a bit chilly now, isn't it?' she said conversationally before wandering over to the radiogram that Danny had mistaken for a sideboard. Flipping open the lid, she took a few minutes to choose an LP from the bundle contained within. Kicking off her shoes, she strolled over and joined Danny on the couch, while the mellow strains of Autumn Leaves by Nat King Cole started to fill the air.

'There, that's better now, isn't it? Isn't that song a dream?' Danny looked at her as she sat with her legs tucked up on the couch, with one hand behind her head, a glass of red wine in her other hand. Yes, he agreed mentally: this was a dream. This was as far removed from his life as he could imagine. When he leaned over to kiss her, she did not resist.

Chapter Eight

Sarah was wakened by the sound of her neighbour's door slamming shut, followed closely after by the sound of the alarm clock. She raised her head slowly and looked at the chicken pie and the beer still sitting on the table. The events of the previous night smacked into her consciousness. 'Danny? Danny?' she called, sitting further up and patting the bed. She looked round the room. Part of her brain told her it was useless: you couldn't hid a cat in that room, never mind a full-grown man. She did not want to admit to herself that Danny had not returned home last night. He had never stayed out all night, not since they first started living together four months ago. She pulled on her robe and made for the bathroom, not caring if anyone saw her. It was empty. She returned to her room slowly, not even bothering to close the door behind her, and slumped back down on the bed. She did not cry.

Danny was wakened by the sound of singing. For a moment he was confused. The golden light streaming in through the gauze-covered window seemed to bathe the room while the pillows felt soft and warm under his head. A smile spread across his face. He remembered. He turned on his back and placed his hands behind his head, replaying the scene in his mind. From the long, intimate, sensual kiss on the couch next door, to Barbara leading him, with eyes full of promise, to the bedroom across the hall. She had lifted his shirt over his head, then, gently but insistently, pushed him on to the large double bed. She had disrobed slowly, tantalizingly, allowing him to get acquainted with every curve and line of her slim, pale body. She had not so much surrendered to him as merged into his soul. They had made love passionately, slowly, fiercely, gently, completely, for most of the night, finally falling asleep entwined in each other's arms just as dawn was threatening to break over the horizon. He had never been happier.

Barbara appeared at the bedroom door, dressed in a long silk robe: 'Get up, lazy bones. Scrambled egg and toast OK?' Danny groped around the floor until he found his trousers and pulled them on. Bare-chested he sauntered into the living room, then through to the kitchen, where Barbara was stirring eggs in a saucepan. His years on the building site had given him a physic worth displaying. Wrapping his arms around her, he gently kissed the nape of her neck Her voice was light and teasing as she chided him and ordered him to behave. When he sat at the teak drop-leaf table, she poured out a mug of strong dark tea for him. 'Help yourself to sugar', she urged, indicating a covered glass sugar bowl. They breakfasted together as naturally as if they had had years of practice. Eventually, however, reality had to be confronted.

'What about Elvis?'

'Never mind about him; he's not pregnant. What about Sarah?'

It was only then that Danny started to feel guilty. Everything had seemed so natural between him and Barbara that he had not given a thought the entire night to the circumstances that had brought them together.

He swirled the remains of the tea at the bottom of his mug. 'I don't know. Honestly. I'm really fond of her, … and I know I should do the right thing, but now, after last night, … I never felt that way about Sarah. How can I marry her, knowing you're the part of my life I've been missing all these years? Surely it wouldn't be fair to any of us?'

'That all sounds very poetic', jeered Barbara, 'and is that what you're going to tell your son or daughter when they ask why people call them a bastard?' Danny flinched. Yet in the core of his moral fibre, he knew she was right. 'But what about us?' he protested.

'Danny', she said softly, 'I think I fell in love with you the first time I saw you. If it hadn't been for that cheesy chat-up line we'd probably be married by now. But that's never going to happen. Still, part of me will always love you. And I wanted my first time with a man to be very special and you made it, well, wonderful and unforgettable and everything I hoped it would be. But now we have to get back to our real lives. You know you have to marry Sarah - make an honest woman of her!' she joked. 'And I'll stay with Elvis until someone else – who isn't spoken for – comes along.'

They spent a long time saying their final, private, goodbye. It was almost three in the afternoon before Barbara, standing at her living room window, waved as she watched Danny walk away, and felt her heart crumbling.

By the time Danny arrived back to a bed-sit that seemed to have shrunk in size in comparison to Barbara's spacious apartment, he had resigned himself to his fate. Marriage to Sarah would not be exciting or glamorous or passionate, but it would provide a home and a name for his unborn child. He had only himself to blame. He could have stayed to speak with Barbara that first night, before Elvis moved in: he should never have visited Sarah that night: or gone back time and again for the sex: he should never have got her pregnant. He had to face up to his mistakes and be a man about them. Sarah turned to face him as he stood in the doorway. Her expression reminded him of a whipped puppy and, for some reason, he found that it irritated him.

'OK, OK, I'm sorry', he said, more roughly than he had intended. 'I just got drinking with the lads and, you know, one thing lead to another. I ended up sleeping on the floor at Roddy's flat'. It worried him how easily the lie came tripping from his mouth. He made a mental note to relay the lie to Rod, Elvis and the rest of them. He needed to cover his back. And then he would also have to lie to Elvis about where he had really been. Life was getting complicated.

'I thought you weren't coming back' Sarah said softly, and he could almost feel the effort it cost her to say that through the lump in her throat.

His attitude softened. 'Of course I was coming back. How could I stay away?' he claimed, moving swiftly to take her in his arms. She was such a tiny little thing. She needed him to protect her.

'Where did you put the coach tickets? If we're going to get married, I need to go to Belfast.'

Chapter Nine

Danny stepped off the trolley bus just after the Albert Road intersection and headed left towards Servia Street. It felt strange to be back in Belfast again. He had grown up in these streets, knew every one of them like the back of his hand, yet they seemed smaller, older and at a distance to what he had become accustomed to. He remembered the names of all the streets in the area: Balaclava Street, where his best mate, Micky, lived; Slate Street, where he had gone to school; McDonnell Street, where he and his friends had, when auld Ma McGuigan hadn't come out to shout at them, played football, hurling, and a host of other street games. The houses were all small, consisting of two rooms and a scullery downstairs and two room upstairs, while an outside yard provided space for the coal, the bin, and the privy. He grinned at the memory of those cold winter mornings when waiting his turn to sit on the toilet had left him with chattering teeth and shaking hands that had not warmed up until after breakfast. And Sarah complained about having to share a nice heated, indoor, bathroom!

Thinking of Sarah reminded him of why he was back and his mood became more sombre. He had still to work out how he was going to break the news to his mother. As he turned the corner into Servia Street, he noticed a young woman on her knees at the front door of number twenty six scrubbing the pavement. He had never understood this strange custom among the women of the Lower Falls to compete with each other as to who could have the cleanest and whitest half-moon of pavement outside their front doors. Practically every house had one, and those that did not were considered 'dirty halyens.' He had no idea was a 'halyen' was, but it was, among the women, the lowest term of abuse they could hurl.

The young woman looked up at his approach.

'Danny!' she screamed, dropping the scrubbing brush and nearly overturning the tin bucket. She jumped to her feet and flung herself at him.

'Danny, Danny, when did ye get back?' It took Danny a moment before he realised he had been assaulted by his youngest sister, Anne-Marie.

'My God! Wud ye luk at ye?' said Danny, suddenly reverting back to the broad Belfast accent he had had to try to lose when he lived in London.

'What happened to the pigtails? And is that lipstick you're wearing?'

'Ach, Danny,' she tutted, 'sure I'm nearly sixteen now. I'm not a wee girl anymore.'

She had been fourteen and still at school when Danny had left. A lot had happened in just over a year.

'Is me mam in?' he asked, ruffling Anne-Marie's hair with his hand, knowing it would irritate her. He received his hoped-for response. 'Ach! You!' she cried indignantly. 'I'll tell ma mam on you!'

Grinning, he stepped inside to face his mother.

Mary Ann McAllister was enthroned in her seat beside the hearth. She was forty-five years old but, thanks to several missing teeth and a disinclination to wear make-up, which in her opinion was reserved for trollops, she looked closer to sixty. Her once thick black hair had turned white and she did nothing to disguise the fact, simply pulling it back into a tight white bun at the base of her neck. She had taken to wearing black clothes since her husband had died, and, now that her children were old enough to do everything for her, she was starting to run to fat. These days, she rarely moved from her chair from sunrise to sunset yet, despite her apparent isolation, she knew everything about everything that happened in her square mile of the planet.

She rocked slowly in her seat, fingers intertwined across her stomach as she assessed her second oldest child.

'Don't be telling me they've given ye the sack.' she stated by way of a greeting.

'Don't be daft, ma. Sure I'm the best worker they've got there.'

'Mam, our Danny's back' said Anne-Marie, delightfully, stating the obvious. 'How long ye staying for? Did ye bring us back a present? I'm going to be an auntie!'

Danny started. The birth of his child would, indeed, make Anne Marie an aunt: but how did she know? He had not told anyone else; certainly no-one who would have got the news to his family so quickly.

He stared at his mother, awaiting her reaction.

'Away an put the kettle on: your brother will be needing a cup of tea after his trip. Is that your washing?' she asked, indicating the holdall Danny had dropped to the floor.

'What? Oh no. It's all clean. I'm just over for a couple of days. Bit of a holiday. We're not that busy at work at the moment' he lied.

'I've put the kettle on,' stated Anne-Marie coming in from the small scullery, 'do you want another cup, ma?' she asked, which was a bit of a rhetorical question as Mary Ann was rarely without a cup of tea by her side.

'Aye, ye may make a pot. Yer brother Seamus will be in soon.'

As Anne-Marie disappeared again, his mother continued: 'You know he got married last Christmas? Well, she's due any day now.' she sniffed, as though in disapproval. 'Doing alright for himself is our Seamus. He moved in with her parents, her being an only child, like. And he's working for her da now too, at the slating and roof tiling. Plenty of work going so they're doing all right. And what about yourself? You moved to new digs I hear.'

'How did you know that?' he asked astounded. He was not much of a letter writer. In fact, during his entire time in London he had sent only two very short letters home: one was to let his mother know he had arrived safely, and the other letter was to wrap round some cash he had sent her for Christmas.

'Mrs Molley's son, Jamie, was home for a while about two months back. He was saying you weren't living in Kilburn anymore.'

'No, I've moved to Victoria. It's handier for getting to work.'

His mother gave him one of her 'I can read you like a book' stares but before she was able to say anything, the front door opened again and in walked Seamus.

Seamus was a slightly older, paler and smaller version of Danny. During their formative years there had been a great deal of sibling rivalry but that had evaporated once Seamus starting courting. He had been walking out with Mairead since he was sixteen and it was clear that neither wanted anyone else. They married when Mairead turned twenty-one, just a week after Christmas.

'Hey, kid! What about ye?' cried Seamus, smacking Danny on the arm, all smiles, truly delighted to see his younger brother again. 'How long ya over for? Here, forget about that tea.' he instructed Anne-Marie who had just appeared again carrying a tray. 'We're off to Mullen's for a drink. Come on, now. No argument. This is the best excuse I've had for a drink in months. Don't get married, lad. They'll only chain ye to the kitchen sink. I hadn't been out for a drink in I can't remember how long!'.

Ignoring his mother's warning about not coming home drunk, Danny let himself be swept along with his brother's enthusiasm and headed for the bar at the corner of the street. The barman, who had worked there for over twenty years, greeted them both by name and indulged in some banter while he poured their drinks. As they went to sit down at one of the small tables, he called over, 'Oh by the way, Seamus, you left your cap in here yesterday. Don't be forgetting it today again or I'll give it to the rag man!'

'So you don't get out much then, eh?' teased Danny.

'Ach, you know what it's like. Ye have to play hard done by or everybody would slag ye. No. I've no complaints. Mairead's the best. An' her family's lovely. Her ma and da can't do enough for us. They're even talking about putting the house and business into our name. We'll be set for life. And they're really delighted that the babe's on its way.'

'So married life suits you then?'

'I've no complaints. You should try it yourself', he grinned, slapping Danny on the arm.

'I might have to,' Danny confided woefully.

The smile faded from Seamus's face. 'What'da mean?'

Danny sighed, and signalled to the barman to bring them over a couple of whiskeys. He looked round the small shabby bar. Old Paddy Flynn sat on a stool at the bar nursing a half pint of Guinness. He would be there all afternoon and probably most of the night as he had no-one to go home to. Manny Stevens was studying the Racing Post, though he had never been known to win anything of account, and old Bobby Maguire was sleeping in the corner. It was unlikely that any of them would be interested in the brothers' conversation. Nevertheless, Danny kept his voice low as he confided in Seamus.

'There's this girl, Sarah, well, she's, Oh God! Well, I got her pregnant.'

'Me ma will murder ye.' stated Seamus simply.

'That's not the worst of it' continued Danny.

Answering his brothers inquiring look, he sighed again before admitting, 'She's English and she's a protestant!'

'Oh Fuck!' Seamus put his elbows on the table and his right hand over his mouth. He shook his head slowly several times before repeating, 'She'll murder ye, she'll fucking murder ye'. He took a long swig from the pint in front of him before continuing: 'You know what she was like when I started going out with Mairead. She was dead set against her because she came from Beechmount and not the Lower Falls! "Never marry away from yer own!", she used to say as if Mairead wasn't a Catholic from less than three mile away.'

There was silence as both Danny and Seamus tried to take in the full implication of breaking the news to their mother. To have fathered a child outside wedlock was sinful, but forgivable: to marry an English woman was not.

Mary Ann's intolerance, indeed, hatred, of all things English had a long incubation period and all her children were well aware of the reasons behind it. 'Hadn't they murdered you're poor uncles, Peter and Micky, God grant them rest.' They had grown up with the stories, and in fact, when Mary Ann was reciting the tales again, the boys often re-enacted the gory bits, with exaggerated pantomime gestures, behind her back, though heaven help them had she caught them at that.

According to Mary Anne, her brother, Peter, had joined the British Army, aged just seventeen, in 1914, when Mary Ann was little more than a babe in arms. He had served overseas for eighteen months and was heading home on leave when he lost his rucksack. As it contained his pass and ID card as well as his belongings, he went to the local recruiting station and reported his loss to the sergeant in charge. The sergeant, after berating him for not putting his documents somewhere safe, had advised him to go home and stay there until new documents could be issued, but a month later, Peter was arrested as 'absent without official leave'. He protested his innocence, claiming that he had never gone on the run, that the army knew where he lived and could have sent for him at any time, and that during his time at home he had continued to wear his uniform. 'Now was that the action of a deserter?' Despite the evident truth of this, he had, nevertheless, been summarily tried and condemned, and shot at dawn as a deserter. Mary Ann maintained that this was because he was an Irish Catholic, and no amount of logical argument, such as pointing out the high number of non-Irish, non-Catholics who had been executed in similar fashion, would change her mind.

Her intolerance was fed even further when, during the civil disturbances of the 1920s, another brother, Mickey, was shot dead by the Black and

Tans. The fact that he had a shotgun with which he intended to shoot a policeman was neither here nor there as far as Mary Ann was concerned. Mickey was fighting for Ireland's freedom, while the policeman in question was a lackey of the state and, as such, deserved everything he got. In fact, such were the irrational tales told of the awfulness of the English, that Danny had been rather concerned about going to London initially. He had been quite shocked to discovered how normal English people really were and how little religion featured in their day-to-day lives.

Religion! The thought suddenly occurred to him: 'What if I ask Father Hanson to help?' Danny suggested.

His brother nodded slowly. 'It could work. You know what she's like when he's around – it's "Yes, Father", "No, Father", "Three bags full, Father". He's the only one she'll take any notice of. If we talk to him first, he could help you break the news to her and she might not go off on one if he's there.'

Buoyed at the prospect of having a plan, the brothers downed their drinks and headed out of the pub and over towards Saint Peter's pro-Cathedral to look for the Parish Priest.

Father Hanson was a tall man, standing almost six foot four, with a frame to match. His wiry red hair was starting to recede and he had the thick neck of a man used to hauling heavy weights, as indeed, his upbringing on a Fermanagh farm had required. He had served as an army Chaplin during the war and, although a non-combatant, had seen action in some of the worst of the front-line battle zones. His hearing had been damaged by proximity to too many explosions and now, when he talked, the volume of his speech ranged from barely discernible whispers to full-blown roars. This had a very disconcerting effect when he was preaching from the pulpit but even more so when speaking on a one-to-one basis. Despite this, most of his parishioners held him in high esteem, while more than one grown man would also confess to being scared stiff of him. Among his many duties as Parish Priest, Father Hanson also took it upon himself to uphold the law in his parish. A summary cuff around the ear from him had been enough to curtail any further thought of criminal behaviour in the mind of many young people, and woe betide the child stupid enough to complain to their parents that Father Hanson had given them a kick up the backside. That would be the signal for the father to loosen his belt and dole out another hiding for disgracing the family: 'If Father Hanson hit ye, ye must have been up to something!' ran the one-sided argument.

Danny knocked on the door of the parochial house, while Seamus whipped off his cap. The housekeeper answered after only a short pause. Mrs Morrow was a widowed lady whose sole purpose in life now was to prevent people bothering the priests under her care. She guarded the parochial house like Cerberus guarded the gates of hell. Her unwelcoming stance as she glared at them could have daunted a lesser man. Compared to the imagined wrath of his mother, however, this woman was a pussycat.

'Could we have a word with Father Hanson, please?' Danny asked politely.

Without a valid reason to refuse, the housekeeper paused a few moments before ordering them to stay where they were while see went to see if the Father was available. As she had just cleared away the tea table in order for them to play a hand of cards, she knew none of the four priests of the parish were busy at that moment, but it would not do to let every Tom, Dick and Harry know that.

On being informed that two young men were waiting to see him, Father Hanson sighed and threw in his hand of three kings and two nines. It was further proof, if it were needed, that God existed. Every time he had a winning hand, someone called demanding his services.

'Bring them into the front sitting room' he commanded as he reached for his cigarettes. Young men coming to the door was rarely a good sign. He took up a stance by the fireplace and faced the door. He was quite surprised when Danny and Seamus McAllister walked in. These were two young men of good character, unlikely, he would have thought, to get into trouble.

'Danny, Seamus', he greeted them, indicating for them to sit down. 'Your mother's well, I trust?'

The brothers glanced at each other, not quite knowing what to say.

'What can I do for you?' encouraged the priest.

'It's Danny here' said Seamus, taking on the responsibility of doing the talking on Danny's behalf, as he was the elder brother.

'He's got himself into a bit of bother.' He paused while Father Hanson nodded encouragingly. 'With an English girl.'

'And is this girl a Catholic?' roared the priest.

Danny simply shook his head, while his brother fumbled with the cap he held in his hand, feeling that he had done all the talking he was going to do for his brother.

'So this bit of bother. Is she with child?'

Danny nodded, wishing fervently that the volume of Father Hanson's voice would drop to a whisper.

'Your mother will fucking murder ye! Ye stupid wee bastard!'

Danny squirmed. The whole street must have heard that.

'I know that, Father.' he admitted. 'That's why we're here. We were hoping that you would break the news to her.'

83

Father Hanson paused, scratching his head. He knew Mary Ann McAllister well, often calling in two or three times a week to visit her when he was doing his rounds. Despite the seeming poverty, she never let him leave the house without putting in his hand 'Something for the souls in purgatory, Father'. He remembered her as a young bride, and as a young mother, almost every year without a break, bringing another one of her increasing brood to be baptised, but ever since her husband had died, she seemed to have lost all joy in life. It had been a tragic accident, although he and Father O'Malley, with the graveyard humour that seemed inherent in his vocation, had secretly chuckled at the thought that it was politeness that had killed Joe McAllister. Always a polite man, drunk or sober, Joe had lived by the maxim 'manners maketh the man'. One evening, having had a few drinks in town, Joe had taken the trolley bus home during the rush hour. When a young women tried to board the crowded bus, he had gallantly stepped aside to let her on, not realising he was already at the edge of the platform, and had fallen onto the road. He never recovered from the skull fracture. They reckoned if Joe had not been so polite, he would have pushed his way further up the bus and maybe still been alive today.

And now, here were his grown up sons, looking as miserable as sin, and frightened to face his widow. Not that they could be blamed. Mary Ann McAllister was a fearful woman when roused and this, he knew with certainty, would rouse her.

'Right. There's no point in me lecturing you now. Your ma'll have more than enough to say on the matter. Let's see. It's Thursday and there's a Novena on tonight that I take it your sisters will be going to. I'll call round about seven and we'll tell her then. In the meantime, if I was you, I'd go to the church next door, light a candle, make a full act of contrition, and pray that your mother won't kill ye.'

Chapter Ten

Sarah was feeling more optimistic. Danny had been very loving and reassuring before he left for Belfast. She had helped him pack the few possessions he would need for the weekend into a holdall and walked with him, hand in hand, to the coach station at Victoria. They had talked briefly about the future while they waited for the Belfast bus and, as she bade him goodbye, he had whispered in her ear that it would not be long before she could start calling herself Sarah McAllister. She had smiled and blown him kisses until the bus pulled out, rehearsing the name in her head. Wandering back to the flat, she climbed the stairs slowly, pausing every few steps as the strain took its toll, thinking to herself that, if the stairs were bad now, what would they be like when she was nearing full term? Maybe tomorrow she would start looking for somewhere else to live. The flat seemed strangely empty without Danny, and the emotional turmoil of the past twenty-four hours had exhausted her. She tossed her hat, coat and handbag on to the bed-settee and flopped down on the chair. Before she knew it, she was fast asleep.

She was not sure what the sound was that woke her from her dreamless sleep. Looking around, everything seemed the same in the dim light. She got up from the chair and lit the table lamp. It was still dark outside but dawn looked to be about to rise over the horizon of mis-shaped roofs. Sarah listened intently, but could hear nothing untoward. Looking at the small alarm clock, she noted it was nearly six, and not really worth the trouble of unfolding the bed-settee, making up the bed, and going back to sleep. Lifting the kettle from the shelf, she decided on a nice cup of tea and quietly, in order not to disturb her neighbour, put the kettle on the stove outside the door and, while waiting for it to boil, splashed some cold water on her face. It was time to start making some firm plans. She found the writing pad and a pencil with an unbroken lead and placed them on the table. Carrying in her tea, she sat down and started to compile a list of things to do.

An hour and a half later, Sarah was at the market stall fingering material for the first item on her list: an outfit in which to get married. The beautiful suit her grandmother had bought her no longer fitted and it would be a shame to try to let it out. Making a dress for herself would be the cheapest option and it would be sure to fit. She used to enjoy sewing when she was younger. Her grandmother had taught her how to cut and adapt a pattern as well as all the different types of stitching, from a simple running stitch to ruching, from blanket stitches to backstitches. She had often complemented her on her neat fine sewing, so Sarah was confident it would be possible to make something presentable in the coming week or two if she kept it simple. She settled for five yards of a pale pink cotton, three yards of a flower trim in deep pink, and a spool of cotton. It came to eight shillings in total but Sarah was confident that, when it was finished, it would look better than anything she could have bought for three times that price.

Moving through the bustling market place, populated, it seemed, with people from every corner of the world, she made her way to a second-hand jewellery stall. The fat old woman sitting behind the mountain of glittering tat eyed Sarah inquisitively as she examined a tray of second-hand wedding rings. 'For yourself, is it dearie?' the stall-holder rasped through broken discoloured teeth. Sarah blushed. She felt as though this repulsive-looking old woman could see into her mind. There was no point in telling a story about losing her wedding ring down the sink as it would only be met with a smirk and she did not want complete strangers smirking at her. She took a deep breath: 'Yes.' she replied as firmly as she could muster. 'I need to get married in a hurry and I want something cheap.' She was slightly startled at her own audacity but, as her granny always told her, "It's always better to speak the truth and shame the devil". The old crone shuffled inside the multiple layers of dark indistinguishable clothing she wore. 'Aye, and you're not the first by a long chalk. You know', she continued conversationally, 'I'd be out of business if it wasn't for the number of careless gals that lose their wedding rings down the sink.' Sarah blushed again but the stallholder, with a crooked smile and a wink, fetched something from below the counter and handed it to Sarah. It was a plain gold band that looked like new. 'Try this. That should fit you nicely or my name's not Pudden Peg.'

'Pudden Peg?' queried Sarah. 'That's an unusual name.'

A wheezy laugh escaped the stall-holder.

'They calls me that 'cos I've been in the pudden club more times than I've had hot dinners!'

'Pudden club?' queried Sarah.

'Up the duff. Bun in the oven. Family way. With child. Call it what you will, it all adds up to the same thing - another mouth to feed. An' I've 'ad more than most'

'How many children have you?'

'Eight still living, three as died as young uns, and five as never came full term.'

Sarah was astounded: having a brood of sixteen children seemed incredible to her. It was also hard to imagine this dumpy, withered old crone had once been an attractive, sexually active girl, in very much the same situation as Sarah now found herself in.

'This is my first' she offered shyly, sensing some sort of intangible bond between them, however unlikely that had seemed at first sight.

'Ah well, the first is always the hardest. But it will get easier, dearie, trust me. Afore you know it, it'll be like shelling peas'

Sarah smiled and hoped she would never find out the truth of that statement.

Trying on the proffered ring, she was struck by the symbolism of it. She and Danny were to be one. When Danny would put it on her finger at the ceremony, she would be a married woman. Sarah McAllister. Mrs Daniel McAllister.

'Have you been married a long time?' she inquired of the prodigious mother in front of her.

Pudden Peg let out another wheezy laugh. 'Bless ye, child. I ain't never been married at all! Why settle for one fish when ye can have a whole river full, eh?'

Although she was quite shocked, the old woman's evident enjoyment of life made it difficult for Sarah to refrain from smiling. Here she was, worried about being pregnant before she was married, while the stall holder showed no embarrassment at all over an outsized brood of illegitimate children. Looking at her with new respect, Sarah pondered on how hard it must have been for her to go through life without the support of a husband. And to lose so many children: that must have been heartbreaking.

Taking the ring off with just the right degree of difficulty, Sarah enquired about the price.

'Five bobs what I usually charge, dearie, but seeing as how you ain't one of those careless types that lose things and you need to get married quick, I'll knock a bit off. Give me three and six and we'll call the rest my wedding present to you.' Sarah could have kissed the old woman as she handed over the coins and popped the ring into her purse. Thanks to Pudden Peg's good nature, it was much less than she had expected to pay, which meant that she could now afford the hat she had seen in the window of the C&A department store. As she moved away from the stall, Peg called after her: 'Gord bless you dearie, and good luck'. She did not hear the muttered 'You'll need it!' that the stallholder added.

Buoyed up by her purchases and feeling in holiday mood, Sarah decided to treat herself to a cup of coffee in a small café close to the market. It would pass the time until the estate agent's office opened. A bigger flat was now a necessity, she thought, and she may as well make a start on that even though she would have to wait for Danny to sign the lease should she find anything suitable. The waitress arrived while she was studying the menu and wondering if she could afford to treat herself to a cake as well. Deciding against it, she looked up, smiled at the waitress and ordered a white coffee. The waitress looked at her, sniffed audibly, and turned away without a word. They obviously don't like small orders here, thought Sarah but then noticed that the waitress was talking to and laughing with a colleague and looking in her direction. Sarah started to feel uncomfortable. Were they having fun at her expense? She checked that the buttons on her blouse were fastened and took out her compact to check she had not smudged her face. Everything seemed fine. The buttons strained a little over her stomach as was to be expected at this stage in the pregnancy which was decidedly noticeable now. As she was not working she had decided there was no point trying to hide her condition with oversized jumpers and she was dressed in one of the few outfits suitable for a summer's day that still fitted her. The waitress returned with the coffee which she put down heavily, managing to spill a good deal of it on to the saucer. 'There you are, Miss. That will be thrupence, Miss. Will that be all, Miss?'

Sarah blushed deeply again. The repeated and escalating emphasis on the 'Miss' told Sarah all she needed to know. Delving into her purse, she drew out the three coppers, then, in a burst of heaven-sent inspiration, asked the waitress: 'Do you know of any good jewellers around here? My wedding ring doesn't fit me anymore, now I'm pregnant, and I need to get it widened.' She left her purse open so that the girl could see the wedding ring laying among the small change. The waitress's attitude changed immediately. 'Oh yes, mam. You could try Gordon's on the corner, mam – just turn left as you go out and it's only a few doors down.' Sarah thanked her in what she hoped was a haughty manner and turned her attention to her coffee. It took some determination to sit there, knowing she was the focus of gossip, while pretending not to care and leisurely sip her coffee. The incident, however, taught her a lesson. Being pregnant without a wedding ring on her finger meant she was open to criticism and hostility by all and sundry. From now on, whether it was legal or not, she would wear the wedding ring she had just purchased.

Chapter Eleven

Father Hanson stooped slightly as he crossed the threshold of the McAllister's home. 'God bless all here!' he boomed. Mary Ann graciously acknowledged his presence and sent Anne Marie off to make yet more tea. Danny and Seamus stood by the door in an exaggerated display of casualness. When the tea was served, Mary Ann, widely accepted in the neighbourhood as nobody's fool, ordered her daughter off to church. 'Well, Father, enough chit-chat. What's the real reason you've called this evening?'

The priest took a deep breath, shooting a quick look towards the two brothers, before explaining: 'There's been a bit of a problem, Mary Ann, but it's nothing too serious and nothing to get too upset about. Heaven knows, it happens often enough and in the best families, too.'

'Danny!' his mother's voice rang out sharply. 'What have ye got yourself into?'

Danny looked appealingly to the priest, who did not let him down.

'Calm yourself, Mary Ann. He is a young man now, and working away from home. Sure he hasn't got the guidance he would have if he was here and you know what young men are like. Easily lead. And sure, he's going to do right by her.'

Mary Ann moved more quickly than any of them had ever thought her capable. Almost before he could raise his hand to protect himself, his mother was beating him about the head and shoulders.

'You stupid idiot! What have I told ye? Bringing shame and disgrace on the family! And who is this dirty halyen you've taken up with, eh? Some no-good trollop, I'll be bound'.

Seamus and the priest moved in to protect him from the onslaught. It took both of them some time before they could manage to stop Danny's mother lashing out at him. Father Hanson indicated with a nod of his head that the victim should leave the room while he and Seamus propelled Mary Ann back to her chair.

When she was capable of listening, Father Hanson tried again. In his best conciliatory voice, he told her how Danny had taken up with a young English girl and now the girl was expecting his child and it was only right that they marry and give the child a name. 'After all, Mary Ann, it'll be your grandchild too, you know.'

Mary Ann almost spat. 'I'll have no English bastard as a grandchild of mine!'

Father Hanson knew when he first talked with the boys that this task would be difficult but even he was surprised by the viciousness of her stance. An hour later, when he left the house, he left behind no improvement in her attitude.

Walking into Mullen's bar, he found Danny seated at the counter, nursing a pint of Guinness.

'I'm sorry, lad, but she's taken it hard. If I was you, I'd leave it for a while. Give her a chance to calm down.'

Taking a swig from the complimentary pint of stout the barman had set up for him, Father Hanson continued: 'Do you have anywhere you could stay tonight?'

'I'll ask our Seamus to put me up. You're right. I don't think I can go back there tonight. But thanks for all your help, Father. It was good of you to do my dirty work for me.'

'Ah, well', the priest said, sighing. 'If I hadn't been there I dread to think what would have happened. I could be presiding over your funeral instead of your wedding.' He shot Danny a sideways look: 'You are getting married in a Catholic Church, aren't you?'

The next day, having spent the night on the sofa in his brother's home, Danny prepared to face his mother again. Seamus had to work that morning and so was unable to go with him to lend support. They both hoped that, with a night to think it over, their mother would have calmed down and that a reasonable conversation could take place. 'She's not all bad you, know, and you were always her favourite. Sure, you'll be able to talk her round in no time.' Seamus tried to reassure his brother and hoped he sounded more confident than he felt: Mary Ann was not one to let a grudge go lightly.

It was nine thirty when Danny walked into his mother's house and, as usual, his mother was sitting in her chair by the fire.

'So you're back then?' she asked rhetorically. 'You'd better tell me all about this woman then.'

Relieved that she was at least willing to listen, Danny explained how he had met Sarah at the train station when she had first arrived and, skimming over certain events, told how they had started walking out together. He tried to explain to his mother how sweet and nice Sarah was and how good a cook and how much his mother would like her when she got to know her and ...

His voice faltered under Mary Ann's silent, icy stare.

'So, this woman ...'

'Sarah' Danny prompted

'This woman, how old did you say she was?

'Nineteen'.

'And she has no family of her own?'

'Just her grandmother in Yorkshire.'

'So', sniffed Mary Ann, 'she'll be expecting us to raise her bastard will she?'

Danny bristled. 'No, she won't. For one thing, I can take care of my own and for another, it'll not be a bastard if we get married!'

Mary Ann seized on the slip: '*If* you get married. So it's not definite then?'

Danny blushed. 'I meant *when* we get married.'

The pause after his statement grew longer and colder with every passing second. Eventually, after what seemed like half a lifetime, his mother spoke again.

'So what you've told me is, that this Sarah is a lovely wee girl, that I'd like her, so I would, that she's hard working, and a good cook, that she's nineteen, she's from Yorkshire, that she's carrying your child and that you intend marrying her.'

Danny nodded his agreement. It was a pretty fair summation of what he had told his mother.

'There's one thing you haven't told me.'

Danny looked puzzled: 'What else is there to say?'

'You never said you loved her.'

Looking at his evident discomfort, Mary Ann leaned forward in her chair as she continued: 'When your brother Seamus started going out with Mairead seriously and started talking about marriage, I told him I didn't like her. You know what he said? He said that it didn't matter if I liked her or not, he loved her and if it came to a choice, he would cut me out of his life forever, rather than give her up. And I've never told him this but that's just what I wanted to hear. Married life is hard. God knows, it can be tough as hell at times, and if you haven't got love to fall back on, then you have no hope. Seamus and Mairead will make it through hard times and good because they've got each other to lean on. Just like me and your Dad. Oh, I know people say that love goes out the window when poverty comes in the door, but when you're poor to start off with, it's the only thing you have to cling to when times are tough. Love is your life raft in a sea of troubles. Me and your Dad would still be happy now, if he was alive, God rest his soul, and Seamus and Mairead will be happy until they die of old age. But you and Sarah, you have no hope.'

She leaned back again. Another few moments passed in silence save the loud ticking of the mantle clock.

'All right.' she said in the manner of one who had finally made up her mind. 'We'll raise the child. Your sisters will help. It'll be good practise for them.' she added grimly.

Before Danny could even make an attempt at a protest, she held up a hand to silence him.

'It'll be best all round. I'm not letting any child of mine be trapped into a loveless marriage no matter what people think. You'll be able to get on with your life without your mistakes dragging you down and that girl Sarah, God help her, will be able to get on with her life and maybe find a man that loves her for herself and not just because she's a good cook!'

'I can't just leave her in the lurch!' Danny protested. 'I promised her I'd marry her and take care of her. I have to keep my word.'

'Very commendable' sneered Mary Ann, 'but it's like this. You marry that girl and you can say goodbye to your kneecaps. And don't think for one moment I wouldn't give the word.'

Danny stared at this mother, horrified. He realised it was no idle threat. She had the means at her disposal. There were several men in the neighbourhood who could arrange a nasty accident if requested to do so by the right people. Danny was convinced that his mother would rather see him crippled for life than married to Sarah. The thought of it scared him.

What scared him even more, however, was the sense of relief he felt now he had an excuse not to marry Sarah.

Chapter Twelve

That Sunday morning, as Danny prepared to go to mass with his mother and his sisters, Sarah rose sluggishly from a troubled sleep. The top floor bed-sit trapped the heat of the day and it had been stifling hot during the night. Added to that, the baby had been very active, kicking and moving around so that now it seemed as if it was leaning an elbow against her backbone. She rose awkwardly and reached for her robe. Her head started to throb so she decided to make a cup of tea before getting washed or dressed, and hoped that she would not bump into her neighbour. As she sipped the tea, she made her plans for the day. Danny was due back about seven that evening and she wanted everything, including herself, to look nice for him. Deciding on a quick shower before starting on the housework and the shopping, in an effort to wash away the heavy sluggish feeling, she lifted her wash-bag and bathrobe and headed for the bathroom. She did not mind if the water was cool, it would freshen her up and, anyway, it was another penny saved towards their future.

After a refreshing shower in tepid water, she made her way back to her room. It was then she noticed a strange smell. Probably the milk gone off in this hot weather, she thought. Getting dressed in an old shirt of Danny's, one of the few things that fitted her comfortably, and a pair of stretchy slacks, she tied her hair up with an old scarf, and reached for the Ajax. She was halfway through cleaning the food cupboard, tossing out anything she felt may have spoiled in the heat, when there was a knock on the door. They did not often get visitors, so Sarah opened the door rather apprehensively. On the other side stood a young boy of about thirteen, dressed in a badly fitting uniform. It took Sarah a second or two before she recognised it as a telegram delivery. She stared at the buff-coloured envelope, making no attempt to reach for it. A telegram never portended good.

'You have to take it, Missus.' explained the young man, obviously used to this reaction. 'It might not be bad news.'

Wordlessly, she accepted it from his out-stretched hand. Aware that a tip would not be forthcoming, the delivery boy made for the stairs, taking them three at a time. Sarah closed the door and moved to the chair, letting herself sink into it slowly, the envelope still in her hand. Her slow motion movements were in direct contrast to the seething, teeming mass of images going through her mind. Anything could have happened to Danny or to her grandmother. Taking a deep breath, and telling herself that her fears were probably more frightening than the truth, she finally tore open the envelope and unfolded the single sheet of paper. The words danced before her eyes:

NOT ABLE TO RETURN AS ARRANGED DANNY

What did that mean? she asked herself. Could he not get his documents? Had he lost his ticket? Was there something wrong? Was he ill? Maybe he was getting another coach tomorrow or the day after. Maybe he was getting a lift back with someone else and had decided not to take the coach. When would he be back? He was coming back ... wasn't he? She turned the telegram over and over in her hands, desperately searching for some clue that would help her make sense of the curt, ambiguous message. She counted the words. While she had never had occasion to send a telegram herself, she knew that you could send up to ten words for the basic rate. Danny had sent seven. That meant that there would have been room for those three little words. The three little words that would have reassured her so much, but whose absence send shivers down her spine.

The throbbing in her head returned and, again, her mind swam with swarms of unanswered questions. She had no idea when, or indeed, if, Danny was going to return. Putting aside her feelings, she forced herself to be practical, if only for the baby's sake. She took an inventory of her situation. She had very little money left. Buying tickets to Belfast, the material for her wedding dress, the hat and the wedding ring, had left very little in her savings account. The hat she could return to the store, but that was only a few shillings. She had no source of income. The rent would be due on Friday and there was no-one she could turn to for help. She had not made chums with any of the people at work, nor did she know the other tenants of the house. The people they socialised with were Danny's friends and workmates and, even though she quite liked

Barbara and Elvis, she did not consider them close enough friends to go to in times of trouble. Sarah's practical streak started to assert itself. Normally malleable and accommodating when Danny was around to take care of everything, Sarah still possessed a grounding of common sense instilled in to her by her grandmother and a Yorkshire upbringing. Rent had to be paid and food put on the table no matter what the crisis. Tomorrow she would go to the dole office. It went against the grain, against everything her grandmother had taught her about standing on her own two feet, but there was nothing else for it. If Danny did not return (soon, she added as an afterthought), she still had to pay the bills.

In the meantime, the flat needed a good turn out. She could clean the place while composing in her head a letter to Danny. She wanted to frame the question of his return carefully, asking him about coming back without sounding like a scolding wife. Maybe if she joked about him being on holiday or suggested that he tell her when to kill the fatted calf. She dismissed that notion. She was not sure if Catholics knew about the parables and, anyway, the fatted calf was for a returning son, not a returning boyfriend. A sudden thought struck her: did she have the address of Danny's mother's house in Belfast? Drying her hands on an old towel, she moved to the top drawer of the dresser. That was where the rent book and all the other important papers were kept. She started rifling through it. Danny was not a great letter writer, nor it seemed, was his family. She remembered Danny showing her a Christmas card he had received from his mother but could not remember if he had kept it or thrown it out. She cursed herself for being so stupid as to let Danny walk out of her life without so much as a forwarding address. Obviously, she knew his family lived in Belfast, and she had often heard him refer to the Falls, but she had the impression that the Falls was an area bigger than the entire village where she grew up, with numerous warren-like streets. She could not remember the name of the street where his mother lived, never mind the house number. How could she let Danny know when his child was born if she did not know where to reach him.

It dawned on her that, with that thought, she had already accepted that Danny would not be coming back. Leaning on the dresser, she asked herself why she was so convinced of this. Again, images poured into her head: Danny's reluctance to talk about the baby, how he changed the subject every time she mentioned getting married, how he did not seem interested in finding somewhere else to live, how he seemed to prefer going out with his mates to going out with her. She forced herself to think of the intimate times. Whenever she snuggled up to him and whispered 'I love you', he had replied with a 'hmm' or a 'me too'. Even when she had asked him outright, 'You do love me, don't you?', he had answered 'Of course'. She had fooled herself into thinking that it was enough and that it was 'just his way'. Now she realised, with blinding certainty, it was because he had never really loved her but was not prepared to lie openly about it. This was why, she realised, the telegram had not contained those three little words: 'I love you'.

Chapter Thirteen

Monday was one of the worst days of Sarah's life. The stifling heat remained unabated, making sleep all but impossible. This gave her more time to think of a future without Danny. She rose early from a fitful sleep and arrived at the dole office just as it was opening. She was, nevertheless, far from being first in the queue. By the time she emerged from the dole office, Sarah was close to exhaustion. She had been forced to stand for hours while waiting her turn to be seen, then there were the forms to fill out, the embarrassing, personal questions to be answered, more waiting to talk to sharp-tongued, disinterested clerical officers before, finally, they had agreed to grant her dole money. She would have to go back on Friday to sign for it, but at least there would be something in time to pay the rent.

From the dole office she had gone to the building site that Danny had last worked on, hoping to find some of his workmates there. She hovered awkwardly at the edge of the site, unsure who to approach when, luckily, Elvis, who had been working on the scaffolding at the front of the building, noticed her standing on the pavement looking lost. Shinning down the framework with practiced ease, he led her to a sheltered corner. Looking at her drawn face, he became concerned.

'What's up, ducks? You and Danny had a row? Is that why he didn't turn up for work today? The foreman's going mad, you know. Says he'll sack Danny if he's not here tomorrow.'

Sarah shook her head.

'I'm not sure when Danny will be back. I'm not sure that he's even going to come back at all. He's gone home to Belfast and .. and... and I don't even know his address.' The last few words were spoken through a flood of tears. Elvis put his arms around her and let her cry herself out.

When the sobbing had subsided somewhat, he led her to a small park just across the street and sat her on a bench. 'Now,' he commanded, 'tell me what's happened.' Sarah managed, in a disjointed and semi-incoherent way, to appraise Elvis of the situation. Finally grasping that Danny had left a pregnant and practically penniless Sarah in the lurch with no forwarding address, Elvis muttered 'The bastard!' to himself before taking control. 'Ok Sarah. You stay here. I'll be back in just a minute. Sean McAuley's on site today and he's from the Falls. He'll know where Danny's folks live.' With a final injunction to 'Stay there!', Elvis headed back to the building site. Sarah was, by this stage, too exhausted both physically and emotionally to do anything else. She closed her eyes and let the warmth of the sun dry her tear-stained face. It was nice in the park. The traffic sounded a hum that melted into the cooing of some pigeons and, from a distance, the sound of children playing added to the background symphony in a way that she found restful. She let her mind go blank. Before long, however, she was brought back to reality when Elvis reappeared with a scrap of paper.

'Sean says he's not sure about the number, but that it's definitely Servia Street. Just ask anybody in the street and they'll know where the McAllister's live. And if you're sending a letter, not to worry 'cos the postman knows everybody and will make sure it gets to the right place.'

He handed her the piece of paper which Sarah stared at wordlessly. It was her only link with Danny.

'Are you going to be all right?' The sound of Elvis's voice reminded her of her manners. 'Thank you, Elvis, thank you! It was really good of you to get this for me.'

Elvis blushed. 'I'm just sorry I had to. I never thought Danny would be the sort of bloke who would do a runner. I've a good mind to give him a thump next time I see him. Listen', he added, 'if you need anything – anything at all – you've just got to ask. Here!' He took the scrap of paper off her again and, on the back, scribbled his own address. 'If you need me, I'll be there. Anytime.'

Sarah's grateful smile added fuel to Elvis's anger. How could anyone, he fumed internally, least of all his mate Danny, leave a lovely girl like Sarah stranded. She certainly did not deserve to be treated in that way and it made his blood boil just to think about it.

'Will you be all right going home now? Do you want me to come with you?' he asked, solicitously. Sarah reassured him she would be fine: 'And anyway, I think your boss is looking for you.' She nodded her head towards the building site, where a large man in dungarees was standing on the scaffolding looking in every direction. 'I don't want to get you into any trouble. Honestly, I'm fine. I'll be in touch soon.'

With a final, 'Let me know how you get on', Elvis bounded back to work. Getting sacked would not help.

Carefully folding the scrap of paper into her purse, Sarah headed for home. It was a distance of over four miles and a very long walk in the early afternoon sun, but she felt that she had to be practical. The dole would make sure she could keep a roof over her head, but she would have to watch every penny. At least she did not have to hurry home: there was no-one to rush home for, no dinner to prepare and, she realised, nothing to look forward too. Her steps were slow and heavy, weighed down even further by thoughts of Danny's desertion. By the time she reached the bed-sit, it was almost four in the afternoon. She dragged herself up the stairs, pulling on the banisters for support. Distracted as she was, Sarah was struck by an odd smell before she reached the halfway landing. The further she climbed, the worse it became. Letting herself into her room, she started searching for anything that could cause such a stench. She found nothing. Hoping a rodent had not died under the floorboards, she stepped outside to put the kettle on. That was when she noticed that the smell was even worse outside. In fact, it seemed to be coming from her neighbours room. She knocked, tentatively, not really expecting an answer: after all, he never came home until after six. Carrying in the boiling kettle, she made herself some black coffee before opening the window as wide as possible, then sitting down at the table to write to Danny.

Two hours and nine crumpled pages later, she was finally satisfied with the tone of the letter. She addressed the envelope, hoping that Servia Street, Falls Road, Belfast, would find him, and affixed the stamp. Deciding to post it immediately, she lifted her handbag and made for the door. The stench that hit her on opening it almost made her retch. She started to bang on her neighbour's door. He must be home by now and something had to be done about that smell. It was unbearable in this heat. Although there was no answer, she continued to knock. The banging eventually attracted the attention of the couple in the flat below.

'Hello, there. Is there a problem?'

A timid-looking man was peering up the stairs between the banisters. Behind him, a plump, blonde-haired girl appeared to be egging him on.

'It's the smell' explained Sarah, 'it's coming from his room and I can't get an answer.'

'Are you sure it's coming from there? We thought it was the sewers. They can get pretty bad in this heat and we haven't had rain for a while.'

Sarah went closer to the man, who would have backed away had his wife not been so close behind him.

'I'm sure it's not the sewers because it's not so bad when I have the window open and if it was coming from outside then it would be worse.' Sarah explained.

'Well you're not going to get any answer from him by the looks of it.' offered the blonde woman. 'Why don't you call the landlord?'

'Good idea', agreed her husband. 'I've got his telephone number if you want to call him.'

Sarah felt a little uneasy about this, but after some discussion, finally agreed it was the only thing to do, although she felt slightly resentful that the couple expected her to do the calling rather than phoning themselves. She had walked home to save the bus fare and now she was going to have to spend the money she had saved on a phone call. As they pointed out, however, indicating the envelope in her hand, she was on her way to post a letter anyway and the telephone box was right beside the post-box, so it made sense for her to call and besides, she was the one doing the complaining.

It was another two hours before the landlord, whose tea she had interrupted, eventually arrived with his bunch of keys. Normally an amicable man, David Bleasdale was a bit annoyed at having to make the trip over to the flats when he had planned to play bowls that evening. However, the young lady on the telephone had sounded very distressed and so insistent that the problem was serious, that he had decided to forego his game that evening. He noticed the smell immediately as he entered the front door. It became stronger the more stairs he climbed and he began to get seriously alarmed. Sarah and the couple from downstairs opened their doors as soon as they heard his footsteps and both sets of tenants started describing the already obvious problem. He silenced the babble of voices by asking Sarah when she had first noticed the smell.

'I think it was yesterday morning – but I thought at first the milk had gone off.'

'We thought it was the sewers!' piped up the timid couple.

Mr Bleasdale unlocked the door and immediately a wave of obnoxious smelling air hit them. Sarah had to run to her room where she threw up in the sink.

As she rinsed her mouth she could hear him asking where the nearest police station was. It was obvious that her neighbours did not know so Sarah forced herself to speak to him.

'What's the problem?'

'He's dead.' said the landlord, not mincing his words. 'Looks like he's been dead for a while. I'll have to get the police to look into this. Don't let anyone near this room until I come back, hear me?'

Sarah was stunned. As the landlord disappeared from view, she let her gaze fall on the couple downstairs who immediately turned and scuttled back into their room, closing the door firmly behind them. She never saw them again.

Chapter Fourteen

The familiar smell of frying bacon was the first thing Danny noticed when he woke on the Monday morning. The next was how shabby the wallpaper was. Not surprising, it had been on the wall as long as he could remember and, as he had been born in this house, that was well over twenty years ago. The room was never a large one and sharing with two of his brothers had not made if feel more spacious but even so, it seemed to have shrunk in the intervening years since he had last slept there. Realising he was alone, he got up, pulled on his trousers and wandered downstairs. He was greeted by his mother:

'Still keeping those fancy London hours, are ye? You know it's nearly nine o'clock and everybody's at work except you. And don't think you can lie about here all day either. I've had a word with Packy Boyle and he says he'll give you a start with his lads in the morning. Here, sit yourself down.'

She indicated a folding table that had been set up by the window upon which was a brown crockery teapot, a mug, a plate and a knife and fork. She disappeared into the kitchen to return momentarily with a large frying pan from which she started to dispense sausages, eggs, bacon, potato bread and black pudding.

'There! Nothing like a good Ulster fry to get you started. Bet you didn't have anything like that in England.'

Danny tucked in gratefully. He had not realised how hungry he was and his mother's cooking was a rarity to be treasured. He did not like to dampen her palpable pride by explaining that the Full English, as it was called in London, could be purchased from any pub or café, where they simply substituted toast for potato bread.

Once he had mopped up the last of the eggs with the last of the bread, his mother spoke again.

'You can stay here as long as you like. It'll be good to have you home again. Packy says he's got lots of work for a good joiner. There's an new development of houses up by the Whiterock gully that'll keep him in work for years, he says. I told him you'd start tomorrow. Thought I'd let you get settled today.'

Danny decided to bite the bullet. 'Look Mum, about Sarah', he began.

His mother interrupted him. 'I thought we'd discussed this.' she said coldly.

'Yes, but, surely you can't be serious. I can't leave Sarah just like that. It's not fair.' He held up his hand to stop his mother's imminent protest.

'Ok. I know you're right. It's true that I don't love Sarah and I should have realised that earlier instead of leading her on. But she is a lovely girl and it's not all her fault she's pregnant: I had something to do with it as well you know and if I hadn't been so stupid, it would never have happened. But it did. And I do feel responsible. So I was thinking. What if I ask Sarah to come over here?'

He could tell by the look on her face that his mother did not think much of the idea but he ploughed on regardless.

'Mrs Murray takes in paying guests and Sarah could stay with her till after the baby's born. That way the baby will be born in Ireland so it'll be Irish.' He was trying to play against Mary Ann's prejudices. 'And once it's born and living with us, Sarah would be free to stay or go as she chooses. And

Mam', he added, pitifully, 'I need to do something for her. I can't just abandon her.'

Mary Ann looked at the handsome young man in front of her. No longer her baby, he had grown into a fine young man, the image of his father, and she was pleased to see that he did have the same sense of right and wrong. It was clear to her that Danny and Sarah had no future together but she could tell that he did not want to abandon his child and that he was prepared to take his responsibilities seriously. It went against her principles – after all, no good ever came of consorting with the English and this latest episode simply proved the truth of that – but she found it hard to refuse his request without disclosing her callous side. While she had, reluctantly, agreed to raise the child as her own, she wanted nothing to do with the child's mother. After a moments reflection, she nodded. 'All right. Why don't you write to her and invite her over?'

Danny grinned in delight. His mother wasn't that bad really, he told himself. Everything would turn out fine for everyone in the long run.

Rummaging around in the dresser drawer he found some faded notepaper with matching envelopes and a pen that still had some ink in it.

Dear Sarah, he started. He was not much of a hand at the letter writing he mused, as he struggled to put pen to paper.

> *I hope this finds you well. I am well as is my family. I am sorry I did not come back on Sunday. I hope you got my telegram. I am not able to come back to you. I will explain it when I see you. I am sending you some money so that you can come here. Mrs Murray will put you up until the baby is borne. Let me know when you are coming and I will meet you at the station.*
>
> *with best wishes,*
>
> *Danny McAllister*

He considered putting a few 'X's to represent kisses at the bottom but thought better of it. Sealing the envelope, he called to his mother, 'Mum, have you any stamps? I want to get this away as soon as possible.'

Mary Ann came in from the kitchen where she had been making herself another cup of tea.

'Put it behind the mantle clock. I'll get Anne Marie to go to the Post Office when she gets back from work.'

Feeling better now that everything had been taken care of, Danny decided to visit the building site where he would be working and re-introduce himself to Packy Boyle. Leaving the house, he sauntered up the street, hands in his pockets, whistling happily to himself.

He would have been a lot less happy had he known what his mother was up to. He had no sooner left the house than she steamed open the envelope addressed to Sarah. Having a kettle always on the go had more than one use. Removing the five pound note Danny had enclosed, she put it in the zippered pocket of her handbag. No point in wasting good money on an English strumpet, she thought. Taking out the notepaper and pen again, she sat and composed her own letter to Sarah.

I hope this finds you well. I am well as is my family. I hope you got my telegram. I am not coming back to you. Let me know when the baby is born.

Faking Danny's signature, she placed it in the original envelope, re-sealed it and returned it to its place on the mantelpiece. Let Anne Marie post that, she thought smugly, as she ripped Danny's original letter to shreds before consigning it to the fire.

Chapter Fifteen

Two police constables had arrived within twenty minutes of the landlord's discovery of the tragedy. It took another two hours before the pathologist arrived and another hour before the undertakers were allowed to move the body. During this time, Sarah had to give a statement to the policeman but found herself unable to answer many of the questions. She did not know her neighbour's name; she did not know if he had any relations; she did not recall him having any visitors; she could not remember the last time she saw him; she could not remember anything untoward, and she had no real information to give. This worried her. They had inhabited different rooms in the same house for almost a year and had never so much as said 'good morning' to each other. The first time she had ever seen him properly was as he lay on his back on the floor of his bed-sit, his dressing gown gaping open to reveal a grey-haired chest and clean white underpants. Sarah felt an overwhelming sorrow and a weird sense of relief that at least his undergarments were clean. How humiliating it would be to be found wearing dirty pants.

After everyone had gone and the house had settled into a strange empty-feeling silence, Sarah sat by the open window. She let the dark envelop her as she brooded on past events. She compared her life to that of her deceased neighbour. Now that Danny had gone, and she knew in her heart he was never coming back, she was in exactly the same situation. She had no friends, no relations, no one knew anything about her. She could die and no-one would miss her. If her neighbour had died in the middle of winter instead of high summer, his body could have lain for weeks before anyone noticed. What made it even worse was the attitude of the policemen who had attended the incident. According to them, this was nothing unusual. Rarely did a week pass without someone from their station having to attend to a corpse that had been discovered only after someone noticed the smell. Or the rats, they had added as an afterthought.

Sarah shuddered. This was not going to be her future, she decided. Rising awkwardly due to the turmoil in her womb, she manoeuvred her suitcase down from the top of the wardrobe. She moved around the small flat slowly, packing up everything she owned. Her grandmother would understand. They could concoct a story to tell the rest of the villagers and she would continue to wear the second-hand wedding ring she had purchased from Pudden Peg. A further flash of empathy with the old market stall holder went through her. They had something in common after all.

She put the rest of Danny's things in a neat pile on the bed. She was not sure what to do with them. Maybe one of his workmates would collect them. She no longer cared. Everything else in the room she cleaned or discarded. The landlord would have no difficulty re-letting the bed-sit – probably at an even higher rent. Sitting down by the window again once everything was to her satisfaction, Sarah succumbed to exhaustion and fell asleep in the chair.

It was mid-morning before she awoke, feeling achy and befuddled. Her sleep had been plagued with strange life-like dreams in which she had been running around a giant building site in her underwear looking for something she could not find. As she rose from the chair she was cut by a sudden sharp pain in her abdomen. It caught her so intensely that she could not even cry out. It subsided after a few moments, leaving her gasping. Hoping it did not portend something amiss with the baby, she went to make her morning tea. No longer needing to worry about bumping into her neighbour, she nevertheless felt his nearness; he seemed more present now he no longer existed than he ever did alive. Telling herself she was being silly, she carried her tea into her room and had just left it on the table when the pain struck again. Again, it only lasted moments. Worried now, Sarah decided to dress quickly and visit the doctor. She did not want to lose the baby as well.

The pains struck three more times before she managed to see Dr Henderson. After that, things happened in a dream-like, slow-motion, flash-before-your–eyes sequence of events. After a cursory examination, he informed Sarah that she had gone into premature labour and, despite her protests that she could not be in labour as she was only seven months gone, insisted she lay on his examining table while he telephoned for an ambulance. She felt so embarrassed being carried past the other patients in the waiting room, wrapped in an open-weave blanket and strapped to the folding chair the ambulance men had arrived with. She barely noticed the ten-minute drive to the hospital, engrossed as she was with her own confused thoughts. There she was carted to a bed and fussed around by nurses taking her clothes, her temperature, her details, her blood pressure. Then she was abandoned to await the arrival of the doctor. Alone in the small side ward, with the heavy starch sheets tucked tightly around her, Sarah felt bewildered and frightened. Thankfully the excruciating pains seemed to have stopped and now there was just the feeling of tingling at the base of her stomach.

After what could have been hours or may only have been minutes, the doctor arrived with two nurses in tow. Without a word of greeting he pulled back the bedclothes and started his examination, firing statements and questions at the nurses who took turns giving short respectful answers that always ended with 'Doctor'. So this is the doctor then, Sarah mused wryly, I'd never have guessed. His examination over, the doctor looked at Sarah, patted her hand, and pronounced: 'Not long now. We'll soon have you nursing your young 'un.', before spinning round and matching out, the two nurses following at an semi-run.

Another interminable wait followed, interspersed with the occasional cramp, before another nurse finally appeared to talk to Sarah.

'Doctor says you're in the early stages of labour and that because you aren't full term, we have to keep an eye on you. You're to have full bed rest, so if you need to go to the lavatory you must ring for assistance. This buzzer here will alert one of the nurses and they will come for you as soon as they're free. Now, on no account are you to get out of bed on your own, hear me? Tea will be coming round shortly. I expect you could do with a cup, eh, love? Now, is there anyone you would like us to contact for you? Your mum, your husband? Anyone?' Sarah's eyes started to moisten as she realised she had no-one to call on. Then she remembered: Elvis. He had said she could call on him for anything and right now, any familiar face would be welcome. The nurse recovered Sarah's handbag from the locker where it had been stowed and waited while the search for the slip of paper with Elvis's address on it was carried out. 'Here', declared Sarah eventually, handing it to the nurse. 'Can you contact him? Let him know where I am?' The nurse looked at the scrap of paper she had been given, turning it over in her hand. 'Which one?

There are two names on this.' 'The London address' said Sarah. 'The other one's not important.'

Chapter Sixteen

The events of the past five days finally caught up with Sarah. Despite the harshness of the sheets and the firmness of the bed, she sleep like a baby for the next twelve hours. When she awoke, it took her some few seconds to remember where she was and why. As she struggled to raise herself onto the pillows, a familiar voice startled her.

'Are you all right? You had me worried for a while.' Elvis moved from the chair in the corner of the room to sit on the edge of the bed. 'How you feeling?' he asked gently. Sarah gripped his proffered hand. 'Oh Elvis. It's so good to see you. Thank you so much for coming. I'm sorry to drag you here but I couldn't think of anyone else to call. I don't know anyone else. I hope you don't mind.' He cut her short. 'It's OK. I told you to call me if you needed anything. And given that you're lying in a hospital bed, I'd say you needed something.' He grinned, and she managed a weak smile in response. It was reassuringly good to see Elvis. Although she had never felt that close to him, she always liked his ability to make her laugh.

She clenched his hand as another heavy cramp seized her. Elvis panicked. 'Are you all right? Will I call a nurse? Are you OK?' Sarah tried to nod through the pain, still holding his hand so that he was unable to leave her side. 'It's OK', she said as the pain started to subside. 'I've been having these pains on-and-off all day. The doctor says I'm in labour and that the baby should be here soon.'

Still feeling uselessly at a loss, Elvis was unsure what to do next. 'Do you want me to get in touch with Danny? Let him know what's happening?' Sarah shook her head as another wave of pain started to rise. 'No. I don't want him to know.' In between the spasms, she discussed her future plans with Elvis, a future that did not include Danny McAllister.

They chatted for a while about their respective homes in Yorkshire and in Scotland before the nurse arrived with a tray and chased Elvis out.

'Visiting hours are three thirty to five and six thirty to seven thirty. and I'm sure your young lady will be happy to see you then. In the meantime, we've got work to do.'

Elvis was just about to say 'She's not my young lady' but thought better of it. Instead, he grinned, kissed Sarah on the forehead, instructed her to keep her pecker up, and assured her he would visit later in the day. Eating the slightly congealed breakfast of egg, sausage and toast, Sarah reflected that she did feel much better knowing Elvis was around.

After the nurse had escorted her to the bathroom and helped her back into the freshly made bed, Sarah asked how long she could expect to be in hospital.

'That depends.' replied the nurse. 'If it turns out that it's just a false labour, then you could be out tomorrow. But if it is your time, then we usually keep new mums in for a week or so after their confinement so you could be with us for a while yet.' She smile reassuringly. 'Don't worry, love. Things will be fine. Shall I fetch you some magazines to help pass the time?'

Sarah was leafing through an old copy of Woman's Own, disinterestedly reading how to fashion a tasty family meal out of inexpensive cuts of meat, when she felt an unusual sensation around her upper thighs. Pulling the bedclothes back, she realised with horror that she had, without realising it, wet the sheets. In a panic, she called the nurse, pressing the buzzer repeatedly as she clambered out of bed. The nurse bustled in. 'What are you doing out of bed?' she scolded. Sarah simply pointed to the bed, too embarrassed to speak.

'I see' said the nurse, in a more kindly fashion. 'Your waters have broke. That means it won't be long now until the baby's born. Here.' She lead Sarah to the armchair in the corner of the room, sat her down and put a blanket over her. 'You sit there while we change the bed. Then once we get you all comfy again, we can let Doctor know.' She scuttled off again to fetch a colleague while Sarah tried to come to terms with the situation.

The baby was on its way and she was not prepared for it, mentally or physically. She had meant to lay in nappies and baby clothes, to knit yellow and white matinee coats with matching mittens and bootees, but had not quite felt the time was right. She realised now that it was probably because Danny had shown such a lack of enthusiasm that she had put off doing anything that may have made the baby seem more real in his eyes. The baby had no clothes, she had no decent nightdresses or dressing gowns for the hospital stay – in fact, she did not even have a change of underwear with her. If she could not take care of simple things like that, she asked herself, how on earth was she going to cope with a baby? It was not just the contractions that made her break out in a sweat.

Returning with clean bed linen, the two nurses set to work stripping and remaking the bed. Sarah watched in fascination as they smoothed every wrinkle out until the blankets were taut as a drum. 'There you are, Mrs Trafford, let's get you back into bed before Doctor comes. Nurse Armstrong here is going to stay with you until then, just in case.' She did not say in case of what but Sarah did not care to ask: she was frightened enough already. Nurse Armstrong drew the chair Sarah had vacated closed to the head of the bed. 'Is this your first baby?' she asked conversationally. Sarah admitted it was.

'You may be a bit worried then' suggested the nurse with, to Sarah's mind, the epitome of understatement.

'Yes, I am' declared Sarah. 'I'm not ready, I've nothing prepared for the baby and I don't know what I'm going to do!'

'There, there,' reassured the nurse. 'Babies don't need much of anything except love. You'll be fine. And now that your waters have broken, you'll probably find that your contractions come a bit more often and probably a bit more intense. Don't be worrying. It's all very natural. Just try and breathe through the contractions. If it gets really bad, the doctor will probably give you some gas and air to help you.'

Sarah stared at the nurse as if the poor woman had lost her mind. Get worse? How could these pains get any worse? She was in agony already. Two hours later, she knew exactly what Nurse Armstrong had tried to warn her about. The pain was excruciating. No longer able to lie in the by now messed up bed, Sarah was on her knees, trying to clutch both stomach and back at the same time as the baby threatened, it seemed, to burst through her backbone. Nurse Armstrong had run off to fetch the porters and to alert the delivery room staff that another imminent mother was on her way. Sarah had been warned that childbirth was painful and difficult – 'that's why it's called "labour"' the midwife had wryly informed her – but this amount of agony could not be normal. If it was this bad, Sarah reasoned through her distress, no-one would have more than one child. There must be something wrong. Sarah was frightened. As they wheeled her along the corridor to the delivery room, she feared for the life of her child.

Chapter Seventeen

Nurse Armstrong woke Sarah some six hours later. 'I've brought you some tea and toast. I expect you need something after what you've been through, eh? But wasn't it all worth it?' she cooed as she turned to the cot beside the bed. 'You have a beautiful baby girl. Have you a name for her yet?'

Sarah turned her head to look at her daughter. Her Daughter. Even the words seemed strange. She rolled them over in her head. My Daughter. She was a mother to a genuine, real person. Until now, the baby had just been an abstract notion, something that belonged to an unforeseeable future. Now, however, it was here and alive. Everything about the baby was as it should be, with the correct number of fingers and toes. She had undergone a normal delivery, apparently, although Sarah grimaced at the mere thought of it. How could anything that painful be normal?

'When you've had something to eat, it will be time to feed baby. Now the doctor says that because baby is underweight by a few pounds she'll have to be fed a special formula.' She indicated to a small clear cup on the tray. 'You're to take those tablets after food. They'll help dry up your milk. Nurse Cartwright will be round with the bottles in a few minutes, so hurry up and finish your tea.' Sarah did as she was told, too confused, tired and bewildered to do anything else.

When the bottles arrived, Sarah put the tray aside and picked up her daughter. The feelings that welled up inside her were overwhelming. Love such as she had never known flooded over her, but so, too, did sadness. This poor little mite had no one to depend on but her and Sarah was not sure she was up to the challenge. It also felt strange to look at this child and see another living being with a personality of its own, even though it was only hours old. Sarah had imagined that, somehow, the baby would simply be an extension of her, and this separateness came as something of a shock. The baby started to mew and writhe around in her arms. Sarah reached for the feeding bottle Nurse Cartwright had placed on the bedside locker. As she held the formula towards her child's mouth, and watched in wonder as it found, clamped on to and started sucking from the teat, she made herself a promise. No matter what happened, her child would have the best she could possibly give it.

Sarah and her baby adapted quickly to the routine of hospital life. Getting up at six thirty did not present a problem for Sarah and the baby enjoyed waking up every four hours anyway. All the babies were taken out of the ward during the night but the mothers were still expected to tend to them when they cried. Sarah discovered, to her own amazement, that she could sleep through the general noise of a maternity ward but as soon as her own child started to cry, she awoke in an instant. She became friendly with some of the other mothers as they sat up during the wee small hours, nursing their children. The atmosphere lent itself to quickly-made close friendships that would have been almost impossible outside the hospital. It was during this period that Sarah learned more about life, men and child-raising than any book could have taught her. The experiences of the women were varied and, Sarah was convinced, exaggerated for effect. Thirty-six hour labours, contractions that never eased, babies delivered that ranged from two pounds to fourteen, cords tangled around the child's neck – the horror stories seemed to be a source of particular delight to the more experienced mothers.

It was when the talked turned to husbands that Sarah tried to fade into the background. As far as she knew, she was the only unmarried mother on the ward and it was a source of embarrassment to her. As she still wore the wedding ring she had bought in the market, the other women assumed she too was married. At first, as no-one but Elvis ever visited, they had taken him to be her husband but when he brought Barbara with him one visiting day, and they had held left holding hands, this aroused the curiosity of the others. Sarah felt forced into lying. Even so, she tried to keep as close to the truth as possible.

'Danny, my husband, had to go back to Ireland. His mother is very seriously ill. Maybe dying', she added, crossing her fingers behind her back and wishing no ill will on Danny's mother. 'He can't leave her just yet, so we'll join him when we're ready to leave hospital. We thought he would have plenty of time to go to Belfast and still be back for the birth, but baby decided to come early.' She hoped people believed her but the absence of cards and flowers on her bedside locker, as opposed to the proliferation of foliage elsewhere, seemed to give the lie to her story. Still, she reasoned, she would not be in hospital for long and the chance of meeting any of these women again were slim, so it did not really matter.

In fact the women, whatever they thought privately, accepted her as one of them. So much so that when the doctor finally announced that both Sarah and the baby would be able to leave hospital the following day, she had some genuine regrets. During the entire time she had spent in London, the maternity ward was where she had felt most accepted as one of the gang. There was also the frightening prospect of managing alone. Having a baby in hospital, surrounded by other, more experienced, mothers and a team of trained doctors and nurses, made it relatively easy to cope. How would she manage with just her grandmother to help? Sarah still felt rather unsure of her own ability to bring up a child.

When Elvis came visiting that evening after work, he volunteered to help her home with the baby. After only the briefest of protests, she agreed that his help with getting the baby home, especially taking into consideration all those stairs to her room, would be very welcome. After he left, she gathered the items she had accumulated, together with items for the baby that the hospital almoner had given her, ready to leave. She had asked Elvis to bring a bag with him when he came to pick her up. She was so grateful to him for all the help he had given her. She had always considered Elvis and Barbara to be friends of Danny, mates that he met in the pub, rather than friends who would help in times of need. Yet Elvis had visited as often as he could and brought with him articles of clothing that Barbara had bought for Sarah: some underwear, slippers, two nightdresses and a bed-jacket. And for the baby they had given Sarah a beautiful pink and white pram set, consisting of a dress, cardigan, hat, mittens and bootees. It just goes to show, she thought, you should never judge people by appearances.

Sarah did not plan to remain in her bed-sit for more than a few days. She simply wanted to gather her things, pay her bills, and return the keys to the landlord. When she and Elvis reached the room, however, there was a problem. 'My key doesn't fit.' Perplexed, Sarah removed it from the lock, checking to make sure it was the correct key.

'Give it here.' commanded Elvis, in a "locks-are-too-complicated-for women" tone of voice.

Unfortunately, he too was unable to open the door. Before he could ask if it was the right key, the door was opened from the inside by a dishevelled looking man who looked none too pleased to see them.

'What are you doing?' he demanded.

Mouth agape, Sarah stared at him wordlessly, before turning to Elvis, who, equally flummoxed, simply repeated the man's question back to him.

'I live here.' came the unexpected answer.

'No, you're wrong. This is my flat.' Sarah insisted.

'Oh, are you called Trafford?'

Sarah nodded assent.

'Yeah, the landlord said you'd disappeared, owing him three weeks rent. So he's let the room out to me.'

He looked at the small group in front of him. Sarah was holding the baby in her arms while Elvis carried a small suitcase and a bag of groceries.

'Have you come to collect your things?'

Sarah thought it one of the daftest questions anyone had ever asked her.

'No, I've just got out of hospital. That's where I've been all this time. I expected to come home. As he continued to stare at them in a puzzled way, she added 'Here! I live here!'

'Not any more, you don't. I've paid my deposit and four weeks rent in advance so it's my place now. Look,' he continued in a more consolatory voice, 'You can pick up your stuff. To be truthful, I was going to throw it out anyway. There's not enough room in here as is without holding on to other people's stuff.'

He went back into the room and retrieved Sarah's suitcase from the top of the wardrobe. He also pulled down a brown paper parcel, tied up with string. He deposited them both at Sarah's feet: 'There you go, that's all the stuff that was left here when I moved in. Oh, and there's some post.' Fetching some envelopes from the top of the dresser he handed them to Sarah. 'I think that's everything. Nice meeting you.' And with that, he closed the door, leaving them on the stairwell.

Stunned, Sarah turned to Elvis. 'What am I going to do now?'

'Come on.' said Elvis, more determined than he felt, 'Let's get out of here. There's no point staying where we're not wanted.' Picking up the suitcases and parcels, he lead the way downstairs. 'Sure this place is a dump anyhow. We'll find somewhere better.' By the time he reached the bottom of the stairs, Elvis had a plan. He knew money was a problem for Sarah right now, so a guest house was out of the question, and he knew he could not bring her back to his digs, as the landlady insisted on letting to men only. 'Barbara will put you up. It's only for a few nights. I'm sure she won't mind.'

Chapter Eighteen

Danny enjoyed being back at home. He had forgotten how much his mother and his sisters liked to fuss around him. He never had to do anything for himself at home. As soon as he walked in to the house one sister would hang up his coat for him while another would make the tea and hand him the newspaper. The money he was making on the building site was not as much as he would have earned in London but on the other hand he did not have the same expenses. His mother took something towards the housekeeping but it still left him enough in his pocket to have regular nights out, save a few pounds and he had even treated himself to a new suit. Admittedly it was from Burton's and he was paying for it weekly, but it still felt good to walk out in something smart on a Saturday night after wearing shabby old dungarees the rest of the week.

Life would be good, thought Danny, if it was not for the people he had left behind. He was surprised that he had not heard from Sarah. He honestly thought that bringing her to Belfast to have the child and letting his mother raise it was the best possible solution for all concerned. His mother and sisters would love the child, he would pay for anything it needed and Sarah would be free to go back to work and maybe find herself a nice young man. Someone who would appreciate her more than I did, thought Danny ruefully. He had waited ten days before writing again, just in case his first letter had not reached her but had still not received a reply: not even a postcard. He was unaware that Sarah's carefully composed letter had been received but his mother had chosen not to tell him. In fact, seeing it was addressed to Danny and postmarked London, she had taken it upon herself to open it and read the contents.

Dear Danny,

> *I hope everything is all right at home. I am fine. I was concerned to get your telegram. I hope nothing bad has happened to you or to any member of your family.*

If you can let me know when you plan to come back again I will have your favourite supper ready. You always did like your food. Ha Ha.

The weather here is still very hot. I hope it is warm in Belfast too.

With lots of Love

Sarah XXX

Mary Ann had scrutinised the letter, trying to read between the lines for any hidden meaning. When she was satisfied that there was nothing untoward in the epistle, she placed it carefully on the hottest part of the fire. No point in bothering Danny with inconsequential chit-chat, she told herself. Better that he forgets all about Sarah and the child.

Danny, however, was not prepared to forget. He decided to write to Barbara. It had been playing on his mind that, now he was free, in a manner of speaking, maybe Barbara should know that he was available. He was not quite sure what he expected. His daydreams had Barbara jumping on to the coach and joining him in Belfast but his rational streak knew that it was never going to happen. Still, he reasoned, writing to her and asking her to find out if Sarah was all right wouldn't do any harm. In fact, it would give him the excuse he had been looking for.

On his way home from work one evening he stopped at a shop and bought some writing materials. He did not want anyone to know he was writing to Barbara. He had not mentioned her to his family as it would raise all sorts of awkward questions. Hiding the package inside the bib of his dungarees until after he had his supper, he then went to his room and placed his purchases under the mattress. As he never normally spent time in his room, except when sleeping, Danny figured he would need some sort of subterfuge so as not to arouse suspicion. He wanted plenty of time to compose a letter that would say all the things he wanted to say to Barbara without being too blatant about it. Picking up a library book left on the shelf by his sister Bernadette, he informed his family that he wanted peace and quiet to read it. Mary Ann guessed that something was up. Danny had never been fond of books and she did not believe that the time he had spent in London had changed him that much. There was nothing she could do however, except hope that whatever he was up to did not involve Sarah. Had she known exactly what he was doing, she would not have been any happier.

Writing the letter to Barbara was a difficult task for Danny. After the words 'Dear Barbara', he sat and chewed the end of the pen for twenty minutes, trying to compose the next sentence. Various clichés were considered and rejected. Finally, he decided to take the plunge and simply write what was in his mind.

> *I am back in Belfast. I have told my mother all about Sarah. I told you how she feels about English prodestants. She will cripple me if I go back to England and marry Sarah. I have written to Sarah to tell her sorry and tell her I will not be back but that she should come to Belfast. My mother will rase the baby as her own and Sarah will be free. I have written two times but she has not got back to me. I am worried that something bad has happened to her. I would like to ask you a favour. Can you make sure Sarah is*

all right and tell her she should come to Belfast were I will be waiting for her even if we arnt getting married. I dont want to leave her in the lurch. I sent her money for the fare but if she needs more money I will send that too.

Yours sincerely,

Danny McAllister

PS. I still think about the night we had.

Danny decided to post the letter immediately. His exit was stalled by his mother's voice: 'And where do you think you're going?'

'Just up to Mullen's for a pint. I won't be long.'

'What about that book you wanted to read?'

'What book?' Suddenly remembering his excuse for being on his own, he quickly added 'I changed my mind. It was a rubbish book anyway.' and was out the door before his mother could ask anything else.

After posting the letter, Danny decided to go to Mullen's for a drink. That way, he reasoned, he wasn't actually lying to his mother. Besides, he did feel the need of one after the emotional wringer writing that letter had put him through. Walking into the smoke-filled bar, Danny was hailed by the parish priest who was holding court at the counter.

'Daniel, my boy! How ye doing? C'mon let me get ye a drink!'

Danny would have preferred his own company at that moment but there was no gainsaying Father Hanson when he was in a sociable mood. He joined the group at the bar. Most of the men were regulars, glad of the chance of a free drink while the priest was in the chair. They would slope off if it looked like they had to buy their own. There was one of the younger priests in the congregation as well as two blokes from a few streets away that Danny recognised.

'So Danny' whispered Father Hanson. 'What's happening with that young English lass of yours then? Isn't she coming over?'

Danny shook his head. 'Doesn't look like it Father. I've written her twice and she's never answered.'

'Ach well, perhaps it's for the best. Your mother would never rest easy knowing you were married to an Englishwoman.' The volume of the priest's voice was starting to rise again and Danny prayed fervently that the conversation would change to something that did not involve him. Unfortunately, the racing and the football had already been thrashed out so Danny's love life was now the chief topic of debate.

'Have you not found a nice Irish girl to go out with? A good-looking young man like yourself, with a decent job. You'd be a fine catch for some nice young girl. Could your sisters not introduce you to one of their friends?'

'Can you not introduce me to one of your sisters?' asked one wag, to a general wave of laughter and banter.

Danny said nothing. He had already decided that he did not want to be introduced to any nice young girl, Irish or not. He had had a nice young girl – you couldn't get nicer than Sarah, he thought. But I never loved her. I want someone who would never in a million years be described as nice by either my mother or the parish priest. I want Barbara.

Chapter Nineteen

Elvis settled Sarah, the baby and the luggage in a small greasy-spoon café while he went to inform Barbara about her new house guests. He naively believed that Barbara would be delighted to have Sarah staying with her. Even though Clare was back, there was still plenty of room in their flat and, being women, he reckoned, they would love to have a baby to fuss over. Barbara was surprised when Elvis turned up at her place of work. It was something he had never done before so she was immediately concerned. On learning the reason behind the visit she did as Elvis had expected her to do: she agreed that Sarah could stay as long as she liked and went to fetch her house keys. She also pressed a ten shilling note into his hand.

'Make sure you get a taxi to my place. You can't expect Sarah and the baby to take public transport after what they've been through. I'll try and leave work early and meet you both there.'

Elvis, touched by his girlfriend's consideration, went off happily to collect Sarah, leaving Barbara wondering how she was going to cope with Danny's discarded family. Elvis had told her all about Sarah's abandonment, something she found hard to fathom. The about-face was puzzling. She, too, was worried that something had happened to him. The last time she had spoken to Danny, before he went off to Belfast, she was convinced he was going to do the right thing by Sarah. Barbara had made it clear it was what she expected of him.

Barbara had never experienced guilt about the night she spent with Danny. She knew that, sooner or later, she would give in to Elvis's pleading and have sex with him. Unfortunately, despite all his bravado, Elvis was still a virgin. Barbara, while curious to find out what all the fuss was about, did not want her first time to be with someone inexperienced and, besides, she had felt a certain bond with Danny, ever since the first night they had met. She felt sure that had the chat-up line not been so silly and her response so flippant, it would be her and Danny who would now be a couple. Every time they had met, usually in the bars where Elvis was playing, she had been engulfed with a desire to throw herself into his arms. Common sense had told her to restrain herself. When she had discovered that he and Sarah were an item, she was kicking herself for not seizing the opportunity when she had the chance. The night she did finally spend with Danny was, she believed, her due. Now, however, she felt she owed Sarah something.

By the time Barbara finished work and made her way home, Elvis had gone and Sarah was settled in the flat. The baby was asleep on the spare bed, surrounded by pillows and rolled up blankets that were doing duty for cot rails, while Sarah's nightwear was laid out at the bottom of the bed. She herself was sitting, quite primly, at one end of the sofa sipping a cup of tea.

'I hope you don't mind.' she asked anxiously as Barbara entered the sitting room. 'Elvis said it would be all right to make some tea.'

'Of course it's all right!' Barbara replied, as reassuringly as she could muster. 'This is your home now, for as long as you like.'

'Would you like a cup?' Sarah's eagerness to please was touching, if a little irritating.

'No thanks, Sarah. You don't have to run after me, you know, and anyway, I think I'd prefer a G&T.'

Sarah sat back again. She did like Barbara, and it was really good of her - and Clare – to put her up in their flat, but she had always been slightly in awe of her. Barbara seemed so grown-up and sophisticated. She was only two years older that Sarah but, having grown up in London, Barbara appeared much more cosmopolitan. The flat on its own was enough to intimidate Sarah. Like Danny before her, she had never been in such a stylish, modern home and was feeling very out of place.

Barbara returned, nursing her gin and tonic.

'How's baby?'

'Sleeping like a – well, like a baby', finished Sarah lamely, feeling rather silly for stating the obvious. Barbara laughed. 'Silly question, I suppose.' It was at that moment, as they laughed at the silliness of the exchange, that the two girls bonded. Barbara liked Sarah's no-nonsense, call-a-spade-a-spade approach, while Sarah was charmed by Barbara's ability to laugh at herself. They exchanges a few more pleasantries before Barbara, taking a seat opposite Sarah, became more sombre.

'Sarah', she started, tentatively. 'I'm really sorry about Danny. I can't believe he's treated you in this way.'

'Thanks Barbara. I couldn't believe it at first either. But, look. This was among the post that was in the flat.'

She handed Barbara the letter Danny's mother had forged. 'As you can see, it's short and to the point. So', she shrugged and let out a sigh, 'I just have to accept that he is not coming back and get on with my life.'

Barbara cast her eyes over the brief note. This was not the Danny she knew and loved. The text was heartless and, whatever else he was, Danny was a nice person who hated to hurt anyone. That was partly his problem. Had he been the uncaring creature this letter made him out to be, he would not have worried about hurting Sarah or Elvis and she and Danny would be together now.

She sighed and returned the letter to Sarah. It would not be to anyone's advantage to confess her secret love now. Instead, she turned to Sarah: 'What are your plans now? Do you have any?'

'Yes. I've decided, if it's okay with you and Clare, to stay here until Saturday. That will give me time to go back to the dole office and get some money, pay off some bills, and get baby registered before I go back home to Yorkshire. My gran will get the shock of her life when I turned up with a baby, but it can't be helped.'

'Your gran doesn't know, then?'

Another sigh escaped Sarah. 'No, not yet. I kept putting it off in the hope I could write and tell her I was married first. But, as that's not going to happen' Sarah stuck out her chin; 'I'll just have to bite the bullet and hope she won't disown me.'

Barbara's heart went out to Sarah. Sarah was trying to put on a brave face but it was clear that she really was frightened. Trying to lighten the atmosphere, she asked again about the baby.

'Do you have a name for the baby yet? We can't just keep calling her "it" or "baby".'

Sarah shook her head. 'Not really. We, and mean I, had planned on calling her something Irish, like Maureen or Patricia or something, if it was a girl. Because of Danny's background and, of course, if we'd married, we would be called McAllister. But now as it's just plain old Trafford, I don't know what to call her.'

They spent a pleasant few minutes thinking of girls names for the baby, rapidly going from the sensible and acceptable to the ridiculous and absurd, before they were interrupted by the sound of the doorbell. Barbara went to answer it and returned with Elvis following behind her, arms loaded down with bundles wrapped in newspaper.

'I didn't think you girls would be too keen on cooking or on going out tonight so I've brought fish and chips for everyone. That OK?'

'Oh Elvis! You love!' cooed Barbara, quickly relieving him of his burden and heading for the kitchen. Elvis waited until Barbara was engrossed in dividing the fish and chips onto separate plates before speaking, quietly, to Sarah. 'Everything all right? Do you need anything?'

Sarah grasped his hand and squeezed it gently as she shook her head. 'No, I'm fine, thank you. I honestly don't know what I would have done without you. And Barbara,' she added almost as an afterthought: 'She's been great.'

'Dinner is served!' Barbara announced in mock grandeur from the kitchen doorway and, with a laugh, Elvis and Sarah went to join her at the table.

'So', asked Elvis jocularly, as he tucked into his fish and chips, 'What have you girls been gossiping about – or do I not want to know?' Barbara pretended to stab him on the hand with her fork before replying 'Well, if it's any of your business, we were talking about names for the baby.' Turning to Sarah, and spearing one of her chips, he asked through the food in his mouth, 'Haven't you decided yet?' Sarah repeated her explanation, as well as offering some of the more outlandish suggestions put forward by Barbara.

'I don't particularly fancy calling her Hermione or Ermetrude or Fedelma, thank you very much. I prefer plain, simple, straightforward names.'

'OK, if you want something plain, what about Anne? You can't get plainer than that.'

Sarah giggled . 'That's a bit too plain. I know, I should call her Barbara. After all, you have both been so good to me that it would be my way of thanking you.'

'Good God, No!' interjected Barbara. 'I hate my name! And I wouldn't want it inflicted on anyone else. No. We can do better than that.'

'Do you have a second name?' asked Sarah, not willing to let go of what she thought of as a good idea.

'Actually, yes. I don't mention it to everyone, but I'm actually Barbara Jean' she admitted.

'Jean?' exclaimed Elvis. 'That's my mother's name.'

'Well, that's settled it then.' declared Sarah, delightedly. 'I'm going to call her Jean.'

Barbara uncorked a bottle of wine and poured out three glasses. Holding her glass in the air, she announced: 'To Jean Trafford! Long life and prosperity!' The others raised their glasses and joined in the toast.

'To Jean!'

In her sleep, the newly-named baby flinched.

Chapter Twenty

Two weeks after Sarah and Jean had left hospital, Barbara, Clare and Elvis had seen them onto the north-bound train. Sarah had not intended to stay with the girls longer than a few days. Complications when she registered with the Unemployment Bureau, however, meant that she received no money until she was able to produce evidence that she had been in hospital. Even then, it had involved almost daily trips to the dole office to sort things out. Most of her day seemed to be filled with feeding, changing and dressing the baby, packing a ton of nappies, bottles and garments, just in case, and standing around for hours in one queue or another as she endeavoured to obtain enough money to pay for her ticket home. Clare, Barbara and Elvis had been very good to her. The girls had insisted that she was a guest and refused to take anything from her, not even for food, and Elvis had slipped her some money 'to be getting on with', assuring her that she could pay it back whenever it suited. Sarah knew he did not expect to ever see the money again, but she was determined that it would be the first debt she paid off, no matter what. She had intended to pay the landlord of her bed-sit the rent she owed him but as Barbara wisely pointed out, she had paid a deposit when she had first moved in that covered four weeks rent so, really, she owed him nothing.

This was a relief to Sarah and a great weight off her mind. She hated being in anyone's debt. Even so, she was rapidly running out of money. Baby formula and the launderette seemed to eat up so much of her cash. Although she washed the nappies by hand there was nowhere to dry them in the flat and she did not like to leave them hanging over the balcony. Therefore she would cart the wet nappies and baby clothes to the nearby launderette to be spun and tumbled dried before going to the dole, the hospital or the baby clinic or wherever she had to go that day, picking up the dry bundle on her way back to the flat.

Evenings were the best times. Once she got Jean settled, Sarah would prepare dinner for Clare and Barbara, as her way of saying thanks. Then, when dinner was over, Clare and Barbara would argue over whose turn it was to feed the baby. Barbara was displaying a very surprising maternal streak and was amazingly good at getting the baby off to sleep. If the girls were not going out, they would laze around talking or playing cards together, discussing clothes and men and film stars and everything else young women normally talk about. If Clare and Barbara went out, Sarah would lie on the turquoise settee listening to music and reading trashy novels, though she usually fell asleep, book in hand, before the first side of the album finished. Living with other girls of her own age was a new experience for Sarah and one she found she enjoyed. It was with some regret, therefore, that Sarah finally left London.

Elvis helped her on to the second class carriage with her bags, and reminded her that he would be available if ever she needed him. Barbara waited until everything was stowed away and Sarah was settled before handing baby Jean over.

'You know, if things don't work out for you up north, just let me know and we'll make up the spare bed. Honestly, any time. You and Jean are always welcome.'

Barbara had been surprised how affectionate she had felt towards baby Jean as she had never considered herself the least bit maternal. She put her feelings down to the fact that it was Danny's child and, somehow, that made it different. Had fate not pointed its fickle finger elsewhere, Jean could have been hers.

Sarah blinked back tears of gratitude. 'Thank you, Barbara. You've been such a good friend to me.'

As the train huffed out of the station, Sarah waved to her friends, as she now thought of them, while they waved back, exhorting her to take care and to write soon. Finally, withdrawing her head and settling back down, Sarah looked at baby Jean, sleeping contentedly on the seat beside her. 'Let's hope we don't have to go back, eh?' she whispered.

Seven hours later, Sarah had walked in to her grandmother's house without knocking. Like everyone else in the village, Lizzie Taylor never locked her door. Sarah stood for a moment, a silhouette framed in the doorway, that her grandmother, with her failing eyesight, could not decipher.

'Who's that?' Lizzie had queried, more curious than frightened. People arriving unannounced was common in the village. Friends would call with the latest gossip, the minister would drop by looking for donations for his latest charity and even the odd peddler would call, trying to sell worthless knick-knacks. Lizzie would normally buy some trinket that shortly afterwards found its way to the local jumble sale, as she found it hard to refuse to help anyone trying to help themselves.

'It's me, gran', said Sarah softly. 'I've come home.'

'Sarah? My Sarah? Why didn't you let me know you were coming? I'd have had summit ready. Well, what are you standing there for? Get yourself in and have a warm. You must be foundered on a day like that.' The early October day had been a cold one, with a hint of frost in the air. As Sarah moved forward, it became clear that the bundle she was carrying in her arms was a baby.

'What's this?' Lizzie stopped, halfway to hugging Sarah. She looked from the child to Sarah's face and back again.

'Aw no! Don't tell me. Please,' she begged, 'tell me it's not yours.' Sarah remained mute, and Lizzie, correctly taking her silence for assent, moved back towards her chair, which she sank into in a state of shock.

Sarah sat down in the chair opposite her. 'Gran! Gran!' she implored, 'Look at me!'

Lizzie shifted round to face her granddaughter.

'How could you do this? Did I not bring you up right? I thought you would have known better. Bringing disgrace to my door like this! I'll not be able to look anyone in the eye after this! My own granddaughter!'

The diatribe would have continued unabated for some time had not Jean chosen that moment to wake up and cry hungrily. Immediately, the focus of the two women changed to meet the demands of the wailing child.

'She's on formula. Can you hold her while I heat up a bottle?'

With the baby placed on her lap, Lizzie, reverting to type, started to hum a lullaby and gently rock her great-grandchild.

When Sarah returned with the bottle, Jean had settled down and was staring silently up at her great grandmother.

'She's just like you were at that age.' offered Lizzie. 'The same big blue eyes and the dark black hair. You took after your mother.'

Removing the baby from Lizzie's lap, Sarah settled into feeding the child. At the same time, she answered her grandmother's questions as to how she had come to find herself in such a state.

'You remember I told you all about Danny in my letters? Well, we were going to get married, but he's left me and gone back to Ireland.'

'Haven't you tried to get in touch with him? Make him face up to his responsibilities? In my day he'd have had to marry you.'

'No, Gran, there's no point. If he was ever going to marry me, he'd have done it by now. And anyway,' she added, with a bit more spirit, 'I don't want to be married to him!' She continued, more softly, 'Gran, I know you think I'm awful, some sort of wanton woman, but I realise now that Danny and me, well, I thought at first we were in love but we weren't really. I liked him a lot, he was easy to get on with, but if I haven't been so lonely I don't think we would ever have been together for so long. I know now that he never really loved me, but I think I just clung to him so that I wouldn't be alone and he was too nice to leave me on my own.'

'Until you had his baby, that is!' added Lizzie, grimly.

There was no denying the truth of this so Sarah said nothing as she continued to feed her child. 'So, are you back for good, then?' Lizzie asked after a few minutes.

'If you'll have me.' Sarah had replied. 'There's just one thing, gran. I've already experienced what it's like to be a unmarried mother and it's not nice. Not only that, but I think a lot of our old friends would shun us if they knew. So I'm asking you to lie for me. It's not really that big a lie,' she coaxed, as she saw the disapproval on her grandmother's face. 'If anyone asks, I'm Mrs Danny McAllister and this is our daughter, Jean McAllister. That's the name I put on her birth certificate. I'm going to tell everyone that I got married in London, but that my husband died soon after in an accident on the building site. No-one around here will ever know any different, and, anyway, as far as I'm concerned, Danny may as well be dead.'

Chapter Twenty-one

It felt good to be home in Yorkshire again. Her grandmother had reluctantly agreed to adhere to the story Sarah had concocted. In fact, when the milkman had called the following morning, Sarah heard her grandmother ordering extra milk and repeating, with embellishments, the tragic tale of her widowed grand-daughter and of the poor wee mite that would never see its father. When the door had shut behind him, Sarah remonstrated with Lizzie: 'Why on earth did you tell the milkman all our business? And what's this about Danny falling four storeys, almost landing on a woman with two kids and nearly killing them as well?'

'Sarah, you've been away too long. Don't forget this is a village and everyone will know soon enough that you're back living with me, if they don't know already. You can't keep anything secret here, and the more you try, the more suspicious people get. By telling Harry, our version of the story will be round the neighbourhood before you've had your breakfast. And people want details, the gorier the better. They won't believe it otherwise. Now when you go out with young Jean, people will sympathise with you on your loss, but they won't feel the need to ask too many questions.'

Sarah looked at her grandmother in admiration. She had taken the initial shock of Sarah turning up with a baby in her stride, and had done a sterling job in spreading Sarah's cover story. Now, however, as Lizzie shuffled off to warm the baby's bottle, Sarah noticed something odd.

'What's that on your feet, gran?' she asked in curiosity.

'Me slippers. What else would you expect?'

'But you've got your socks on over them.'

Lizzie looked at her feet. 'So I have!' she exclaimed in surprise. 'I thought floor were a bit slippery! I must be going daft in me old age!'

They both laughed at the notion.

Once Jean was fed, changed and put back down to sleep again, the two women sat chatting over a cup of tea and talked of the future. It was agreed that the income from Lizzie's pension and Sarah's dole money would not be enough for all three of them to live on but Sarah was reluctant to go out to work and leave Jean. Although she did not like to say so aloud, she believed her grandmother was too old to look after such a young baby. Yet it was her grandmother who came up with the solution to their financial problems.

'Do you mind when you were young, I used to take in stitching? My eyes are too bad for it now, but I could ask at factory if there's any work going. It doesn't pay that well, especially at first, when you're just getting into the way of it, but it's enough to make a living on, and with my bit of pension as well, we'd make do.'

It seemed the ideal solution. They decided to go to the Driffield factory that morning and enquire about the possibility of piece work.

The factory supervisor remembered Lizzie and greeted her warmly.

'Lizzie Taylor, as I live and breathe! Come for your old job back? I could certainly use a good machinist!'

'Ach Sam! You were always a one, even as a lad! I doubt I'll ever be working again. No, it's for me daughter here. She needs to work from home.'

'That's never your Evie!' exclaimed Sam, looking rather perplexed

Sarah stepped in. 'She meant to say granddaughter. I'm Evie's daughter, Sarah.'

'Aye, and a widow now.' added Lizzie. 'Life's not been kind. Can you fix her up with some outwork?'

Sam looked Sarah up and down before nodding. 'Aye, I'll send the lad over tomorrow with the makings.' Turning to Lizzie, he added, 'And I suppose you'll be needing a new machine – the one you have must be at least forty year old.'

Lizzie agreed and between them they settled on a fair rate to be deducted from Sarah's wages to pay for the new sewing machine.

Leaving the factory, the women called into Abraham's pawn shop. Uncle Ab, as he was known in the neighbourhood, was a life saver to the factory workers who, getting their wages on a Saturday, would be penniless by Wednesday. Items of clothes, furniture and household appliances would be pledged during the week and redeemed at the weekend, for it would not do to be seen out on a Sunday without one's best suit on. Uncle Ab's assistant produced a second-hand pram from the back of the store: 'Best one in the shop!' he informed them when they asked for a good quality baby carriage. Showing just the right degree of lack of enthusiasm, Lizzie was able to have the asking price reduced by a few shillings before handing over the cash.

They waited until they were out of the pawn shop before spreading the blanket Jean had been wrapped in on the base of the pram and placing her carefully on it.

'We can buy a new mattress for it and I can cut down and hem some old blankets and it'll be good as new. Fit for a princess.' Lizzie said the latter bit in the strange voice that adults use for babies while rubbing Jean's belly at the same time. Together, the women walked home at a leisurely pace, enjoying the crispness of the autumn air.

Reaching their own village, Sarah was delighted to recognise one of her old school friends.

'Hannah! How are you? It's lovely to see you again.'

'Hello Sarah! I heard you were back. Can't say I'm surprised. I went to London once. It was awful! All that noise. And the traffic! And far too many people for my liking. Is this baby Jean?' she asked bending over the pram.

Sarah was taken aback by the speed of the village telegraph. 'Yes. This is her. Jean McAllister' she added for good measure. Sarah noticed Hannah's eyes move from the baby to her left hand. To ensure Hannah had the opportunity to check it out properly, Sarah started fussing with Jean's cardigan buttons, offering yet another prayer of thanks to Pudden Peg and her inexpensive wedding rings.

'I was sorry to hear about your husband.' offered Hannah mournfully, 'Such a tragedy.'

'Thank you Hannah, but if you don't mind, I'd rather not talk about it. It's just too painful.' She took out her handkerchief and blew her nose. 'God, what a liar and an actress I've become!' she chided herself silently. The ploy worked, however, and soon Sarah and Hannah were talking about the good old days.

Lizzie decided to leave them to it and went to buy a few more groceries at the village store. As she disappeared into the shop, Hannah turned to Sarah with a serious look on her face. 'Sarah, I am glad you're back. And please don't think I'm meddling, but I'm worried about your gran.' Seeing the look of genuine concern, Sarah enquired anxiously as to why.

'Last Sunday you gran came to the Meeting House wearing her best coat and hat' she paused for emphasis, 'but with no shoes or socks on. And Harry, the milkman, was telling my mam that two weeks ago your gran had told him not to call on her any more as she was going to marry Herbert instead.'

'Herbert was my grandfather's name.' proffered Sarah, 'That is a bit strange.'

'There have been one or two other silly things but you know, everyone does something stupid once in a while. It's just that, well, your gran seems to be doing quite a few daft things lately.'

'Is there anything else I should know?' Sarah asked worriedly.

'Well, you know the war memorial in the Market Square? She was having a conversation with it one day. Look Sarah', she added. 'It's not my place, but if I was you, I'd ask Dr Harrington to take a look at her.'

Sarah nodded, biting her lower lip. 'Thanks Hannah, it's good of you to let me know. I'll keep an eye on her and maybe I will have a chat with Dr Harrington.'

Sarah and Hannah parted as Lizzie emerged from the store.

'I got a couple of nice lamb chops for our tea. We can have them with those carrots and potatoes I have growing out back.' She took hold of the pram handle and started pushing it in the direction of home, chattering inconsequentially all the way. She did not appear to notice how quiet Sarah had become.

Dr Harrington had been born in Halifax and educated in Leeds. While doing an internship at the General Infirmary, he had met the nurse who was to become his wife. Together they had moved back to the village of her birth once he was qualified, and he had opened his surgery in Victoria Street, just off the Market Square, in the heart of the village. For the past thirty years he had tendered to the health of the surrounding population but, in true village tradition, he was still considered a relative newcomer, a 'blow-in' in the local parlance. Sarah, however, had known him all her life. He had been present at her birth, despite the protests of the local midwife. As a baby Sarah had threatened to present breech, but thankfully, at the last minute, had turned and arrived naturally. There had been no need for his services after all, but Sarah believed this devotion to duty was one of Dr Harrington's main strengths.

Sarah knew there would be no point in asking her grandmother to visit him in his surgery: Lizzie prided herself on being in the best of health, despite her age. Subterfuge was needed. She called into his surgery the next day to arrange for Jean's vaccinations but while there, confided her concerns to the doctor. She repeated what Hannah had told her, and added some concerns of her own.

'She keeps calling me Evvie. That was my mother's name. Now she's started to call Jean Evvie as well. Yesterday, she bought lamb chops for dinner. She put them on the plates raw. She didn't realise she hadn't cooked them. And last night, I got up to feed Jean and there was gran, sitting in her nightdress at the parlour table, piling all the crockery up into a tower, with the cups and plates upside down. When I asked what she was doing, she told me she had just cleaned them and didn't want the dust to get into them. This morning, I found Jean's bottle in the coal scuttle. Doctor, I'm seriously worried about her.'

'Let's not worry ourselves too soon.' advised Dr Harrington soothingly. 'We all get forgetful at times. I'll tell you what: I'll call in on you later this afternoon, pretend I'm asking about Jean. If she thinks I'm calling to check up on her, I'll be shown the door before you can say Jack Robinson. But there's a few little tests I can do to help us decide whether or not it's anything to worry about.'

Chapter Twenty-two

A week after her grandmother had been diagnosed with senile dementia, Sarah got a letter from Barbara.

Barbara had received Danny's letter three weeks after Sarah had left for Yorkshire. At first, she was not sure what to do for the best. Sarah had made it clear that she wanted nothing more to do with Danny. Yet, here was Danny, acting like the man she knew and loved, offering to take care of Sarah. The tone of the letter was so different from the brief note he had sent to Sarah that it was hard to believe it came from the same person. She spoke to Elvis as casually as she could about Danny and his home life to see if her suspicions were justified. He was able to repeat what he had heard on the building site: Mrs McAllister was a force to be reckoned with, by all accounts. Barbara started to put the pieces together. She was convinced that, if Danny had written the original letter, then he had been made to do so by his overbearing mother.

Barbara grappled with her conscience for several days. Danny was a free agent: Sarah had given up all claim to him. If nothing was said or done, then there was a chance, albeit a slim one, that Danny might return to London some day and would be free to take up with her. It would mean splitting up with Elvis but, increasing, that was becoming less of a problem. He seemed to have other things on his mind recently and was not the funny, madcap person of whom she had been fond. Eventually, however, reason won through. Barbara had to accept that there would be no future for her with Danny. Furthermore, she liked Sarah and had actually become quite good friends with her when she had stayed at the flat. Sarah ought to be told, she decided. It may be that even knowing the truth, Sarah still may not want anything to do with Danny.

It took a while to compose the letter to Sarah. The post script Danny had added in his note to her made Barbara reluctant to simply pass his letter on. Eventually, she was satisfied with the finished article:

Dear Sarah,

I hope both you and baby Jean are enjoying the best of health up there in the Yorkshire dales. All that fresh air must be a bit of a shock to the system after living in London for so long.

Well, I have another shock for you. I received a letter from Danny. In it, he wonders why you never replied to any of his letters. He said that he wrote to you explaining why he didn't come back to you, and that he sent money for you to go to Belfast. Did you ever get any of these letters?

He also asks me to look after you and to let him know when the baby is born, so I take it that you have not told him about Jean or that you have moved back to your grandmother's house. Do you want me to tell him? Or would you prefer to answer him yourself? I'm not sure what to do for the best, but if it's any consolation to

> you, I have the feeling that somebody may have interfered with his letters to you.

Without proof, Barbara was unwilling to put a name to her suspicions. She finished her letter with the usual good wishes and a final postscript:

> PS. Don't forget, anytime you want to come to London there will be a room here for you and Jean.

Sarah read and re-read the letter. Danny had not totally abandoned her. But if he did write to her and send her money, why did she not receive his letters? Thinking back, Sarah tried to put two and two together. Of course! she reasoned. That man who took my flat! He must have got the letters while I was in hospital and stole the money! That was probably what Barbara was alluding to. How dare anyone interfere with my mail! Sarah was infuriated.

Upon reflection, however, she calmed down. It would not really have mattered that much if she had received them. It was highly unlikely that she would have followed Danny to Belfast. And now, seeing so clearly with the benefit of hindsight, she knew it would have been a mistake for them to marry anyway. They would have grown further and further apart, staying together only for the sake of the children. Still, it did give her some consolation to know that he had not intended to simply cut her off from his life. And, it seemed, he was taking an interest in his daughter. She had intended to write Danny out of her life entirely, but now decided to write to him instead.

Dear Danny,

Barbara has written to me to say that you have been in touch with her and that you wanted to know how we are. I say 'we' because you now have a beautiful baby girl. I have named her Jean and given her your surname. I've also told everyone I am a widow, so please do not do anything that would give the lie to that.

I only ever got one letter from you. It was very short and to the point. It simply said you were never coming back. I did not get any money either. I think the man who moved into my flat after me may have stolen it.

I moved back to Yorkshire to my Grans after Jean was born as I thought you had deserted me and even though Barbara and Elvis and Clare were very good to me and to baby Jean, I did not want to stay in London.

Now I cannot leave here even if I wanted to. My Gran is very ill and needs looking after.

Danny, I do not bear you any ill-will. I hope you go on to have a good life. Me and Jean will not be part of it. I think there is no point in you contacting us again as we are happy here.

With best wishes,

Yours sincerely,

Sarah 'McAllister'

She considered putting an 'X' after her signature but decided against it.

Chapter Twenty-three

Danny was getting bored with Belfast. At first, being home had been fun, seeing all his old friends and neighbours again and being fussed over and spoiled by his mother and sisters. After six or seven weeks of it, though, it was starting to feel claustrophobic. Every time he went out, his mother wanted to know where he was going, who with, and when he would be back. She treated him like a twelve-year-old, he moaned to his brother. The other thing he was getting bored with was the social life. It seemed to revolve around two pubs and the Plaza on a Saturday night. Having lived in London, Danny felt very restricted. There was so much more on offer there, even if he had not always taken advantage of it. Going back, however, was not an option. His mother was firmly against it and her threats were not to be taken lightly.

It also looked increasingly unlikely that Sarah was coming to join him in Belfast. He was surprised he had not heard from her. She had not even written to say she would not be coming. He wondered if perhaps she was waiting until after the baby was born before travelling, but quickly dismissed the idea. She would have written to tell him so. The letter he had written to Barbara had not been answered either. As he could think of no logical reason for this silence, he assumed that both Sarah and Barbara had decided to cut him out of their lives. The thought of it depressed him. He realised that Barbara had only ever been an impossible dream – after all, she, too, was an English Protestant. Although it dawned on him that it would not have mattered: he would have given up everything for her. Not that she would ever have him now, after the way he had treated Sarah. And Sarah was lost to him too, as was their baby. The baby would be due about now, he mused. A little girl would be nice, but a son would be good too. His face clouded over as he realised that somewhere out there would be his child and he would never get to meet it. He would never know whether it was a boy or a girl. He did deeply regret that. He reached a decision. He would give it another two weeks and, if he had heard nothing from England after that time, he would move on. He had had enough of working on building sites and even the thought of another winter working in freezing conditions made him shiver. If he was not going to be part of his baby's life, then he would make a new life for himself.

Danny was unaware that just as he had reached that decision, his mother was reading Sarah's latest letter to him. Mary Ann was curious as to who Barbara was and why, when or how, he had written to her. She thought she had censored all Danny's post. That, however, was simply a sideline to the main thrust of the letter. So, she pondered, her first grandchild was an English bastard. After all her years spent uttering that curse, she ended up connected to one. The irony was not lost on her. She shook her head. At least the girl (Mary Ann did not even wish to say her name) had the sense to see that Danny was never going to be a part of her life and, it seemed, wanted nothing more to do with him. 'And that makes two of us!' she said to the empty room.

Just at that moment, the door open and in walked her neighbour, May McCormack. Mary Ann hastily stuffed the letter into the pocket of her apron.

'Mary Ann, you cudn't spare us a bit o' butter till the weekend?'

'Go and help yourself, May. Do you fancy a cup of tea while you're here?'

'I won't say no.' answered May agreeably and, after helping herself to her needs, settled down on the over-stuffed brown couch.

'So any news of your Seamus's wife? She must be due by now.'

'Overdue more like.' retorted Mary Ann.

'Ach, well, I wouldn't worry,' said May, 'When the apple's ripe it'll fall.'

Both women nodded sagely. They spent an agreeable half hour discussing childbirth, the difficulties thereof, and the latest gossip of the neighbourhood. Yet, despite May McCormack being her oldest friend and closest neighbour, Mary Ann mentioned not a word about the newest addition to her family.

Danny, however, could think of little else. Although he had not actually wanted a child, and had tried to ignore its imminent arrival as much as possible, the idea of never seeing it when it was born caused a knot to form in the pit of his stomach. It was made worse by the evident joy his brother was experiencing. Seamus and Mairead were obviously delighted and looking forward eagerly to their impending parenthood. Seamus had rarely left Mairead's side, not even for his usual drink in Mullen's, since a week before her due date. By the time she was eight days overdue, Seamus was feeling the strain. Every time his wife so much as burped, he was running for the midwife. Danny had got into the habit of calling in to see them on his way home from work.

As he turned into Beechmount he could see his brother walking up the street. Seamus looked distracted. Danny had to call his name before he noticed. When he recognised his brother, he ran to him.

'Danny! Danny! She's started! She's started! The baby's on its way!'

Danny laughed at his agitation.

'Calm down, calm down', he exhorted him. 'Is the midwife with her?'

'Yes, that's why I'm out here. She chased me out of my own home.' he added dolefully.

'Don't worry. Look, I'm sure everything's under control. She'll be fine.'

Just at that, a piercing scream rent the air and Seamus ran into the house again, only to be pushed out seconds later by his mother-in-law.

'Here, Danny', she commanded. 'Make yourself useful. Take this one down to the pub out of the road or we'll never get this child born.'

Danny man-handled a reluctant Seamus up the street towards the Beehive.

'Come on, Seamus. You're better off out of the way. Let's leave it to the womenfolk. Anyway, it looks like you could do with a drink to settle your nerves.'

Seamus was not really the best of company that evening. His thoughts were, understandably, elsewhere. He did not even notice what he was drinking, downing whatever was put in front of him with a gulp. Every five minutes he would ask anxiously : 'Will she be alright? Should I go home now? What if there's a problem and I'm not there?'

Danny tried his best to be supportive, saying with a confidence he did not feel: 'She'll be fine, women do this all the time. You're better off staying here. And sure, what good would you be if something did go wrong? Not that it's going too!' he added hastily, as Seamus looked stricken. Coping with Seamus was hard work. He sincerely hoped that Mairead's labour would not be a long one.

It was almost nine o'clock before the pub doors opened and a young urchin shouted in, 'Seamus McAllister! If yer here, me ma says you've to come home right away! And to hurry yerself!'

Seamus jumped up immediately.

'I'm a daddy!' he cried, just before the alcohol hit him and he collapsed in a drunken heap on the floor.

Chapter Twenty-four

Danny slowly poured the jug of water the barman had presented him with over the prone body of his elder brother.

'Come on, Seamus! You can't lie there all night. Get yourself up.'

Seamus finally sat up with a splutter. A stupid grin started to spread across his face as memory flooded back.

'Here, Danny. Lend me a hand.'

As his brother stooped to help him up, Seamus remonstrated with him.

'What did you let me get into such a state for? Mairead'll kill me for being so drunk.'

'It was hardly my fault. You were knocking them back like they were going to ban drink tomorrow! Come on, now, let's get you home.'

Staggering as they walked, Seamus continued to regale Danny with his plans for the future.

'If it's a boy, we're going to call him Joseph John. Joe after me Da and John after Mairead's Da. And if it's a girl, it's gonna be called Margaret Mary. Margaret after Mairead's Ma and Mary after my Ma.'

'Yea, yea, I get the picture, you've only told me about a hundred times before.' Danny replied, struggling to keep his brother upright and on the pavement.

'Joe or Maggie May! Not Peggy! Maggie May!' Seamus said emphatically, with the usual staunch conviction of the truly drunk man.

Danny was relieved when they reach the corner of Beechmount as, having taken more than a few drinks himself; his efforts to support Seamus were becoming more difficult with every step. He was looking forward to collapsing onto a chair for a while before making his way home.

Turning the corner, Danny pulled up short. His brother, slower on the uptake, muttered a slurry 'Wha's up?' before his eyes, too, focused on the ambulance further up the street.

'It might not be your house Seamus.' Danny offered reassuringly, yet knowing, beyond all doubt, that it most definitely was.

'Mairead!' cried Seamus, launching himself towards the small crowd who had gathered around the ambulance. They stood aside silently, to let him pass. Margaret, his mother-in-law, grabbed him as he tried to peer into the back of the vehicle.

'Seamus, there's been a problem. The doctor's been and he says she has to go to the hospital.'

Before he could ask any questions, a murmur from the bystanders turned their attention to the doorway, where Mairead, wrapped in blankets, was being carried out on a stretcher. The overwhelming fear for his wife's safety had rendered Seamus as sober as a judge. As he leaned over the stretcher, calling her name, she appeared to be in too much pain to respond but her hand sought his and he grasped it tightly.

'It'll be alright! Everything will be fine!' he practically shouted at her in his earnestness for it to be so. Still holding her hand, he clamoured up the ambulance steps and sat beside her, continuing to utter reassuring sounds. Margaret turned to Danny before she too, climbed into the vehicle. 'They're taking her to the Royal. Let your mam know.' Danny continued to stare blankly as the doors closed and the ambulance took off, sirens blaring.

'What happened?' he asked in bewilderment to the person at his side.

'Not sure, mate. You'll have to ask the midwife. That's her there.'

Danny followed the direction of the pointing finger to where a middle-aged woman stood, buttoning her coat.

'Excuse me. That's my sister-in-law they've just taken away. What's wrong with her?'

The woman shook her head. 'I'm sorry son. I did all I could. Just the baby's head was too big and she wasn't opening enough. As soon as I realised she was in distress I sent for the doctor. But even he wasn't able to do anything. That's why he sent for the ambulance. Listen', she continued as Danny continued to stare blankly at her. 'I'm sure it'll be fine. Sure they can work wonders nowadays up in the hospital. Why don't you go on home and let your family know what's happening. They'll be worried.' As Danny turned to go, the midwife called after him: 'I did all I could, you know. It's not my fault.'

Digging his hands deep into his trouser pockets, Danny headed for home. Normally he would have walked the few miles to his mother's house but on this occasion he hopped onto a passing trolleybus. The quicker he got home the better. At that time of night the traffic flowed freely and he was home within ten minutes. He steadied himself and took a deep breath before opening the front door.

'Mam?' he called needlessly, as his mother was sitting in her usual chair. She took one look at his face and knew something was wrong.

'What is it? What's happened?'

'It's Mairead. She's been taken to hospital. There's something wrong with the baby.' Danny explained as succinctly as he could. Mary Ann fire a few questions at him, most of which he could not answer. All he could add was that Mairead had been taken to the Royal Maternity Hospital. Reaching for her handbag and her hat and coat, she called up the stairs:

'Bernadette! Anne Marie! Come here!' As the two girls appeared on the staircase in answer to their mother's summons, she continued to issue instructions while stabbing her hat with pins: 'Bernadette: you stay here and look after Kevin. Ann Marie, get your coat, you're coming with me. Where's Catherine? Is she still at Jim McKeever's house? Well, when she gets home send her round to Seamus and Mairead's house. She might be needed there.'

'Where we going, Mam?' queried Anne Marie.

'I'll explain as we go.' replied Mary Ann grimly.

It took them ten minutes to reach the hospital and another twenty before they could find the right ward. Finally, they spied Seamus, pacing up and down a corridor in agitation, worry and frustration. On hearing his mother's voice, he ran to her, throwing his arms around her neck and burrowing his head in her ample bosom, the way he had done as a child whenever something had caused him pain.

'Mammy, mammy! What am I going to do?' he wailed.

'There, there, shush, shush', soothed his mother. 'It's all going to be alright, you'll see.' She continued to make comforting sounds while patting his back until the sobbing subsided.

'Anne Marie, go and get your brother a cup of tea. One of the nurses will show you where to get it. Here', she dug into her handbag. 'Here's some money. Hurry back.'

Anne Marie was glad to have something to do. It scared her to see her big brother, who always seemed so grown-up and cheerful, lose control in that way.

By the time she returned with two teas in green Bakelite cups, Seamus and Mary Ann were engrossed in conversation with what looked like a very senior doctor. His white coat was open to reveal a brown tweed suit and a stethoscope hung round his neck. Anne Marie hurried over, mindless of the slopping tea.

'Unfortunately, the child's heart gave out. It was just too much of a struggle for too long. Had we got her here earlier we might have been able to do something but I'm afraid… well. All I can say is that I'm sorry for your loss.'

'And Mairead? How is she?'

'She's exhausted, obviously, and to be truthful, she has been torn pretty badly inside, due to the baby's struggles, and she's lost a lot of blood.' He paused, then added more cheerfully, 'But we're hoping she'll pull through.'

Seamus's face had drained of all colour. The doctor's words seemed so callous, so everyday, as if he did not mind one way or another whether Mairead lived or died. Suppressing a desire to punch him repeatedly and forcefully in the face, Seamus asked instead, 'Can I see my wife, Doctor?' His request was uttered in a strange, strangled tone, as if he was struggling to keep from screaming.

'You can see her for a moment but please don't mention the baby. Let's wait until she's a little stronger, eh?'

As he followed in the doctor's wake, Anne Marie looked after her brother with sympathy. She noticed he had his hands clenched tightly by his side.

So tightly in fact, that his nails had dug into his palms and had drawn blood. He did not appear to notice.

Chapter Twenty-five

The priest's sermon centred on the theme of 'suffer little children to come unto me and hinder them not', and was preached to a packed congregation. Relatives, neighbours, friends, even people not directly connected to the family, had crowded into the church to pay their respects to the parents and to honour a child they had never known. The McAllister and the McCann families stood side by side in the front pews, trying hard to support each other through this trial. In the end, however, watching Seamus carry the tiny white coffin, barely bigger than a shoe box, in his arms, tears sliding unchecked down his cheeks, the emotion of the moment overcame them all. They tried coping in their different ways. John McCann started ordering people about, directing his wife, daughter and Mary Ann towards the funeral car, ordering the funeral directors where to place the flowers and generally doing anything that would block the thought that he was attending the funeral of his first grandchild. Taking control of the mundane helped subdue the raging anger inside him at not being able to control the most important thing of all. Danny kept pinching the bridge of his nose and coughing through clenched teeth in an effort to stem the tears, while around him the women of the congregation, friends and strangers, were weeping openly.

As they proceeded slowly towards the cemetery, Seamus walked in front bearing his dead daughter. Behind him, Danny and Joe McCann walked silently and blindly, locked in thoughts of the bitterness of life. The officiating priest had been joined by Father Hanson and they had taken up a position, one on each side of the funeral car. Inside the vehicle, Mairead was flanked by her mother and her mother-in law, all dressed in black. Behind streamed a long line of men, most with hands clasped reverently in front of them. There was little conversation. This was not the usual funeral of an old friend; someone they knew who had lived a full and, most likely, decadent, life. Someone they could tell tales about, tales that usually started: 'Do you mind the time…?' and culminating in some embellished embarrassing incident. There was no laughter, no anecdotes, no low-key conversations about the next horse race. This was a serious and solemn occasion.

At the graveside - a huge gaping hole, far too big for the tiny little coffin - the priest delivered the Catholic rites for the un-baptised child. No-one really heard. Even had the mourners been listening, the wind would have whipped the words away, or they would have been drowned by the cawing of the hooded crows, whose territory the graveyard was. Eventually, one of the funeral directors stepped forward and relieved Seamus of his burden. He let it go without demur, too dead inside to raise a protest. The diminutive casket was laid to rest. As the first clods of earth thudded against the wooden box, a heart rending wail rent the air. Mairead fell to her knees and would have toppled into the grave had not Margaret and Mary Ann been at her side to grab hold of her.

Seamus and Danny moved quickly to her side. On feeling her husband's presence, Mairead turned and started thumping his chest. 'My baby! My baby! Why? Why?'

Seamus could do nothing to comfort her. He simply held her close until exhaustion set in and she could struggle no more. He lead her back to the car in almost total silence, save the harsh mocking call of the crows. The journey home was much quicker but seemed interminable as Mairead, beyond speech now, rocked to and fro, lost in her world of grief, beyond the reach of comfort.

Back at the McCann's house, Anne Marie, Bernadette and Catherine had prepared the traditional funeral tea. The best china had been brought from their house to marry up with that of the McCann family, as well as some crockery borrowed from neighbours. Friends had brought round additional foodstuffs: a shank of ham, some roast chicken, extra tea, a home-made cake. At such times as theses, the community rallied round in a show of support for the bereaved. A small group of women and children had gather around outside of the house, waiting to pay their respects. As the funeral car drew up, they parted respectfully to make way for the bereaved.

When the chief mourners were ensconced at the head of the table, the rest of the mourners drifted in: 'I'm sorry for your trouble.' 'It's a sad loss.' 'We must accept God's will.' Mairead, Seamus and the rest of their family members accepted these trite comments in the spirit in which they were meant. What, after all, could anyone say to help heal a hurt that cut so deeply to the core of your being, that changed not only your life, but the lives of those around you and even the way that you viewed life and the future. The future should have contained sleepless nights worrying over teething, childhood illnesses, school results, and the hundred and one other problems that plague ordinary parents. Instead, an emptiness that nothing could dispel stretched darkly ahead.

Few of the mourners stayed longer than politeness demanded. The death of a child was too painful for them to stomach. The men left for the pub, as was traditional, leaving the womenfolk to clear up the remains of the funeral tea. Eventually, all that remained were three or four women, not including the bereaved. These women, despite other demands on their time, were not going to leave any time soon. If need be, they would stay all night. They were the ones who did know what it was like to lose a child, either in similar circumstances or in a later incident. They knew how deeply that pain cut. How dark the future looked. They knew that 'accidents' could happen to distraught mothers at these times. They knew, also, that the childless mother needed to talk about her loss. It was more than the loss of a child: it was the loss of a future, of a role, of all the dreams and plans. It was the shock that life could be so cruel.

They talked of their own losses, offered as proof that life did go on, that it was, present circumstances notwithstanding, still worth living. 'Sure you're young, Mairead. Plenty of time for you to have more wee 'uns. Look at me. I lost my first two, but the next four were all fine.' The other women nodded in a chorus of agreement. 'Aye, you're young yet.' 'Plenty of time' 'You'll fall again before you know it.' Mary Ann and Margaret exchanged silent glances over Mairead's head. Although they said nothing, they communicated everything. The other women stopped talking. Had it been lit up in neon it could not have been more obvious. The sympathy in the room was almost tangible as they realised that all Mairead's chances of motherhood had died with her child.

Chapter Twenty-six

It was a cold, bleak, late November day when Danny McAllister packed up his tools and walked off the building site. He ignored the threats that Packy Boyle fired after him and headed for the nearest bus stop. He climbed to the top deck and immediately lit a cigarette. It was a habit he had only recently acquired but he enjoyed it. Smoking gave him the air of having something to do when he had really nothing but thoughts chasing themselves around his head. He did not know if his own child was alive or dead, and it seemed, he never would. And it was no-one's fault but his own, he reproached himself. While there was Seamus, wanting a child so much, so eagerly looking forward to it and now likely to remain childless forever. Life had a nasty habit of promising so much and delivering so little.

Ever since the death of his niece, Danny had been unable to focus on anything properly. His work suffered, he argued with friends, snapped at his sisters, and he used any excuse to avoid meeting with his brother. He was overwhelmed by feelings of guilt and helplessness. When the men at work had started talking about Christmas and complaining about how much the 'little bleeders' were going to cost them, Danny could take no more. He decided it was time to move on.

Dismounting from the bus, he walked the few streets to the Merchant Navy recruitment bureau. He paused for a moment or two outside reading the advertising posters: 'It's a great life!' they promised. He had his doubts on that score but entered into the office anyway. Although he had no naval experience and his academic work record was poor, he was signed up immediately, subject to physical. As neither he nor the recruiting officer had any qualms on that issue, Danny was convinced he would be sailing away from the troubles of Belfast before long. Now, all that remained was to let his mother know.

She would not be happy, he was certain of that, but it could not be helped. He could no longer remain in Belfast: he could no longer return to London. By joining the Navy, he would be safe from romantic entanglements, which at this point in his life suited him well enough, and he would be able to see a bit of the world while he was still young enough to enjoy it. His mother was surprised to see him home so early.

'What's wrong, now? You haven't lost your job an all, have you?', she queried, always ready to think the worse.

'No, I haven't lost it. I've jacked it in.'

'What on God's earth have you done that for? Sure that was a great wee job! Set for life you were! And you were making good money. Don't be thinking you can lie around the house all day, for I'm not going to keep any lazy good-for-nothing! If you don't work, you don't get fed!'

Danny let her rant on for a few minutes more before explaining his plans to her. She sat in contemplation for a few minutes. Finally, she spoke: 'I'm not happy, Danny. I don't want you going far away for months at a time. But I can see you're not happy here at home. It's been building for a while, and with the baby …'. She did not finish the sentence. 'Well, I'll not stand in your way. Have you any idea when you'll be leaving?'

They sat and discussed his future plans for a while until Bernadette, returning home from work, interrupted them.

The next few weeks flew by. There was more to joining the navy than Danny had realised. Apart from the medical, there was the aptitude test, then he had to see Father Hanson for a character reference, and soothe things over with Packy Boyle in order to obtain a reference from his last employer. That took three pints and half a bottle of whiskey before Packy agreed: 'You wasn't the worst in the world. Come and see me tomorrow. I'll tell some decent lies about you, lad.' He also had to do the rounds of the friends and acquaintances he had collected since he had come back to Belfast. There was rarely a night that he was not in Mullen's bar. His sisters were upset he was leaving, and set to work planning his going away party, while young Kevin, despite originally being delighted at having his big brother living at home, was more delighted at the prospect of having a room to himself again.

As the day of his departure drew closer, Danny knew he could not leave without visiting Seamus and Mairead. He had been avoiding them, simply because he could find no words to express his feelings of rage and anger and regret and despair and sorrow for their loss. Yet he knew he had to face it. He could not leave without at least saying goodbye. They were just finishing Sunday lunch when he arrived.

'My timing's off! A while back I'd have made sure I was here in time for dinner!'

The response was a weak smile and an invitation to sit down and join them in a cup of tea. Danny refused. 'Is it all right if I take this one out to the pub?' He directed the question at Mairead. 'It's his last chance to buy me a drink before I'm off on my travels. And he owes me plenty!'

Mairead set down the plates she was holding. She looked older, thinner, more drained of life. 'I suppose it'll do no harm. Don't be getting him too drunk, now! I want him back in time for tea.' Even Danny could see the effort it cost her to try and act like a normal wife would under the circumstances. 'Don't worry, Mairead. He's safe with me.'

The brothers chatted aimlessly as they made their way to the public house and ordered their drinks. It was only after they were halfway through the first pint that Danny broached the subject that had been hanging over them.

'So. How are you holding up?'

Seamus shook his head, probably in an attempt to force back the welling tears.

'It's hard.' he said at last. 'Mairead's taking it very hard. I don't know what to do for the best. I don't know whether to talk about it or ignore it. Whether I should suggest we visit the grave or not. As it is, she cries herself to sleep every night. At first she used to cry in my arms but now she waits until she thinks I'm asleep before she starts. It's as if she doesn't want me involved. But I'm not sleeping either and even though I feel like screaming, I keep my mouth shut for her sake. I don't know what to do for the best because nothing I can say or do is going to comfort her and make up for the loss of our baby.'

Danny said nothing. Encouraged by the silence, his brother gave vent to his pent-up feelings.

'I blame myself. If I hadn't been getting drunk in the pub I'd have known things were going wrong. I could have made sure she got to hospital earlier. I wasn't there when my wife and child needed me!'

He put his head in his hands in an effort to hide the tears.

Danny was dumbstruck. How could Seamus think it was his fault? It was Danny who had taken him to the pub at Margaret's suggestion. 'And what', he asked Seamus, 'do you know about childbirth? Are you a doctor? Or one of those gynocolist thingies? Experts? How could it be your fault? You did as you were told, what countless fathers have done before you and will, no doubt, do in future. You are not to blame.'

Taking his brother by the shoulders, he looked him steadily in the eye: 'Look at me Seamus, Look at me!' he commanded. 'You are not to blame!'

If Danny expected his brother to go, 'Oh, well, that's all right, then', he was doomed to disappointment.

'Of courses I'm to blame! I should have been there for her! I let her down when she needed me most! And now, I'm no use to her at all. I may as well join the navy as well. Get as far away from this place as possible. Mairead would be better off without me.' he added bitterly.

'Don't talk nonsense' urged his brother. 'You'd be lost without Mairead!'

Seamus nodded his agreement. 'You're right. I know Mairead would be better off without me, but I can't live without Mairead. She's my world. When I thought I was going to lose her as well as the baby, I prayed to God to take me instead. I wish to God he had.' he ended fervently.

Danny remained silent. There was nothing he could say.

Apart from goodbye.

Chapter Twenty-seven

Dear Sarah,

As usual, I hope you and baby Jean are keeping in the best of health and that your grandmother is not too poorly.

Quite a bit has happened here since I last wrote to you. For a start, I'll be looking for a new flatmate soon, as Clare has just got engaged! You know she was keen on the branch manager where she worked? Well, turns out he was keen on her too! They got together at the Christmas office party and have been inseparable ever since. Even though it has only been eight weeks since they met, they have both decided not to wait any longer. They are getting married in June and I'm to be bridesmaid! He's a really nice guy and seems to think the world of her and she is completely dotty about him so I'm really pleased for both of them.

On the other side of the coin, Elvis and I have split. Things had not been going very well for a while so we decided to call it a day. He has gone back to Scotland and if you want to write to him, I have his address. Only thing is, you have to address the letter to Robert Campbell as he refuses to answer to Elvis any more. You'll never believe this, but he has cut his hair and shaved his sideburns! He looks so strange without them that you wouldn't recognise him. So now I have no boyfriend and before long, I'll have no flatmate. Are you sure you and Jean don't want to come and live with me? I could certainly use the company. Only joking. I know you can't leave your grandmother. Is she getting any better? Did the last lot of medication help at all? I know you won't mind when I tell you that I laughed out loud when I read in your last letter that she had taken the rubber duck from the bathroom and tried to set it free!

Seriously, though, it must be very difficult for you, trying to look after your grandmother and a baby at the same time, and all on your own. I wish I could be of some help. I don't know how you'll take this, but what if I were to come and visit you for a week or two? I'm due some holidays soon and I could take a room in the village pub. That way I won't be crowding you but we can still get together every day. Let me know what you think. I wouldn't like to impose.

And changing the subject totally, have you heard anything from you-know-who? In your last letter you said you had decided to write to him to tell him about Jean but that he had never got back to you. Is this still the case? I can't believe he could ignore the fact that he has a daughter – and such a pretty one at that! But I suppose it's none of my business so I'll shut up now and get this letter signed off before it turns into a book! Ha Ha! Write back soon!

With all my best wishes. Give Jean a big kiss from me.

Bye for now,

Barbara XX

Dear Barbara,

It would be so lovely to see you again, but why on earth would you take a room at the village pub when there is oodles of room here! I won't hear of you staying anywhere else but with me – if you think you can stand all the crying, the silly goings-on, and the night-time wailing. And the baby and granny aren't too quiet either! Ha Ha!

Seriously, Jean is a love and is now sleeping through the night, which is just as well as Gran appears to be getting worse. I've had to put a lock on her bedroom door to stop her going down to the Market Square in the middle of the night to talk to the war memorial statue. I don't know why it seems to hold a particular fascination for her, but she was found there, wearing nothing but her nightie, on two separate occasions. Now it's easier to lock her in for her own safety. I'm afraid of her falling down the stairs or hurting herself in some way. I'd never forgive myself if something bad happened to her.

Apart from Gran making a show of herself, nothing much happens here. You'll probably find it deadly dull after London. The highlight of the week is the Saturday market, when all the farmers from miles around bring in eggs and vegetables and stuff to sell. Lord knows why when you can buy exactly the same stuff in the local shop every day of the week. My friend, Hannah, says they really come in looking for a wife! So, you never know, you might find yourself a new boyfriend after all!

Sorry that was tactless. I am sorry you and Elvis – sorry! Robert, - have spilt up. I thought you made a great couple but hey! what do I know about men eh? I still haven't heard anything from Danny. I'm not sure that I expected to. But it was strange him sending that letter to you. As I say, I'll never understand men. I do hope Clare has better luck than either of us! Give her my congratulations, won't you. I'll send her a letter separately but just in case, wish her all the best from me and Jean.

Write soon and let me know when you can visit. Anytime suits me, but Easter might be nice if you can manage it then?

All the best for now. Jean sends her love.

Sarah

Chapter Twenty-eight

Mary Ann could see little sign of improvement in her first born son. It was three months since the funeral yet, to judge by his demeanour, it could have been yesterday. He rarely smiled, the usual banter between him and his siblings was missing and he often sat silent for long periods. Another area of concern was how often he called to the house to see her. Not a day passed that he did not drop by to see how she was. The length of his visits gradually increased as well. At first, it had only been for five or ten minutes, then it was half an hour. Recently, he had stayed until Mary Ann was ready for bed. It was as if he did not want to go home. She wondered what Mairead thought of his new behaviour pattern. One thing was for certain: it could not continue. Mary Ann believed it her duty to interfere.

Choosing a time when she knew no one else would be around, she paid a visit to her daughter-in-law. After the usual greeting and cup of tea, and the small talk, Mary Ann finally got to the point.

'So. How's things with you and Seamus, then?'

Mairead looked into her teacup, as if the answer lay there.

'Fine.' she lied.

'Come on, Mairead, I wasn't born yesterday. Things are far from fine. He's avoiding you and you're not doing a thing to change it!'

'What can I do? I can't do anything right! If I nag him, he storms out: if I say nothing, he says I don't care: if I try to talk to him, he says he's busy and if I say nothing he accuses me of ignoring him! So you tell me! What can I do?

'How long has this been going on?' Mary Ann probed.

'Only for the past month or so. At first, after the … you know'. Mairead could not bring herself to mention the death of her child.

'Well, at first, he would hold me and let me cry myself to sleep. But I could see it was upsetting him and so I tried not to cry until after he had gone to sleep. And then he started coming to bed later and later. I would pretend to be asleep so that he wouldn't think he was disturbing me. Now, it's like we're two strangers sharing a bed. And it's not much better the rest of the time either. If he's not working, he's at your house. I don't think he even goes to the pub any more, not since Danny left.'

'I think he blames himself for the child's death.' Mary Ann was nothing if not blunt.

'But that's just silly!' cried Mairead. 'There was no one to blame but me. If I hadn't been so insistent on having the baby at home – if I'd booked into the hospital like Seamus suggested – but oh no! I knew best! I wanted a home birth just like my mum and her mum before her. And it was my silly pride. I'd never been in hospital and I wanted to boast I never would be. And now look at me. If I had gone to the hospital like Seamus wanted, our child would be alive and well, instead of dead and buried! It's all my fault I lost our baby. And worse still,' Mairead's face was streaming with tears by this stage, 'I can never have any more children! What sort of a wife does that make me?'

'Hush, hush', soothed Mary Ann, patting Mairead's knee in a comforting manner.

'What will be, will be. You weren't to know it was going to be a difficult birth. The changes we'd make if we could only see the future! Look', she took Mairead's hand in her own: 'Do you still love my son?'

Through the tears, Mairead looked stunned. 'Love him? Of course I love him. He's my world. But why would he love me? What sort of a wife can I ever be to him?' she wailed, bursting into tears again.

'My Seamus thinks the world of you, too. He's just not good at facing up to things. You're trying to avoid upsetting him, he's trying to avoid upsetting you, and the both of you are only making it worse for each other. But listen up, I have a plan that will help put things right. Seamus needs to see that it's all right for both of you to grieve. Have you been to the grave since the funeral?'

Mairead shook her head. 'I didn't want to go on my own and I didn't want to ask Seamus to go with me in case it upset him.'

'Well, when Seamus calls in tonight, I'll tell him I want to go to the cemetery and that I want you two to come with me. He'll not say no to me.'

With that, Mary Ann stood up and started buttoning her coat with the attitude of one who has just tackled a difficult task and won resoundingly. 'Right', she said as she took her leave: 'I'll see you here on Sunday, two o'clock sharp. Mind you're ready!'

She marched up the street, her head full of schemes for the future. Her first duty, she believed, was to ensure that her son and daughter-in-law supported each other in their grief, instead of each pretending everything was 'fine' as Mairead had initially tried to imply. No good came of bottling up feelings of that nature. Naturally, Mary Ann believed equally strongly that it did not do to wear one's heart on one's sleeve, nor to cry in public, but if there was grieving to be done, best that the people involved did it together, preferably in the privacy of their own bedroom. They would never get to that stage, however, without an honest discussion of how they both felt. Mary Ann intended to ensure that that discussion would take place because, without it, the healing process could not start. And they needed to be strong together again for what she had in mind.

Arriving home, she checked that she had the house to herself before sitting down to write a letter.

Dear Sarah,

I am Danny's mother. You may be surprised to get this letter from me. Danny has gone of with the navy as he wants to see a bit of the world and he says the life is good. The night afore he went we had a party and he got drunk and he told me all about you and showed me the letter what you wrote him. I cannot tell you how shocked I was. He never told me he had a girl-friend, let alone a baby! I am very angery at him for deserting you. Had I knowed he had a baby I would have made him marry you. It is to late now as he will be half away round the world by the time you get this. I am sorry about that but I would very much like to see my first grandchild. I understand that you can not leave your grandmother who I am very sorry to hear is not well. I was thinking that I could come and visit you and my granddaughter if it is all right with you. I will understand if you dont want nothing to do with us after the way my son has treated you but Jean is my family as well now and I would like to aknowlegde her and get to know her and you to. Please do not say 'NO' as I am deeply ashamed of the way my son has treated you and I would like to make up for it.

Yours respectfully,

Mary Ann McAllister.

PS. Please give wee Jean a kiss from her Granny.

Mary Ann read over the letter again. She was pleased with the result. It sounded sincere and apologetic and she believed it would take a hard heart indeed to refuse what seemed like a reasonable request. She was glad now that the last letter from Sarah had not found its way into the flames as the others had. Having been interrupted by May, she had stuffed the letter in to her pinafore pocket where it lay hidden until she had retired to bed. She had placed it in the dresser drawer, intending to burn it the next day but the intervening tragic events had pushed it out of her mind and it had lain, ignored, in the drawer until now. Folding the letter she had just written, she placed it in the envelope and carefully copied the Yorkshire address. She decided to post this letter herself. She wanted nothing to go wrong.

Placing the envelope in her voluminous black handbag, she went to her bedroom where she retrieved a square biscuit tin from under the mattress. She opened it to reveal a number of five and one pound notes. She counted it carefully. The small fortune of one hundred and forty three pounds had taken over thirty years of penny watching to accumulate. She would rather starve than dip in to her savings. But desperate times required desperate measures and, if all went according to plan, it would be money well spent.

Chapter Twenty-nine

When Mary Ann first set foot on English ground, she felt overwhelmed, rather scared and slightly panic-stricken. The sea crossing had been smooth, especially so for March, but Mary Ann still felt a bit shaken by it. Luckily, she had brought Anne Marie with her, both for company and as an accomplice to her plan. Anne Marie was young enough to treat the entire trip as one big adventure. It was she who approached the uniformed official to ask for directions to the train station and her sparkling good looks had encouraged the young man to escort her and her mother further than duty demanded. At the station Anne Marie again came into her own as the guard helped her find the right train for their destination, directed her to the platform and explained carefully where they had to change trains and which platform they would need there. His reward was a beautiful beaming smile from Anne Marie and a grudging nod from Mary Ann: she did not want English people to be nice nor helpful. She wanted to be able to complain about everything.

As the train lurched out of the station, making quite a racket as it rattled over the rails, Anne Marie looked out the window, determined to take advantage of the trip to drink in as much of the view as humanly possible. It was the first time she had ever been out of Ireland. In fact, she had barely been out of Belfast before so everything was new and exciting to her. It was also Mary Ann's biggest adventure but, as befitted her age and dignity, she felt it would not be seemly to look like an excitable schoolgirl, so she sat rigidly in her seat with her back to the engine, clutching her handbag and staring straight ahead. As conversation would have been difficult anyway over the noise of the chugging train, she let her mind turn to recent events.

Accompanying Seamus and Mairead to the graveyard had been harrowing, but necessary. There had been very few people in Milltown cemetery at that time on the Sunday afternoon and it did not take long to reach the freshly dug grave. As they approached, with a degree of trepidation, Mairead groped for and found Seamus's hand. Together, they had stood at the foot of their child's grave. There was no headstone as yet and the wreaths had faded, as had the hand-written messages of condolences attached to them. There was a few moments of utter silence before Mairead, with tears flowing silently down her cheeks, started to mutter, 'I'm sorry. I'm so very sorry.' Putting his arms around her, and with tears filling his own eyes, Seamus cried in anguish: 'It's my fault! It's all my fault! I let you down!' Clinging to each other, they cried like babies until eventually the heaving, heartfelt wailing gave way to softer sobbing and sniffles. Moving to a nearby bench, while Mary Ann pretended interest in a grave some distance away, Mr and Mrs McAllister had their first real heart-to-heart since the death of their child.

They took turns accepting all blame for the tragedy, despite protests, and they expressed amazement that the other even thought for a moment that it was in any way their fault. Each forgave the other for any perceived culpability. Once they realised and accepted how the unexpected death had affected them both, it dawned on them that each had been trying to protect the other by pretending that they were coping; Mairead by crying only when she thought she was alone, and Seamus by avoiding Mairead so that she could cry on her own. They promised to be more honest, open and supportive of each other.

Mairead's greatest concern for the future, however, was her inability to have any more children and, for the first time, she raised these concerns with her husband. She explained that she did not feel like a proper wife, not even a proper woman, if she could not give him children. Seamus, not normally the most eloquent of men, tried to find the right words to reassure her.

'Mairead, ever since I first met you, you were all that I ever wanted. If the rest of the world disappeared, as long as there was you, I would be happy. I never needed anyone but you. Yes, it would have been nice to have had a family of our own, but it wasn't to be and we just have to accept God's will. Who knows why he took our baby from us? Maybe it's the price I had to pay to make up for being so happy with you. But I can't blame God. After all, He was good enough to give you to me in the first place and I am eternally grateful for that. Let's just be thankful we have each other because, at the end of the day, you, and you alone, is all that really matters to me.'

As she buried her head in his chest, Mairead's tears started to mutate from grief to relief. As long as Seamus still loved and wanted her, as long as he did not despise her stupidity and her barrenness, she would get through this trial eventually. Losing her child had been like losing a part of herself: losing Seamus would be to lose life itself.

'I thought you would stop loving me if I couldn't have children.' she confessed.

'Mairead! My love! My Mairead! I could stop breathing easier than I could stop loving you!'

Anxiously, as a thought struck him, he raised her chin until he could see her eyes: 'You do still love me, don't you?'

'More than life itself!' she declared hugging him close once more.

They had clung to one another for some time before Seamus looked up to see his mother approaching. Giving her a quick kiss before gently levering Mairead away from him, he greeted Mary Ann brightly: 'Well, was your friend's grave still there? Come on, let's go home and have some tea.'

Taking Mairead under one arm and his mother under the other, Seamus steered them towards the cemetery gates. As they strolled along, Mary Ann studied their tear-streaked faces and, judging by the way they held each other and exchanged loving glances, was satisfied that the worse was over. Now she just had to wait for a reply to her letter.

She did not have to wait long. On the Wednesday after the visit to the cemetery, the postman delivered Sarah's response.

Dear Mrs McAllister,

It was a delightful surprise to receive your letter. Of course you must come and visit! You are right, Jean is part of your family now and it would be unfair to you and to Jean not to have the opportunity to get to know each other. Let me know when you are coming over and I will have your room ready as, of course, I insist that you stay with us! You must spend as much time with your granddaughter as possible. She is six months old now and a proper little madam but so adorable. I am sure you will love her as much as I do when you meet her.

I should let you know that I do not hold you in any way responsible for Danny's behaviour. He is, after all, a grown man and can make his own decisions. It is a shame he did not tell you about me and Jean earlier but now you know, we can start being a proper family.

I am so looking forward to meeting you – and so is Jean. She sends kisses to her Granny!

With all Best Wishes,

Sarah

The smile on Mary Ann's lips as she read and re-read the letter was far from mirthful. It was more a smirk of triumph. She folded the letter, placed it in her pocket, then called up the stairs:

'Anne Marie! Come here! We're going on a little trip!'

Anne Marie was slightly shocked at discovering she was an aunt. Her mother told her very little, only that Danny had met some girl while he was in London and that this girl had given birth to his baby. She had also been told that the girl had moved to Yorkshire and that they were going to visit her but on no account was Anne Marie to mention anything about Seamus and Mairead's recent tragedy. 'I don't want this girl to know anything about our personal business.' Mary Ann had stated emphatically. It took several attempts on Ann Marie's part before her mother would even admit that the girl had a name and that that name was Sarah.

Chapter Thirty

Had anyone asked her, Anne Marie would have been forced to admit that she had been under the impression that her mother did not seem enamoured by Sarah's existence. She was slightly puzzled, therefore, by this new version of Mary Ann, the one who was graciously accepting tea and scones and being as nice as nine-pence, even with the dottery old grandmother. She had appeared delighted to meet Sarah, was gushing in her praise for baby Jean and deeply sympathetic towards Lizzie Taylor's illness. Anne Marie was young and naïve. She put Mary Ann's former aversion down to the fact that she had only recently found out about Sarah and it was the shock that had made her so disapproving. Now she had actually met her, no-one could fail to warm to Sarah, thought Anne Marie. She was a lovely girl, bright and friendly, cheerful and welcoming. Anne Marie could perfectly understand why her big brother had fallen for her. She would have been happy to have had Sarah as a sister-in-law.

Sarah, for her part, was genuinely pleased to meet Danny's mother and Anne Marie, his youngest sister. She warmed to Anne Marie immediately.

As well as the facial resemblance, she could see traits of Danny in her demeanour. The two younger women formed an instant friendship. There was a four year gap in their ages but they found plenty to chat about, even when they were not talking about Jean. Danny, however, was conspicuously absent from their conversation. Even Mary Ann tried to avoid mentioning his name. It was not until later that night, when the rest of the household had gone to bed, that Mary Ann sat down to have a heart-to-heart with Sarah over a nice cup of tea.

'All this must be very hard for you.' she started, making the statement sound like a question. Sarah half opened her mouth to give the usual, 'everything's fine' answer but changed her mind. This, after all, was Danny's mother – almost part of the family. She decided to trust Mary Ann with her true feelings.

'It has been hard.' she admitted. 'It's hard enough raising a baby – though don't get me wrong! I love her to bits and wouldn't part with her for a king's ransom! And I could probably manage on my own, even if it is difficult at times, like when she's crying in the middle of the night and I can't get her over to sleep again. I don't have anyone to turn to, to take her off me for a while to let me have a bit of a break. You know? And it is quite lonely as well. Like, if she's done something clever, and I want to say to someone but there's no-one to share that with. You know?'

Mary Ann nodded understandingly. Sarah continued: 'At first, it wasn't so bad as my gran was able to help a bit. But now, well, I can't trust her to be alone with Jean. She's got Senile Dementia and it's getting worse. At first, she was just getting names confused or forgetting simple things. Now, she can't seem to remember anything, even whether she's had lunch or not. I'm afraid to leave her alone with Jean in case there's an accident and I have to keep an eye on her all the time. It's like having two babies in the house.'

'That must be so difficult', agreed Mary Ann, compassionately. 'And how are you managing for money?' she queried.

Sarah sighed. 'Again, it wasn't too bad at first. I'm taking in sewing from the factory on piece work. You know, where you get paid according to how many pieces of work you complete satisfactorily. And while gran wasn't as ill as she is now, and with Jean sleeping most of the time, I was able to get through a good deal and earn decent money. But now, I'm lucky if I can manage half the workload.'

Mary Ann clucked sympathetically, then reached into her voluminous handbag. Withdrawing a small bundle of banknotes, she pressed them into Sarah's hand.

'Here you are, dear. That'll help you out a bit.' As Sarah protested that she couldn't possibly take her money, Mary Ann insisted, continuing, 'You take it to buy something nice for my granddaughter. After all, if Danny won't support you, it's the least I can do. That way you won't have to worry so much about getting your piece work done. And I'll see if I can send you a wee something now and again.'

Sarah was so touched by Mary Ann's thoughtfulness that she could feel the tears welling up in her eyes. She was so grateful to this woman. She could not believe that Danny had made her out to be so rigid and bigoted. It simply confirmed what she had come to believe: Danny had never intended to marry her. He had claimed his mother would never tolerate a protestant in the family yet, here she was, not only tolerating one, but being supportive, helpful and generous.

'Oh Mrs McAllister! That is so good of you! I can't thank you enough! I thought you wanted nothing to do with me and Jean!'

'Don't be silly! And call me Mary Ann.' she commanded.

Sarah jumped up and went to hug her child's grandmother. There was the tiniest, barely discernible flinch on Mary Ann's part before she returned the hug.

When they parted there were tears on both sides. Sarah suggested another cup of tea as a pick-me-up while Mary Ann blew her nose on a large white hanky. When Sarah returned with the tea and resumed her seat, Mary Ann stirred her cup reflectively.

'You know, I was just thinking about what you said.'

'What was that?' asked Sarah not following any particular reference.

'About us not wanting to know you and Jean. It's not true, you know. It's just that we didn't know she existed until recently.'

'Yes, but now you do know, we can keep in touch.'

'Of course. I intend to. But I was wondering.' She paused long enough to arouse Sarah's curiosity.

'You were wondering what?'

'Well, no, actually. It's probably not a good idea. You probably wouldn't want us to anyway.'

'Wouldn't want what?'

'Ach no. Forget I even mentioned it.'

'Mentioned what? You haven't actually said anything!' Sarah exclaimed in mock exasperation. 'Come on, tell me.' she coaxed.

'Well', Mary Ann began again in a hesitant voice. 'Well I was wondering if it was possible – but it probably isn't so don't worry about it …'

'What?!'

'Well how would you feel if I took Jean back to Belfast with me? Just for a week or two', she added hurriedly as Sarah's smile started to fade. 'It's just that she has all these aunts and uncles who are just dying to see her and then there's all my other friends and relations that I would love to show her off to. She is my first grandchild after all. And I know everyone would love her as much as I do. Also,' she added, using every weapon in her arsenal, 'it would give you a bit of a break. Give you a bit of a holiday like, with only your gran to look after, you could catch up on your work if you wanted to.'

Sarah said nothing as she tried to take in this latest turn of events. Mary Ann took advantage of the silence.

'I would love it if you could come too, of course. But I suppose with your grandmother being so ill, it would be hard for you to get away. Never mind. Perhaps in a couple of years or so, when circumstances change, it might be possible for you both to come to visit all your Irish relatives.' She paused, mainly for effect, before adding wistfully, 'Jean will probably be all grown up by then.'

Under cover of taking a sip from her teacup, Mary Ann studied Sarah's face. She could tell that Sarah was giving the idea some consideration but was not entirely convinced yet. Putting down her tea cup, Mary Ann delivered the *coup de grace*.

'Of course, if you don't trust me to look after her for a couple weeks, I perfectly understand. No offence taken.'

Chapter Thirty-one

'Are we going on a picnic?' asked Lizzie Taylor.

'No, gran, we're going to the train station.'

'Are we going on a day trip?'

'No gran. We're leaving Mary Ann and Anne Marie to the train. Remember? They're leaving today. Going back to Belfast.' Sarah annunciated every word slowly and carefully in the hope that her grandmother would understand.

'Are we going to Belfast? I've never been to Belfast.' There was a pause while the information sunk in. 'I don't want to go to Belfast.' she protested. 'I want to go on a picnic.'

'It's all right, gran. We'll go on a picnic later. After we've been to the train station.'

Sarah sighed and turned to Mary Ann. 'She gets confused so easily now.'

Mary Ann nodded sympathetically. 'You've got your hands full there, no doubt about it. But at least us taking Jean off your hands for the two weeks will give you a bit of a break.'

'Are you sure you'll manage all right? It's a long journey. And two weeks with a young baby …'

'It'll be fine,' Mary Ann assured her. 'Don't forget, I've raised six of my own and, sure, I've got Anne Marie to give me a hand. Everything will be fine. We'll be back before you know it.'

'I'm looking forward to that already!' laughed Sarah.

Waiting for the train, Sarah inundated the McAllister women with information on how Jean liked her bath, what her favourite toy was, what songs to sing to her at bedtime, what foods she liked and disliked and the hundred and one things that a mother knows is indispensable to her baby's happiness.

'Honestly, Sarah', laughed Anne Marie. 'You'd think we were never coming back, the way you're carrying on!'

'Are you trying to tell me I'm fussing too much?' demanded Sarah in mock indignation.

Lizzie did not join in the general laughter.

'I don't want to go to Belfast.' she said, petulantly, 'I want to go on a picnic.'

Sarah's groan of 'Oh gran!' was drowned by the noise of the train pulling in to the station.

Mary Ann boarded the train first, found an empty carriage, and made herself comfortable. The porter loaded on their luggage, which now included an extra bag containing all the baby's necessities. Sarah, after lifting Jean from her pram and bestowing any number of kisses and hugs on her, handed Jean over to Anne Marie who, in turn, deposited the baby safely into Mary Ann's lap. Anne Marie leaped on to the station again and the two younger women gave each other a final hug before the whistle blew. Anne Marie hopped on board again and rushed to the carriage window. 'See you in a fortnight!' she shouted out the window. Sarah shouted something back but, whatever it was, was lost over the huffing of the train.

'Come on, gran', said Sarah, after the train had disappeared from view, 'Let's go on that picnic.'

It seemed eerie pushing an empty pram. Every time she looked down, Sarah expected to see Jean gurgling up at her. It had been agreed that the pram would be too awkward to manoeuvre in and out of trains and gangways and buses, so it was left behind. Mary Ann had assured Sarah that, once they were back in Belfast, they could borrow whatever was needed from neighbours and friends and that, while they were travelling, she and Anne Marie could between them easily carry baby Jean in their arms. Sarah wished now that they had taken the pram. Without Jean in it, it felt wrong.

It had also felt wrong permitting Mary Ann to take Jean away with her. She could not quite put her finger on the reason. After all, everything

Mary Ann had said made sense. It would be good for everyone if Jean was acknowledged as a member of the McAllister family. Both mother and daughter seemed to dote on the new addition to their family and, Sarah was sure, the extended family she had never met would be equally loving. And for the few days the McAllisters were visiting, they had been perfect house guests. Mary Ann had taken Lizzie under her wing, while Anne Marie played with Jean every moment she could, even feeding and changing her. Once she showed Anne Marie how to make up Jean's formula, Sarah felt quite redundant as Anne Marie insisted on doing everything she could for her niece. Still, Sarah had an uncomfortable feeling somewhere in the pit of her stomach that she could not put a name to. She would be glad when the fortnight was over.

Mary Ann breathed a sigh of relief when the ship finally pulled away from the port. There was no going back now. More to the point, she could stop play acting and pretending to be a doting grandmother. It had taken all her strength of character to fuss over Danny's bastard, while as for that daft old woman! The very thought of Lizzie almost made her feel sick. If ever I get like that, she thought, I hope someone cares enough to put a pillow over my head and put me out of my misery. As for Sarah, she could see what had attracted Danny to the Girl in the first place but to her mind, he should have known better than to get involved. No good ever came of mixing with outsiders, she had told him that often enough. It was all behind her now, though. With a bit of luck on her side, she would never see any of them, nor have to set foot in England, ever again.

She turned to face Anne Marie, who had found a deck chair just outside the engine room, and was singing an Irish lullaby to the baby in her arms. Anne Marie would make a very good mother one day but, please God, not for a while yet, thought Mary Ann, and certainly not until she was married. One bastard in the family was enough for any respectable household.

'Isn't this great, Mum?' called out Anne Marie as she spied her mother approaching. 'I had no idea that England would be so nice. And the English people! I thought they would all be really nasty, but everyone we meet was really, really nice. They couldn't have been more helpful if they'd tried. I can't wait 'til we go back!'

'We'll not be going back, Anne Marie' stated Mary Ann flatly. 'This is a one way trip.'

'Aw Mum! That's not fair! Anyway, Bernadette won't be able to get the time off work and Catherine won't leave Jim McKeever for more than five minutes so she's not going to want to go. And you can't manage Jean all on your own.' she finished triumphantly, as one who had resoundingly nailed the argument.

'Jean's not going back. And from now on, you can call her Sinead. That's Irish for Jean. No matter that she was born in England, she'll be brought up in Belfast and she may as well sound Irish.'

Anne Marie's face was a study in confusion. 'What do you mean? Not going back? But what about Sarah? Sarah's her mother! We can't take Jean away from her mother!'

'We just have.' Mary Ann cut in. 'Now get used to it. And for Christ's sake, will you stop calling her Jean!'

Chapter Thirty-two

It was not often that her mother-in-law summoned them to tea and Mairead was feeling slightly apprehensive as they made their way to Servia Street.

'Don't worry', advised Seamus. 'She probably just wants to tell us all about her big trip to the deepest, darkest, dungeons of Hell, otherwise known as England to you and me.'

Mairead permitted herself a smile. She knew Seamus was trying to cheer her up. Ever since the heart-to-heart in the cemetery they had, if it were possible, grown even closer together. Nothing would ever take away the hurt they both felt, but at least they were learning to live with it together.

'Come on', urged Seamus. 'You know mum hates to be kept waiting.' Taking her husband's hand, Mairead allowed him to drag her at a half-run the rest of the way.

They arrived slightly breathless and dishevelled, Mairead's hat having come loose of its moorings and dangling by one hairgrip. She removed it and her full length navy coat as soon as she entered the house.

'There you's are!' stated Mary Ann, who obviously did not believe in any regular form of greeting.

'Hello, Mary Ann. How are you?' Mairead replied but there was no effort made on either side to kiss or to hug: it was not the done thing in the McAllister family.

'Hello, Mum! What's for tea? I'm starving. This one doesn't feed me, you know!' exclaimed Seamus, indicating his wife.

'Go on with you!' berated his mother. 'You certainly don't look like you're starved, not with that stomach!'

'That's pure muscle, that is!' cried Seamus indignantly, wobbling his stomach with both hands.

'How was your trip, Mary Ann?' asked Mairead politely, as they started ploughing their way through a mound of sandwiches and French fancies.

'Well, I got what I went there for and that's the main thing.'

'So you planning on emigrating to England then, Mam?' teased Seamus.

'I am not!' she retorted, 'and with the help of God, I'll never set foot in that accursed country ever again. Mind you,' she continued, with evident disapproval, 'your sister seemed to enjoy herself there.'

'Where is Anne Marie?' enquired Seamus. 'In fact, where is everybody? I didn't realise it would just be you and us tonight.'

'Anne Marie will be along shortly. I've told the others to stay out of our way.'

Seamus and Mairead exchanged concerned glances. 'What's the big secret, Mam? Is anybody in trouble?' he asked anxiously, reaching for his wife's hand.

'Far from it.' she replied smugly. 'I think I might have the answer to your prayers.'

The puzzled look on the faces of her son and daughter-in-law provided Mary Ann with a rare moment of glee. Before Seamus and Mairead could begin to guess what on earth Mary Ann was alluding to, the door opened and in walked Anne Marie.

'That was good timing.' remarked her mother approvingly. Moving towards her youngest daughter, Mary Ann relieved her of the bundle in her arms. Turning to Mairead, 'Here,' she said, thrusting the bundle towards her. More in an automated response than with any rational thought, Mairead held out her arms and found herself, for the first time since her own child's death, holding a baby in her arms.

Seamus slipped his arms around his wife. He could not decide if his mother was being cruel to be kind or just being cruel and insensitive.

'Are you OK, love?' he whispered.

Mairead simply nodded, not trusting herself to speak. She was trembling with the emotion of holding a baby – any baby – in her arms again and tears were very close to the surface.

Seamus turned to his mother: 'Whose baby is it?'

'Yours, if you want it.' was the unanticipated, startling, reply.

Seamus was sure he must have misheard. 'What? What did you say?'

'I said; it's yours if you want it.'

Seamus was dumbfounded. He turned to his wife as if seeking clarification from her. She was too engrossed in the baby to look at him. He had a feeling that she had not heard the generous offer his mother had just made. He turned back to Mary Anne.

'You can't be serious! You can't just pluck a baby from mid-air and tell us it ours like some sort of belated Christmas present! Babies don't grow on trees you know! Anne Marie!' he appealed to his sister. 'Talk some sense into her. She's clearly gone mad.'

Anne Marie wisely refrained from saying anything. Her mother had already read her the riot act. When she had discovered on the ship home what Mary Ann was planning, Anne Marie had protested vigorously that it was cruel and unnatural to take a child away from its mother. Mary Anne had, ferociously, put her straight:

'So it's all right for your brother to lose a child that was loved and wanted, is it? It's all right for Mairead to cry herself to sleep every night, is it? Are you more concerned about the feelings of some stranger than those of your own flesh and blood? This child', indicating Jean, 'was never wanted. It was an accident. We're doing the girl a favour by taking the child away from her.'

Her tone of voice changed to the epitome of reasonableness. 'Think how happy Seamus and Mairead will be to have a child of their own. They'll give it a good life and it'll want for nothing. And it's not as if your woman can't have any more kids. She'll no doubt get her hooks into some other defenceless young lad and have another one by this time next year.'

It was not often Anne Marie contradicted her mother but on this occasion she felt she could not let her mother ride rough shod over the lives of so many people.

'First of all, mam, she's not an "it", she's a baby and she has a name! A name that was given to her by her mother. And, yes I do feel sorry for our Seamus and Mairead, but you can't snatch Jean away from her mother! That just makes two unhappy families, instead of one. And what about Jean? She'll miss her mother. My God! If I had even suspected what you were going to do, I'd have never come with you. You lied to everybody, including me!'

'It was for a good cause!' Mary Ann thundered, raising her voice in the way that made grown men quake. 'This child is as much ours as it is hers' indicating, with a nod of the head towards the disappearing English shoreline, that she meant Sarah. 'After all, it is our Danny's child. We're just bringing it home.' Mary Ann made the kidnap seem reasonable and righteous.

Anne Marie tried again: 'But surely, if Danny had wanted Jean, he would have married Sarah. It's just not right, taking a child from her mother.'

'Exactly!' said Mary Ann triumphantly, 'If he had wanted her he would have married her, so that proves he didn't want her, so it's our duty to rescue his child from a woman he wanted nothing to do with.'

Anne Marie could not quite follow the logic of that argument, but was at a loss as to how to counteract it. 'It's not right!' she reiterated.

'Look, it's like this.' Mary Ann stated, as if talking to a sleepy child. 'Danny didn't want Sarah: He didn't say anything about not wanting his child. In fact, he wanted me to raise it. It's the truth! Ask him!' she replied in answer to Anne Marie's incredulous look. 'But instead of me raising the child, I'm going to let Seamus and Mairead raise it - her. Think how happy everyone will be. Your brother and his wife will have a child to bring up, Danny will be able to see his daughter whenever he comes home, I'll be able to watch my grandchild grow up, and Sarah will be able to look after her grandmother without having to worry about a baby as well. Now, doesn't that all make sense?'

While Anne Marie was grappling with the morality behind the argument, Mary Ann slammed the lid shut.

'Anyway, it was you who took the child of its mother. Remember, I got on the train on my own. You were the one who carried the baby on to the train and on to the ship. You are the one who abducted Jean.'

As Anne Marie recoiled in horror, Mary Ann reminded her: 'And don't forget. From now on, her name's Sinead.'

Chapter Thirty-three

When people want something badly enough it is not hard to persuade them to accept the most outlandish arguments. Particularly if, unbeknown to them, part of that argument is based on a deliberate lie. Mary Ann steered a path halfway between the truth and fiction. She told the grieving couple that the baby was Danny's, which was true, and that the child's mother did not want her, which was patently untrue.

'How can someone not want a beautiful baby girl?' wondered Mairead in amazement.

'Are you sure it's all right for us to have her?' asked Seamus, half afraid this was some sort of elaborate and cruel test. It would be better if the child was taken away immediately before Mairead became any more attached to it. Bette Davis could not have turned in a better performance than Mary Ann McAllister. 'If the mother had wanted her, do you think she would have given us all her clothes and toys and bottles and stuff? No, no, she was glad to get rid of her. The poor mite was an inconvenience to her. Of course, I still had to promise she would be going to a good home and would be well looked after. So if you don't want her ...?'

Mairead clutched the child tighter to her bosom. She had lost one child already: she was not prepared to lose another.

'What's her name? How old is she?'

'Her name's Sinead and she's six months old.' Mary Ann shot a look at her youngest daughter, daring her to contradict.

'Sinead. That's a lovely name. A lovely name for a lovely girl. Yes, you are. You are a lovely, lovely girl!' Mairead was bonding with Sinead. Another hour passed while Mary Ann related her version of events to Seamus and Mairead, answering their questions and making plans for the future.

'You know I've put our name down with the council for one of those new houses up the Whiterock that our Danny was working on? Why don't you two do the same? Apparently, all the houses have gardens. That'll be nice for Sinead to play in when she's a bit older. And we'll all be on hand to help you baby-sit.' Mary Ann paused before adding: 'And new neighbours won't have to know about Sinead's background.'

As Mairead looked anxiously at her husband, he nodded slowly. 'You're right. I think that might be a good idea.'

As the newly constituted family took their leave, Mary Ann promised to call on them the following day to help them 'get things settled' as she put it. Closing the door, she turned to Anne Marie. 'Did you see how happy they were? Would you deny them that happiness?' As Anne Marie shook her head almost mournfully, her mother continued: 'Well in that case, you keep your mouth shut. I don't want you saying a word to anyone, ever. It's done now, and what's done is done. Let's hear no more about it. Now, I want you to go to the shop and buy some good quality writing paper. I've a wee message I need to write.'

When everyone had gone to bed, Mary Ann retrieved the only surviving letter that Sarah had written to Danny. Taking an old school jotter of

Kevin's, she started to copy Sarah's handwriting. It took a number of attempts but once she was satisfied that the copies would pass muster, she used the new notepad to write a letter to herself.

Dear Mrs McAllister

I now have a baby girl. It is Dannys. I cannot look after her and do not want to. As you are her grandmother I would like you to take her. I can not go to Belfast as my grandmother is ill. Can you come here and fetch Sinead back with you?

Much appreciated,

Sarah

Admiring her handiwork, she folded it and placed it in the envelope that Sarah had used. No-one would doubt that the letter came from Sarah now. The postmark would prove that. She used the poker to ensure that Sarah's original letter reached the dying embers of the fire and watched as it turned to black ash. Satisfied with a job well done, she retired to bed. She planned an early start in the morning.

Seven o'clock mass on a weekday morning in St Peter's Pro-Cathedral was sparsely attended apart from the usual sprinkle of old men and women. If asked, they would have claimed it was a devout love of the faith that had them on their knees at that hour of the morning but Mary Ann suspected it was simply because they could not sleep and had nothing else to do. She, however, was on a mission. As soon as the final blessing ended, she made her way as quickly as she could to the vestry door. She wanted to catch Father Hanson as he left the church.

'Father, can I have a word?' she called as he emerged from the church.

'Mary Ann! What are you doing here at this time of the morning? I hadn't got you down as an early morning altar eater.'

Mary Ann glanced round to make sure no-one had overheard. She hoped he would lower his voice a little.

'I need to speak to you in private, Father. It's about a christening.'

Puzzled, Father Hanson invited her back into the church.

'What's this all about, Mary Ann' he asked, when they were both settled. The volume of his voice had moderated a little for which Mary Ann was thankful. You never knew who could be listening in.

'It's about my grandchild, father' she began.

'A sad tragedy Mary Ann, a sad tragedy.'

'No, not that one, Father.'

In answer to his confused expression, she continued: 'You remember Danny got a English girl into trouble?'

Remembrance flooded his countenance.

'Indeed, I do' he whispered. 'How did that turn out?'

'A baby girl, Father, but now the mother doesn't want anything to do with it. And Danny, as you know, has joined the navy. She didn't want anything to do with him either, Father.'

Father Hansom shook his head: 'These modern young women. They should be horse whipped. That'll knock some sense into them!'

'Yes, Father. But the thing is you see, she wrote to me.'

She produced the letter she had so carefully crafted and handed it to the priest. Watching him closely for any signs of disbelief, she waited until he finished reading and returned the letter to her.

'I don't know what to make of that, Mary Ann. What are you going to do?'

'It's what I've already done, Father. I've been to England and I've brought the child back with me. Seamus and Mairead have agreed to raise it as their own. Now I want it baptised in the Catholic church.'

Chapter Thirty-four

Sarah watched for the postman anxiously. It had been almost two weeks and there was still no word from Belfast as to when Jean would be returning. She could hear her grandmother in the kitchen, demanding breakfast. With a groan, she turned from the window.

'Gran, you've just had your breakfast. Don't you remember? You had a boiled egg and toast. Look, there's the plate. I haven't even washed up yet. Here, have another cup of tea.' Sarah had barely finished pouring the tea when the familiar rattle of the letterbox announced the arrival of the post. Hastily adding milk and sugar, she set the cup down in front of her grandmother and practically ran to the front door.

There were two letters on the mat. Sarah snatched them up, eagerly scanning the postmarks. At last! She breathed a sigh of relief: Finally, word from Belfast. She tore open the envelope and almost tore the letter in her haste to read the contents.

Dear Sarah,

I hope everything is well with you and with your granny. We are all well here. Now I dont want you to worry but Jean is not well. The doctor says he thinks it might be the Measles but that she will be all right soon. As you can imagine, I do not want her to be travelling when she is not well so I will keep her with me for another few weeks until she is better. So dont worry. Everyone here thinks she is very bonny and she has quite won are hearts.

I will write to you again before we come over.

Respectfully yours,

Mary Ann McAllister.

Sarah read and re-read the short note until the tears blurred the words. Her daughter was not coming home. What made it worse, if possible, was knowing that Jean was ill and Sarah was powerless to help her.

Her grandmother's voice cut through her thoughts. 'Evvy, Evvy, I've made you breakfast.' Returning to the kitchen, Sarah was just in time to rescue the bread that was starting to burn under the grill.

'She's not coming home, gran.'

'Who's not coming home?'

'My Jean. She's not coming home for a while yet.'

'Why not? Is there something wrong with her?'

'She's got the measles, apparently.'

'Ah! Dangerous things, the measles' nodded Lizzie, in a rare moment of clarity. 'Better she stays where she is until she's over them.' As she shuffled off to the living room, she added: 'Don't want the baby catching them.'

Realising her grandmother had drifted away again, Sarah tried to think rationally. She was sure Mary Ann and Anne Marie would take good care of Jean. It was unlikely to be their fault that Jean had caught the measles in the first place. Measles were so contagious. It was probably a wise decision not to travel with a sick baby but, nevertheless, Sarah missed Jean so much it was like a physical ache. Now she would have to wait another two or three weeks before she could hold her baby in her arms again.

On the premise that keeping busy would occupy her mind and stop her dwelling on Jean's absence, Sarah sat down at her workbench and started on a bundle of cloth. Lizzie took a seat by the fire and was soon lulled to sleep by the buzzing of the sewing machine. Sarah's thoughts were hammering away as quickly as the needle. It was over an hour before Sarah remembered that there had been a second letter. Finishing off the sleeve she was working on, she went to the kitchen to retrieve it. It was postmarked London. Guessing this letter was from Barbara, she sliced it open with a butter knife and sat down at the kitchen table to read it.

Dear Sarah,

I have finally managed to arrange my holidays! I have a whole week off at Easter so I will be inflicting myself on you on Friday the 9th of April and I will be staying for five whole days. I can't wait to see you and Jean again. I really miss her. I can't believe I'm so fond of someone who can't say a word and who sleeps most of the time. I must be getting broody!

Anyway, I'll be in touch closer to the time to let you know what time my train gets in. Hopefully, you can meet me at the station as I'm sure I'd get lost in the wilds of Yorkshire if I'm left to my own devices. You know I can't go anywhere outside the east end without my A-Z!

Looking forward to seeing you all soon,

Lots of love,

Barbara.

PS. Lots of hugs and kisses to Jean.

In her concern for Jean, Sarah had totally forgotten that Barbara was due to visit. Hoping fervently that Jean would have returned home by Easter, Sarah returned to her stitching. It would be lovely to see her friend again and catch up with all the gossip. She wondered how Clare's wedding plans were going. Somehow, she could not image Barbara in a fluffy pink bridesmaid's dress. The image made her smile. It also made her feel slightly better. After all, it did make sense to leave Jean where she was if she was ill, and the time would pass quickly enough. And maybe, if the timing was right, Barbara could meet Danny's mother and see that she was not the hard-hearted monster people had made her out to be.

Chapter Thirty-five

On Good Friday, when Sarah arrived at the train station to meet her friend, the only female waiting there was a tall sophisticated lady, wearing a beautifully-tailored, charcoal grey suit. Her black patent stilettos with the matching handbag looked expensive and even the luggage by her side reeked of quality. It was not until the woman turned and squealed 'Sarah!', reaching out her arms in anticipation of an embrace, did Sarah realise it was Barbara.

'Barbara! My God!' Sarah gasped in amazement. 'What happened to you? You've got all grown up! I didn't recognise you at first. You look fabulous!'

Barbara laughed. 'I thought I would surprise you! Unfortunately, the beatnik has gone, and I've become all sensible and mature. Come on, I'll tell you all about my metamorphous on the way. Have you a taxi waiting?'

'Afraid not. I just walked here.' Sarah said apologetically.

'Never mind, I'm sure the porter will manage to find one for us.' As she raised a finger in the air, she continued firmly: 'There is no way that I am going to walk anywhere in these heels.'

She smiled at the porter who had arrived at a trot and was slightly breathless as a result. 'Would you be a dear and see if you can fetch me a taxi?' As he scuttled off, she turned back to Sarah. 'Unfortunately, I didn't have time to change out of my work clothes before catching the train but don't worry, I have lots of hiking shoes for long tramps over the moors or the dales or whatever it is you have up here.'

They followed the porter to the roadside where a car pulled up almost immediately. Barbara waited for the driver to get out and open the rear door and, while the luggage was loaded into the boot, she and Sarah made themselves comfortable.

The car was old and the roads uneven which meant that the driver could not overhear the whispered conversation taking place in the rear.

'I take it your friend, Hannah, is taking care of your gran while you came to meet me?' In response to Sarah's nod, Barbara continued: 'And Jean's still not back?'

Sarah shook her head and tried her best to explain the current situation to her friend.

'I think I mentioned in my last letter to you. Just as Jean was getting over the measles, Mary Ann fell over and sprained a ligament in her foot. She can't walk anywhere at the moment so she needs one of the girls to help her out. And she doesn't want any of them bringing her granddaughter back on their own, especially without her there to supervise.'

Barbara gave a long sideways glance at Sarah. She still had her suspicions about Mary Ann. However, she could tell that the entire situation was making her friend miserable even though Sarah was trying to put a brave face on it for her sake. Barbara decided to change the subject in an effort to lighten the mood.

'I must tell you all about my new job.' she began cheerfully. 'It's an absolute hoot! I have the grand title of Second Assistant to the Deputy Fashion Editor. I'm really the lowest of the low, but the job is crazy, and the perks amazing! Everything I'm wearing' she indicated with a sweep of her hand, 'cost me not a penny. Can you believe that? This suit alone should have cost me more than six months' salary but I get all my clothes for free now.'

Sarah demanded to be told the secret of such riches.

'Well, every time the fashion houses put on a catwalk show so that the Deputy Editor can decide on what she is going to choose to suggest to the Fashion Editor, we get to keep all the clothes she picks. Luckily for me, the Deputy Editor is five foot nothing in her stilettos and a size sixteen so absolutely nothing fits her. And the first assistant is fifty if she's a day and wouldn't wear any of the clothes anyway. She only has the job because she's related in some way to one of the top bosses. Apparently, she was there before the magazine even covered fashion. Probably back in the stone age!'

'Maybe she just does the fur coats now' suggested Sarah and, adopting a fake French accent, held up her arms as if modelling a coat: 'Vat ze vell-dressed cave-dweller is vearing zis season!'

Both girls laughed at the absurdity of the notion and were still giggling like schoolgirls when the taxi drew up outside the cottage.

Hannah came out to meet them. She could barely take her eyes off Barbara. Never had anyone so elegant ever set foot in the village. She doubted if they even looked as grand up in Halifax. In response to Sarah's query, she directed her answer towards Barbara, so mesmerised was she. 'Your gran's fine. She slept most of the time and when she woke up we played Happy Families. She got most of the cards mixed up, but she seemed to enjoy it.'

'Thank you Hannah. I don't know what I'd do without you.' Noticing the stare, she continued: 'Have you met my friend, Barbara? She works for a fashion magazine down in London.'

Hannah was overwhelmed. 'Pleased to meet you, ma'm' she replied, bobbing a curtsey.

Barbara burst into peals of laughter. 'I definitely must come up here more often.' Putting her arm round the star-struck girl, she walked with her into the house. 'Sarah tells me that you have been a real friend to her since she's come back to the village. I hope we can be great friends as well.' Hannah grinned in delight: She could not wait to tell everyone about her posh new friend.

Afternoon tea was an extremely jolly affair as Barbara indulged Hannah with all sorts of tales from the big city and about her job at the fashion magazine. Even though Barbara had taken the time to change out of her city suit and into casual capri pants and sweater, she still appeared more elegant and stylish than anyone Hannah had ever seen outside of a Hollywood movie. It was with great reluctance, therefore, that the babysitter finally took her leave. After she had gone, Barbara washed and put away the dishes while Sarah settled Lizzie comfortably in her favourite chair in front of the recently installed television. Barbara then produced a bottle of wine from her luggage and invited Sarah to supply the glasses.

Sitting down at the kitchen table, Sarah took a long draught from her glass. 'Hmm, that's so nice!' she declared. 'I haven't had a glass of wine since I last saw you.'

'That's over five months ago! How on earth can you cope without wine?' Barbara asked in mock horror. Sarah grinned. 'Actually wine isn't the problem. But I'm telling you, I do not know how I could manage without the television. It's been a god-send.'

Barbara make a quizzical face over the wineglass. 'Oh, not for me!' claimed Sarah. 'For gran. As long as there is a programme on – it doesn't matter what it is, from Muffin the Mule to the News – she watches everything. She just sits there and watches and I don't have to worry about her straying off or falling down stairs or anything. It's a few hours of total bliss as far as I'm concerned.'

'She's not getting any better, then?'

Sarah shook her head. 'There's nothing the doctors can do. It's just a matter of time.'

'She seemed to go downhill very fast.' opined Barbara. 'She wasn't that bad when you first went back home. You told me she was just a little forgetful.'

'That's true', admitted Sarah, 'but I didn't know the half of it. She's been suffering for some time now, but I hadn't noticed. She only wrote to me when she was having one of her good days, so I thought everything was all right when I was in London. Even when I did come home, I tried to tell myself it wasn't that bad. But Dr Harrington doesn't hold out much hope. "It's only a matter of time" he says, but whether that's six months or six years, he can't say.'

Barbara clucked sympathetically. 'It can't be easy on you. Even with the TV. I suppose looking after your gran doesn't give you much time to miss Jean?' She was fishing, but even she was surprised by the anguish in the answer.

'You must be joking! I miss her all the time! I can't sleep at night wondering how she is and when she's coming back! She's the first thing I think about when I wake up in the morning! Everything I see reminds me of her. If it's a nice day I'm thinking, I can put Jean out in the garden. If it's raining, I'm wondering how to get the nappies dry. And every time I remember that she isn't here, it's like a knife going through my heart. Not miss her? I would miss my right arm less!'

'Can't you go to Belfast and fetch her back yourself?'

'I'm dying to, but I can't leave gran on her own and, while Hannah's really nice about helping out, she can't look after gran for more than a few hours at a time. She has her own family to see to. I'm stuck here, just waiting on Mary Ann's damned leg!'

A few moments passed while Barbara watched Sarah try to dig the welling tears out of her eyes with the heel of her hand. She had to do something to help her friend.

'What if I looked after your gran?' she offered.

Sarah looked up puzzled. 'That's very good of you to offer, but – and please don't take offence –what do you know about looking after a sick old lady?'

'I've done it before. My aunt Rosie had the same problem. My mum used to send me round to look after her all the time. I used to keep her happy for hours. And we didn't have a TV in those days!'

'But you're on holiday!'

'So? I'm still on holiday. I'm just not seeing quite as much of you as I would like. But at least I'll get to see Jean.'

Sarah tried to think of any other excuse before permitting herself to get excited.

'It wouldn't take that long. I mean, all I need to do is take Jean. I don't have to stay. I could take the overnight boat from Liverpool and be there first thing in the morning and then take the evening boat home. I'd only be away two nights. Do you really think you can cope?' Sarah's brain was whirring at a mile a minute.

'Steady on.' advised Barbara, pouring her another glass of wine. 'Let's plan this out carefully.'

It was decided that Sarah would take the Monday evening ferry to Belfast, in an effort to avoid the holiday rush. Having collected Jean, Sarah would be back Wednesday afternoon, which was when Barbara had originally planned to return to London. She agreed to stay another two days, however, declaring that there was nothing so pressing in London that would take precedence over seeing Jean again. Know that her daughter was only a matter of hours away, Sarah relaxed and allowed herself to enjoy her friend's company to the full. It was almost like old times again.

Chapter Thirty-six

May McCormack was Mary Ann McAllister's oldest friend and, as such, could not be trusted with a secret of any kind. It was for this reason that Mary Ann paid her a visit, bringing with her a few favoured knick-knacks that May had always admired.

'You'll be off soon, then.' said May as she reached her visitor a cup of tea and invited her to help herself to the pink wafer fingers on the accompanying plate. She was nothing if not hospitable.

'Aye.' agreed Mary Ann. 'We'll be off on Thursday. The Council wanted us to move on Saturday but you know what that means.'

'"A Saturday flit's a short sit"' recited May wisely. 'You don't want to be moving then.'

'Exactly. And there's no way I'm moving on Good Friday. So tomorrow it is then, ready or not.'

'Have you much to do?' May enquired solicitously, eying the bundle in her neighbour's lap.

'Nearly all done. Just a few odds and ends. Which reminds me, May,' Mary Ann was innocence personified. 'Would you ever take these off my hands? We haven't room for them where we're going, and I'd like them to go to a good home.'

May's eyes gleamed, but she played the game. 'Well, if you're sure you don't want them. They're too good to throw out. I'll see if I can't find a space for them somewhere.' She made it sound as though she was doing Mary Ann the favour.

Now the ritual was over, Mary Ann got down to the real business in hand. 'I'll miss this place, you know. But I have to look to the future. Where we're going is much better for the children and, if truth be told, it doesn't hurt to be one step ahead of the Tally man.'

'Whatever do you mean, Mary Ann?' asked May innocently, while at the same time pricking up her ears. Mary Ann McAllister in debt? That was a turn-up for the books. May wanted to know more.

'Ach well, May, you know what it's like with a growing family. If it's not one thing, it's another. Kevin would have me ate out of house and home and there's no keeping up with our Anne Marie when it comes to style. And now they're all on at me to get a television set and there's me not even paid off the wireless yet.'

Mary Ann slyly watched her friend lap up all the juicy details. None of it was true. Mary Ann did not agree with getting items on hire purchase. If you could not afford it, you should not get it, was her motto. May, however, like many of her friends and neighbours, was up to her eyes in tick, as such debts were known. Mary Ann leaned forward confidentially. 'If anybody comes looking for me, May, don't let on you know my new address. It'll give me a chance to get meself sorted.' She winked conspiratorially. 'And don't be telling a soul what I've just told you.'

May swore herself to secrecy. Later, she also made Maisy in the shop swear she would not tell another living soul. And her friend, Bridie. And Patsy. And Tessy. And Kitty. And they, in turn, swore all their friends to secrecy.

Satisfied with a job well done, Mary Ann sauntered home. For someone who had allegedly suffered a sprained ligament only the week before, she walked amazingly well.

The next day, Seamus took the morning off work to help his family load the hired lorry with all their worldly goods. It took almost two hours to move the furniture and, with much sweat and swearing, haul everything on to the van. When everything was loaded, Mary Ann gingerly climbed into the passenger seat, commanded Bernadette to be careful as she handed up a prized ruby glass vase, and then settled herself like the Queen of Sheba. Seamus sprang up into the driver's seat, and with much hooting, shouting and cheers, Mary Ann proceeded to her new home. Bernadette, Catherine and Anne Marie were left behind to ensure the old house was swept clean as a new pin and they, together with Kevin, followed later on foot.

On arrival, Mary Ann's first priority was to discover who her new neighbours were. Here, she struck gold. The tenants next door were headed by a skinny little red-haired woman with the beginnings of a hump on her back. As soon as she noticed the van drive up, she was out the front door, pretending to polish the windows, waiting to make her introductions.

'Youse moving in to number eight? How you doing? I'm Sadie Flanaghan. We moved in last week. We were wondering who we'd be getting as neighbours. Here, let me take that off you and come on in for a cup of tea.'

Mary Ann handed the vase to Seamus instead, but followed her new acquaintance into number ten. As she bustled about preparing tea, Sadie introduced the rest of the household.

'That there's me husband, Billy'. She indicated to a small, fat, bald man of about fifty, who had stood up as the stranger entered, removed his pipe from his mouth to mutter a greeting, then sat back down to continue reading his newspaper.

'He's got a bad back', Sadie whispered confidentially, as if he could not hear her perfectly well. 'And those two' she pointed to two young boys of about ten years old playing in what would eventually be a back garden,

'They're the twins, Thomas and Anthony. Our Terry's at work, you'll meet him later, and the girls, Patricia, Deirdre and Pauline, are away to the Irish dancing. They've won medals, you know', she added proudly. 'But here, what am I thinking of. Sit yourself down and tell me all about yourself. I was just saying to Mrs Braniff, in number twelve "I wonder what the new people will be like." I was just saying that, wasn't I, Billy?' Her husband did not acknowledge the question.

Two hours later, Mary Ann emerged from the Flanaghan's home with her head spinning. Sadie had told her the entire history of every family in the street: who they were, where they had lived before, how many children they had, whose husband had a job and where they were employed, and who was married to a feckless layabout. Her own husband was not included in the latter description being, apparently, 'a martyr to his back'. When she had been able to get a word in edgewise, Mary Ann had told Sadie as much as she wanted her to know about the McAllister family. Including the lie that she was only one step away from the debt collector. 'Oh, don't worry,' Sadie reassured her. 'I'm the soul of discretion. I'll not say a word. I'm not one to gossip, you know.'

'I know I can rely on you.' replied Mary Ann truthfully. The whole estate would know before nightfall that the Tally Man might come looking for the McAllisters at number eight. In Belfast sub-culture, the Tally Man was a creature to be feared. Knowing he or his minions were trying to track down anyone meant that if strangers came making enquiries, no-one in the area would have heard of the McAllister family, never mind know their address.

Chapter Thirty-seven

When Sarah disembarked from the Liverpool boat on the cold, grey, overcast Belfast morning, she simply followed the crowd to the exit. Once there, she had no idea which way to go, so decided to take one of the hackney cabs that were waiting in line. Normally, she would have conserved her cash but Barbara had insisted on giving her money for the journey and, anyway, she thought, the sooner I see Jean the better. The taxi fare will be money well spent. The taxi driver, a stout man in his late fifties, tried to chat to her as he drove away from the docks but, as Sarah had difficulty understanding his thick Belfast accent, conversation lagged before they reached the Albert Clock. As he drove though the town, Sarah was impressed by some of the larger department stores. Although the names were different, they reminded her of the main shopping streets of Halifax. These grand buildings quickly gave way to row after row of small terraced houses, interspersed with mills and factories, with a number of tall, red-brick chimneys stabbing the skyline.

Dismounting from the cab outside number twenty-six Servia Street, Sarah paid off the driver, including a small tip for his trouble. She had considered asking the driver to wait but on reflection decided that, as she was arriving unannounced, it would take time to gather together everything Jean would need for the journey. Besides, it would not be polite to simply walk in, take her baby and disappear off again. She would probably have to listen to all the details of Jean's illness and how Mary Ann had damaged her foot. Taking a deep breath in an effort to contain her excitement at seeing Jean again, she turned to face Danny's childhood home.

The sound of the door knocker reverberated throughout the empty house, sending the echoes back to Sarah as she stood on the pavement. Her second knock brought the next door neighbour on to the street.

'There's no point in rapping, dear, they've left.'

'Left?' asked Sarah puzzled. 'Left where?'

On hearing Sarah's English accent, the neighbour appeared to lose interest.

'I've no idea. They just moved.' she stated firmly before slamming her door shut again: it did not do to be seen talking to debt collectors.

Sarah remained where she was, trying to figure out what was happening. Mary Ann had said nothing about moving in her last letter. When had they left, and more importantly, where had they gone to? Realising there was no point in standing outside an empty house, Sarah took stock. There was a shop on the next corner but one and, working on the premise that corner shops were the same all over the world, Sarah decided to make some enquiries there.

Maisie, the owner, was been leaning over the counter talking to a friend when Sarah entered the over-stocked, dusty, shop. The smile of greeting quickly faded when Sarah stated her business.

'I've no idea where they moved to', was the shopkeeper's stony-faced response. Her friend, however, eager to be first with the gossip, piped up:

'They've moved up the Whiterock.' A glare from Maisie immediately silenced her. 'At least, I think that's where they gone.' the helpful friend finished lamely.

Sarah stared at them bemused. She instinctively felt that they were keeping something from her but she also knew that there was no point in forcing the issue. She decided on a different tack.

'Where is the Whiterock from here?' she asked. Reluctantly, having had her hand forced by her indiscreet friend, Maisie gave directions: 'Go back on to the Falls Road, turn left and go straight on until the City Cemetery, then turn right. You can't miss it.'

Sarah thanked them for the information and left the shop. Just before the door closed, however, she heard the shopkeeper berate her friend: 'Bloody debt collectors! Have you no sense!'

With no indication of the distance to be covered, Sarah set off on foot. She used the journey time to try and make sense of this latest piece of information. The McAllisters probably hadn't had much notice of the move, she reassured herself. That's the way those housing bodies work. Mary Ann has probably written to me to explain everything and send me her new address. I must have missed the post, or it's probably been delayed due to the Easter holidays.

All the 'probablys' were making Sarah feel uncomfortable. As she followed the grudgingly given directions towards the Whiterock area, she found it difficult to convince herself that nothing was wrong.

The new Whiterock housing estate, set on the lower slopes of the Black Mountain, was an attempt by the city council to alleviate the severe housing shortage that Belfast had experienced. Many of the slums had to be cleared, as they were unfit for human habitation, while the influx of new workers, attracted from the countryside both by the availability of jobs and the relatively high wage compared to agricultural work, added to the housing pressure. As Sarah gazed uphill towards the Whiterock estate, her heart sank. There were literally hundreds of new homes. Mary Ann could be in any one of them. Gritting her teeth, she forced herself to continue. Selecting a house at random, she rapped on the door. It was opened by a grubby young lad of approximately ten years of age who, before she could say anything, offered the information that his mother was unavailable. Although it did take a few attempts before Sarah could interpret the Belfast parlance of 'Me Ma's not in!' into understandable English. When she tried to enquire if he or anyone else in the house knew of the McAllister family, he shouted something unintelligible into the room behind him. A haggard-looking young woman came to the door. She looked Sarah over very carefully before asking: 'Who's it you're luking for?' Sarah again explained her mission. The woman, obviously the grimy child's mother, shook her head. 'Never heard of them. Can't help ye. Get into the house, Sean!' And with that, she shoved the child into the room behind her and closed the front door.

Undaunted, Sarah tried the next house in the street. This time she received a more civil response but no more helpful than the first. The occupant had no information to offer regarding the whereabouts of the McAllister family. Sarah received more or less the same reply at every other house at which she called. Most claimed, quite a few of them truthfully, that they had only moved in themselves and therefore had no idea who else lived on the estate. Sarah was reminded of her time in London. No-one there knew their neighbours either. She would have been surprised to know that she was being lied to by complete strangers. Suspicious of her English accent, Sean's mother had sent him post haste to the McAllister's house to warn them that some posh English woman was looking for the family. Young Sean also spread the word to an few of the other neighbours he came across: 'The Tally Man's wife is lukin for the McAllisters!' The word spread like wildfire and, therefore, when Sarah came knocking on their doors, the residents believed she was an official of some kind. And an official calling round asking questions never boded well, particularly for the family under investigation. Showing a solidarity that the Trades Unions would have been proud of, the neighbours had rallied round to protect one of their own. Mary Ann, with the aid of Sadie and Sean, had done her job well.

As soon as she had received Sean's warning, Mary Ann took herself and her cup of tea upstairs to the front bedroom. She positioned a chair carefully, close – but not too close - to the window. From that position she could view anyone coming up the garden path while any visitor would be unable to see her. She did not have to wait long for Sarah to come knocking. Sarah rapped sharply on the door and waited for a response. When none was forthcoming, she rapped again. And again. After a few minutes, concluding that no-one was home, Sarah walked away. Watching her retreating back, Mary Ann's smug smile broadened.

As Sarah continued to pound the streets of the new housing estate, the soft, mizzling rain fell persistently. Sarah looked as damp and woebegone as the weather. Her hair clung to her face in thick, flat clumps, her blue woollen coat was soaked through, her feet were cold, sore and wet, her knuckles raw and bleeding from rapping on so many doors, but this was as nothing compared to how she felt inside. Her high hopes of the morning had faded with each passing hour. Eventually, she admitted defeat. She had called at practically every occupied household and still had no clue as to where Jean was. It was as if the McAllisters had disappeared into thin air. She considered the possibility that the shopkeeper and her friend had deliberately misdirected her. If that was the case, then she was simply wasting her time. There was nothing left but to return home and hope that Mary Ann would write to her.

She left it to the last minute before boarding the ship that would take her back to Liverpool. There was a vain, unreasonable hope that, if she stayed in Belfast, Jean would somehow mysteriously appear. Finally, Sarah was forced to give up even that hope. Drying herself off as best she could in the ladies cloakroom, she wandered around the ship, until she finally found a bench in a secluded corner where she sat, hugging her knees, all the way back to England. She was too depressed to eat or drink or sleep. All she could think of was her daughter. Would she ever see her again? The seemingly interminable train journeys passed in similar fashion. It was not until she arrived home where Barbara was waiting with a new doll for Jean, that Sarah broke down into uncontrollable, heaving, anguished, sobs. 'My baby! My baby! I couldn't find my baby!'

Chapter Thirty-eight

Barbara had tried her best to reassure her friend. 'I'm sure it's nothing to worry about. You know what it's like, moving house. Especially at short notice. Mary Ann was probably up to her eyes trying to get things sorted before she moved and then, afterwards, well, that's just as bad. Everything's in boxes and bundles and trying to get it all sorted and into some kind of order takes forever. I'm sure once she's settled, she'll write to you and explain everything.' Barbara sounded a great deal more confident than she felt. She was sure Mary Ann was up to something underhand: but it would not do to voice her suspicions to Sarah who was distraught enough already. Sitting with her friend at the kitchen table, Barbara poured her a very generous glass of wine. Sarah gulped it back unthinkingly as she reiterated her thoughts and questions in the hope that a reasonable answer would eventually materialise. Before long, the alcohol had the desired effect. Worn out by her experiences over the past two nights, and weak from lack of food, Sarah passed out.

Barbara carried Sarah into bed, tucking her up as if she were a baby. A good night's sleep would not solve all Sarah's problems, but it would help her cope better. Making sure Lizzie was asleep and locked in her bedroom, Barbara slipped out of the house. Five minutes later, she was standing in the hallway of Hannah's home. Hannah had been preparing for bed when Barbara called, and was dressed in an floral-patterned, orange-coloured, nylon dressing gown, with rags tied into her mousy fair hair, and a pair of maroon coloured slippers on her feet. Under the Pond's Cold Cream her face glowed red. She was mortified. The most glamorous woman Hannah had ever known had caught her looking like a frump.

'Hannah, I need your help' Barbara began without preamble.

Hannah, essentially a kind-hearted girl, immediately forgot her own concerns and offered her services: 'What's wrong? How can I help?'

Barbara explained as succinctly as she could what had transpired. She also mentioned her own suspicions. Hannah was horrified. 'You mean this woman, Mary Ann, has deliberately stolen Sarah's baby? I don't believe it! No-one could be so cruel!'

Barbara shook her head. 'I can't prove it. Not yet, anyway.' she added grimly. 'But whatever you do, don't tell Sarah what I've just told you. I want you to try and keep her spirits up as much as possible. Call in on her as often as you can. She really needs a friend at a time like this and I can't be here for her. I have to go back to work. If I stay any longer I'll lose my job. Knowing you're here to keep an eye on her will afford me some comfort. And anyway, I know some people back in London who might be able to help.' Hannah was slightly frightened by the look that flashed across Barbara's face. It was a combination of determination and fury and it made Hannah realise that, while Barbara made a good friend, she would make a fearful enemy. She almost felt sorry for Mary Ann: but not quite.

The next day, having slept for almost twelve hours, Sarah felt woolly-headed and tired. The dull ache in her head was not eased by the two aspro tablets she swallowed with her tea, and the dull ache in her heart had only one, unobtainable, cure. Nevertheless, she allowed herself to be dragged out for a walk by Barbara. Lizzie came along with them but, as she tended to trail behind to pick bluebells or the last of the daffodils, the two friends were able to talk to each other in complete privacy.

'I'm really sorry to leave you this upset', began Barbara. 'Hopefully it won't be for long.' Putting her arm around her friend's shoulder, she gave her a hug. 'Look, Mary Ann will probably write within a week or two and, before you know it, Jean will be back, giving you sleepless nights and running you ragged. You'll wonder what all the fuss was about.'

Sarah stopped walking and turned to face her. 'I know you're doing your best to cheer me up and I know you're trying to pretend that everything will be fine. But we both know the truth. For God knows what reason, Mary Ann has stolen my baby, and there's not a thing I can do about it!'

'Don't say that! We'll get Jean back, I swear to you! OK, Mary Ann may have decided to hold on to Jean longer than is good for anyone, but we'll have her back with you before you know it. Trust me!'

Sarah shook her head. 'How?' She asked simply. 'How can we get Jean back when we don't even know where she is? When no-one in Belfast will talk to me? For all I know, she might not be in Belfast. She could be anywhere.'

'I'll find out where she is.' Barbara made it sound like a statement of fact, not an empty promise to reassure an old friend. 'I'll get in touch with Elvis. Or Robert as I have to keep reminding myself to call him. He knew most of Danny's friends and workmates and one of them is bound to know where his family have moved to. I'll write as soon as I get back to London and I'm sure he'll help.'

'But hasn't he moved to Scotland? Will he still be in contact with his old workmates?'

'Well, if he's not, now would be a good time for him to renew old acquaintances, don't you think?'

For the first time, a glimmer of hope appeared in Sarah's eyes. Before she could ask any further questions., however, Barbara, linked her arm and said: 'Come on, let's be getting you and Lizzie home. I've got packing to do.'

Sarah, Lizzie and Hannah went in the taxi with Barbara to the train station to see her off. Barbara and Hannah had become quite friendly in the few days Barbara had been in the village. As they embraced at the station, she whispered into Hannah's ear: 'Remember! Keep an eye on Sarah, and try to stop her from moping too much.' Hannah nodded. She did not actually need to be told: Sarah was her friend too, and she was happy to be able to help her though this, but it was nice to feel that she had a comrade in Barbara. She was sorry to see her leave.

Sarah, however, was distraught, even though she did her best to put on a brave front. It almost felt that, with Barbara's departure, she was losing all connection with her child. No matter how often she rebuked herself for being silly, the nagging hurt in the pit of her stomach remained. As Barbara stepped aboard the train, there were tear-stained goodbyes all round. Even Lizzie cried, and she had no real idea what was happening.

As the train chugged away from the station, Barbara worked on her plan to find Jean. If Robert could find out the address of Danny's mother, she could try writing to Danny again. She dismissed that thought immediately. She had an inkling that any letters written would not reach their intended destination. She distrusted everything Mary Ann had said, including the information that Danny had joined the navy. He might still be at home and it was possible, after all, that Mary Ann was acting in her son's interest, if not with his actual encouragement. No, she told herself, writing is not a good idea. It would have to be a personal visit. Preferably with a big strong man to keep her company. She wondered how Robert was fixed for a visit to Ireland. Come to that, could she get any more time off work? She had been in her job only a few months and still had Clare's wedding to go to. That would use up all her holidays. She sighed. If she could not get the time off work, well, she could always get another job: Sarah could never get another Jean.

Chapter Thirty-nine

Margaret McCann had thought she was seeing things at first. Her daughter had walked into her house carrying a baby. She surely could not be babysitting for a friend, thought Margaret: no-one would be so cruel as to ask that of her. The suspicion that Mairead had stolen a child from its pram was uppermost in her mind. Grief made people do the strangest things. 'What on earth? Where did this come from?' she stuttered.

'It's OK. She's ours.' Seamus reassured her. Mairead turned and smiled at her husband. He gave her a wink before turning to his mother-in-law, who was standing with her mouth open. So many questions had jumped into her mind that she did not know which to ask first.

'It's true.' he insisted. 'Here, let's get baby Sinead settled and then we'll tell you all about it.'

Margaret had to constrain her curiosity until the baby was feed, bathed, changed and put to sleep in the bedroom.

'Right!' demanded Margaret, 'Now she's settled, I want to know everything. Where did she come from? Whose is she? Why have you got her?'

Seamus held up his hand for silence. When he could finally get a word in, he tried to explain: 'She's Danny's. You know, me brother? When he was away working in England, he got this girl into trouble and Sinead was the result. Now the mother doesn't want the child and thought Danny's family should rear her. So we're taking her in.'

'Though how anyone could not want such a beautiful baby is beyond me. The mother must be some sort of monster.' Mairead added indignantly.

'Let's not be too hard on her' advised her husband. 'After all, she's given us Sinead.' Mairead nodded and smiled, squeezing her husband's hand.

Looking at her daughter's face, Margaret held back on the many protests she had planned to make. Taking in another woman's child on a whim did not seem right to her but, for the first time in a long while, her daughter was actually smiling. Mairead's face had softened and lost some of the gauntness that had settled there since the loss of her child. It almost looked like she was coming back to life. That settled it as far as Margaret was concerned. If it made her daughter happy again then she did not care if the child was given, stolen or dropped by a stork. The baby was now family.

'There's just one thing.' Seamus cautioned his mother-in-law. 'Me ma doesn't want everybody knowing that our Danny has been, you know, putting it about, like. So, if anyone asks, we're going to say we got the child from the nuns in Nazareth Lodge. That we're taking it in with a view to adoption. And there's something else.' He glanced at his wife, who nodded encouragingly. 'Me and Mairead are thinking of moving. If we go somewhere where nobody knows us, then nobody will know the child is not really ours. That way we can bring her up without any stigma attached.'

Margaret could see the wisdom in this but, at the same time, was concerned at the thought of losing her daughter.

'Where will you go?' she asked.

'We haven't decided yet. We don't want to rush into anything. After all, we've got a baby to consider now.'

Margaret almost cried with relief at seeing the joy that statement evoked in her daughter and son-in-law's faces.

Later that night, as Mairead and Seamus lay in each other's arms, listening to their newly acquired daughter breathing, and making plans for the future, Seamus put forward a proposal.

'Mairead, I was just thinking. You know the way we're planning on moving away from here?'

'Hmm?' came the sleepy reply.

'What if we moved right away?'

'What do you mean?'

'What about emigrating to Australia?'

'Australia!' exclaimed Mairead, sitting upright, all thoughts of sleep banished.

'But that's miles away! It's the other side of the world!'

'Exactly. No-one will know us there. No-one will ever have to know that Sinead's not really ours. And we'll never have to worry about Sinead's mother changing her mind again and turning up looking for her.'

'Do you think she'd do that?' Mairead asked anxiously.

'Hard to say. But if we migrated then it wouldn't matter.'

'And what about our families? We'll miss them.'

'That's true. But they could always come and visit. And anyway, isn't Sinead more important?'

Mairead was forced to agree but there was still a hesitation about venturing so far away. Seamus reassured her.

'Look, we don't have to decide now. We'll go down to Australia House and find out if we're eligible for the "Australia for Ten Pounds" scheme. We may not be. And we'll read all the leaflets and stuff that we can get on Australia. At the minute it's just an idea. We may not like the sound of the place when we find out more about it. But, you know, it might be something worth thinking about.'

Mairead settled down again. A new start with her new family. It was quite an appealing idea. She drifted off to sleep and dreamt of a bright and happy future, full of laughter and joy.

Chapter Forty

It was the end of a long hard day at work and Barbara was looking forward to going home, kicking off her shoes, and wrapping herself round a large gin and tonic. She was slightly irritated, therefore, to see someone standing outside the door of her flat. Annoyed that one of her neighbours had let him in the front door, she made a mental note to bring it up at the next Resident Association's meeting. She was in no mood to talk to salesmen. It was not until he said 'Hello, Babs' that she recognised Robert.

'Elvis!' she cried, throwing her arms around him. 'Am I glad to see you! Come in! Come in!'

Leading the way into her living room, she offered him a drink and, pouring one for herself, joined him on the settee.

There was something subtlety different about Robert. Although it was only three or four months since she had last seen him, he appeared more grown up, almost sophisticated. He was wearing a navy pinstripe suit that looked far superior to anything that Burton's could supply, and shoes of good quality leather, buffed to a high shine.

'Why are you in London?' asked Barbara as soon as they were settled comfortably. 'Did you get my letter?'

'That's one of the reasons I'm here. What's this about Jean being kidnapped?'

Barbara explained the story in greater depth than in her letter, telling him in more detail of her suspicions and her plans and answering his questions.

'So basically, you want me to find out where this McAllister woman is living now, go there and fetch the baby back?'

'That's a fair summation' agreed Barbara.

'I'm not sure that it will be that easy. If she has stolen the child – and we're still not sure of that' He held up a hand to stem Barbara's imminent protest. 'If she has stolen the child, what makes you think she'll just meekly hand her back to me, that's assuming we can find her. If Sarah couldn't find the woman, what makes you think I can do any better?'

'You found out her address before, when Sarah was pregnant. Ask your friends in the building sites. Somebody must know!' Barbara was becoming increasingly agitated. This was not the response she had been expecting. Robert was supposed to make everything all right, not point out difficulties.

'OK. Assuming I find out this woman's address and assuming it's not just a misunderstanding, wouldn't it be better for Sarah to be there? That way, if we do have to call the police, they would be more likely to give the child back to her than to hand it to me, who, for all they know, could be some sort of mad axe murderer.'

Barbara was forced to agree to the logic of the argument but reminded Robert that Sarah had a sick grandmother who needed to be cared for twenty-four hours a day.

'We'll cross that bridge when we come to it.' asserted Robert. 'Let's see if we can track down the baby-napper first. I have to go to the building sites tomorrow anyway, so I'll ask around and see if anyone knows anything. Let's keep our fingers crossed.'

With that, Barbara had to be content.

Before he took his leave, Barbara gave Robert her phone number at work and Sarah's address in Yorkshire. She made him promise he would contact both of them as soon as he had any news. He agreed, but warned her again against getting too hopeful. In his limited experience, people who wanted to disappear usually proved very difficult to find. He was heading back to his hotel when, on a hunch, he turned and made for the White Swan. It was just possible that some of the workers might still be having a pint or two there, even if it was a Tuesday night. Walking into the pub, Robert felt as though he had never left. Nothing had changed. He was not sure why he had expected it to be different, maybe it was because he himself had changed and therefore he expected other things to be different too. A voice from the corner broke into his musings.

'Well blow me if it isn't our Elvis! Look at ye! All posh and fancy now. I suppose you're too good to talk to the likes of us now?'

Robert grinned. 'How are you, Roddy? Good to see you again. I see some things never change. A pint of mild, is it?'

'I'll not say no. So what brings you back to these parts? I thought you'd gone back to Scotland for good?'

'I'm recruiting. Looking for a few good men that'll be willing to work in Scotland.'

'Tell me more, I might be interested myself. Getting a bit fed up with this place. It's all right for a while but it's not a place to live in for long.'

Roddy and Robert chatted about work for a while before Robert casually started asking about other workers. He eventually worked round to the subject of Danny McAllister.

'All I know about him', volunteered Roddy, 'was that he went back to Belfast. I heard he'd got some girl in trouble then did the dirty on her. Shame. I thought he was a good bloke. He was a good worker, mind you. If you want him to go work for you, you could ask young Bernie McArdle. He's working down Oxford Street. He seems to know everybody. Have a word with him.' Robert bought another round of drinks and continued chatting with Roddy. He had found out as much as he could from his old colleague but, as there was nothing else he could do that night, Robert thought he may as well enjoy the crack.

First thing the following day, he took the tube down to Convent Gardens and walked the length of Oxford Street, looking for building sites. There were a number of them but a casual query soon lead him to the one that Bernie McArdle was working on. Robert had a quick word with the foreman first of all: building site etiquette demanded it. The foreman reluctantly granted him permission to speak to Bernie during working hours. Robert grinned to himself. It was amazing the difference a decent suit made, he thought. Had he walked on to the building site in the sort of clothes he used to wear, no-one would have given him the time of day. Yet now, here he was getting special dispensation to talk to one of the workers.

'Is anything wrong? Is me ma all right?' Bernie asked anxiously as he approached Robert. Robert reassured him quickly.

'No, No, I'm sure everything's fine. I'm actually looking for an old friend of mine. We used to work together but then we went our separate ways and lost touch. I was hoping you might be able to help me find him again.'

Bernie looked doubtful. Men in suits never boded well.

'Why do you think I can help?' he asked suspiciously.

'Roddy said you might be able to help. He said you were the only one to go to for information. Said you knew everybody.'

Bernie preened a little at the praise. 'Well, I might be able to help. Who are you looking for and what do you want with them?'

'I'm looking for Danny McAllister. I've started my own business up north and I want him to come work with me again.'

Bernie peered a little closer at Robert. 'I don't remember you working with Danny.'

'Well, I used to have sideburns and a DA. And I used to wear drainpipes.'

'Elvis!' exclaimed Bernie. 'Lord I didn't recognise a bit of you! I thought you was somebody important! Aye, I know where Danny is. Half way round the world by now! He joined the merchant navy soon after he went back home. Turned out he couldn't stick Belfast either.'

Robert was disappointed but at least, he thought, there was some truth in what the girls had been told.

'Do you have any idea where his family have moved to? I did write to the address in Servia Street but they never got back to me.' Robert could ask anything now he had established his credentials.

'His family's up in Whiterock Avenue now. They're living beside my aunt Sadie. She's in number ten so it's one of the houses beside that.'

Robert could have hugged Bernie. However, he wisely restrained himself as it would not have gone down well on a building site. One more question: 'I hear they've had a new addition to the family. A baby girl?'

Bernie shook his head. 'Don't know about that. Me auntie Sadie never mentioned it. And she loves babies.'

Robert was nonplussed. He thanked Bernie for his information and slipped a half-crown into his hand. Bernie skipped away delightedly. Robert, however, was puzzled. Whatever had happened to baby Jean?

Chapter Forty-one

Every morning Sarah waited for the post. And every morning her hopes were dashed. The longed-for letter from Mary Ann never materialised. She could not stop herself from hoping, but every day without word pushed her further and further into despair. The only thing that kept her going was her grandmother. Now almost totally dependant on Sarah, Lizzie required full-time care. One morning, while struggling to help Lizzie get washed, Sarah found herself thinking: *It's as well Jean's not here. I couldn't cope with two babies!* The shock of the thought made her drop the sponge and run out of the bathroom. *How could I even think that*, she chided herself. *Maybe I don't deserve her! I should have done more to protect my baby, instead of handing her over to Mary Ann as if she were a cup of sugar to be lent out! I was stupid enough to fall for Mary Ann's falsehoods. Everyone warned me about that woman but I thought I knew best! I'm not fit to be a mother!*

She was shaken out of her self-pitying crying fit by Lizzie. 'I've finished washing myself. Can I have my breakfast now?'

Sarah looked at Lizzie who was standing before her, dripping wet. It looked like her grandmother had upended a bucket of water over herself. She should not have been left alone in the bathroom. Wiping away the tears with the back of her hand, Sarah gave herself a shake: there was no use feeling sorry for herself. She had to put her trust in Barbara and Robert and hope that they would, together, work something out. In the meantime, her grandmother needed her.

After her grandmother was dried, changed and fed, Sarah settled her in front of the television. During the day the BBC would broadcast music and that, together with the test-card, seemed to amuse Lizzie as much as any of the programmes. It kept her occupied enough to allow Sarah to get on with some work. While she was stitching, Sarah often held conversations in her mind with her distant daughter, reminding Jean that she was loved and missed and that she would be home soon. She imagined bringing Jean for her first pair of shoes: for her first ice-cream. These thoughts helped keep her daughter alive in her imagination. Hours passed in this manner, with the sewing machine whirring away intermittently against a background of cheery classical music.

The knock on the door was unexpected. Few people in the neighbourhood bothered to announce their arrival in this way. They usually opened the door and walked straight in. Wondering who it could be, Sarah reached for her purse before opening the door. She did not like to send pedlars away empty-handed. Initially, she did not recognise Robert but the instant she did, she threw her arms around him and hugged him as if she would never let go.

'Robert! It's so good to see you!' she exclaimed. 'How are you?' Finally relinquishing him, she took both his hands in hers and stood back a step. 'Barbara said you'd changed! But look at you! You look wonderful!'

Robert hoped he sounded sincere when he returned the compliment but, in truth, he was shocked by Sarah's appearance. Her hair was scraped back into an unflattering knot at the back of her head and her skin, naturally pale, now looked haggard. There were dark circles under her eyes and her normally curvaceous figure looked gaunt.

'How long are you staying for? Oh I hope you can stay for ages! It's so nice to see you again. Barbara said you'd gone back to Scotland. What are you doing there? You can't still be in the building trade – you look far too prosperous!'

'Actually, I am' replied Robert, making himself comfortable as Sarah fussed around him, offering him food and drink.

'Difference is, I'm the boss now.'

Sarah demanded to hear all about his new position and how it had come about.

'I had a real stroke of luck. When I left London, I met this guy on the train. We just got talking, you know the way you do. It helps pass the time on a long journey. Well, it turned out this guy was an architect, down in London for some conference or something. Anyway, we seemed to hit it off together and we were just chatting away when he mentions he's looking for a good building firm for these conversions he's doing.'

'What's a conversion?' asked Sarah.

'It's when you get one of these big old houses that are too big for one family anymore, rip out the insides, and turn them into three or four separate flats. There's good money in it. Well, to make a long story short, he offered me the job. I got some of my mates together, lads I'd worked with in the past, and we finished the first job in six weeks. He was so pleased with the result, not only did he give me a bonus, but I'm now contracted to do a dozen more. And he's recommending me to all his architect friends. That's why I was down in London, looking for more reliable lads who can come and work for me.'

'You were in London? Did you see Barbara?' Sarah did not want to ask Robert if he had found out anything about Jean. She could not stand it if her hopes were dashed again. Robert, however, knew what was on her mind.

'I saw Barbara. I also saw a guy I used to work with. He told me that Danny has joined the navy.' He paused before saying 'He also gave me Mary Ann McAllister's new address.'

Robert watched the light go on in Sarah's eyes. He spoke quickly, before she became too hopeful: 'Mary Ann is there, but there's no word on Jean.'

Sarah was puzzled. 'If Jean isn't with Mary Ann, then where is she?'

'I don't know yet. But I think it might be a good idea if we both went over to Belfast to see her. She's bound to know where Jean is.'

Sarah slumped visibly. 'I can't go. I can't leave my gran. I'm all she's got.'

Robert glanced over to where Lizzie was propped in front of the television.

'Is she all right?' he asked in concern.

Sarah turned and, with a cry, jumped to her grandmother's side.

'Gran! Gran! Are you all right? Gran?'

Lizzie's head was lolling on her neck and, while her eyes were open, it was clear that she could see nothing.

'Stay and watch her!' Sarah commanded Robert. 'I'm going to fetch Doctor Harrington!'

Within ten minutes Sarah was back with the village doctor who made a perfunctory check of Lizzie's vital signs before turning to Robert.

'There's a phone box at the end of the street. Go call an ambulance. Tell them Mrs Taylor has had a serious stroke and they must send someone straight away.'

Robert bounded out the door and down the street, glad of something positive and productive to do. He had felt so helpless sitting holding the old lady's hand, murmuring 'There, There, everything's going to be fine' when he had no idea if it was or not.

Sarah, meanwhile, was pressing Dr Harrington for answers that he could not give.

'I'm sorry, Sarah. I was afraid something like this would happen. It's not unexpected but I can't tell how it's going to go. Some people can recover from a stroke, even worse than this, and go on for years. With others, well …' He let the sentence trail away.

Chapter Forty-two

Since her grandmother's stroke, Sarah had had no more than three hours sleep at any one time. At first there had been the anxiety of travelling in the ambulance to the cottage hospital, where her grandmother had been poked and prodded by various doctors and nurses, injected with medication and hooked up to a drip feed of some sort. Sarah had sat by her bed all night, afraid to leave in case the worst happened. Robert had sat beside her, giving her encouragement occasionally but mostly just sitting there holding her hand. She drew a great deal of comfort and strength from simply knowing he was there. In the morning Sarah had spoken to the doctor but the prognosis was not encouraging. According to him, there was little anybody could do expect make Lizzie comfortable. It was, Sarah was told, only a matter of time.

She had talked it over with Robert, but Sarah had already made up her mind. Her grandmother was not going to die in some anonymous hospital: she would be nursed at home. The hospital insisted on keeping Lizzie for a few days to run some tests and during that period, Robert had stayed by Sarah's side. He had helped her move Lizzie's bed from upstairs to the living room, rearranging the furniture in order to make everything as comfortable as possible for Lizzie. Once they had her home and settled, Robert had taken Sarah into the kitchen to discuss the future.

'Sarah', he began, 'I hate to do this, but I'm going to have to go back home for a few days. I have things I need to sort out and I can't really leave it any longer. I don't like leaving you to cope alone so, I hope you don't mind, but I've had a word with Doctor Harrington and his wife and they have agreed that Mrs Harrington will look in on Lizzie for a couple of hours a day to give you a hand. Hannah says she'll do whatever she can to help as well.'

Sarah flung her arms around him. 'Robert, you have been wonderful! I don't know what I would have done without you! It's funny how you're always there when I need you. Thank you for everything you've done for me and for Lizzie.'

Coming out of the embrace, Sarah took hold of one of Robert's hands and looked up into his eyes. 'I'll miss you.' she said sincerely.

'Not for long', replied Robert. 'As soon as I get everything sorted, I'll call down again – just for a day or two – after all, I have to make sure my favourite girl is being looked after properly. Isn't that right, Liz?' He called the last sentence into the other room.

After he had gathered together the few items of clothes he had brought with him, Robert paid his bill at the inn and paid a visit to Hannah. With her usual good nature, she agreed to keep an eye on Lizzie to give Sarah the opportunity to walk her friend to the train station. They had walked the two miles at a slow pace, talking about nothing in particular and enjoying the beautiful May weather. Seeing him onto the train, Sarah was surprised at the emotion that overwhelmed her. She had not wanted him to leave. She told herself that she was simply feeling particularly vulnerable at that point. Robert had been a very good friend when she needed one and she was sorry to see him go. That's all, she told herself.

When Sarah reached her home, Hannah was sitting on the front step reading a magazine.

'Lizzie's sleeping so I thought I would come out here so that I wouldn't disturb her. Look,' she said, showing Sarah the magazine, 'This is the magazine Barbara works for. Isn't it fabulous?'

The two friends sat on the steps for a while discussing the latest fashions and guessing which of the articles Barbara had been involved with. Eventually, though, Hannah had to go and Sarah was faced with the prospect of looking after Lizzie on her own.

It was much harder work that she expected. Lizzie could do nothing for herself. She had to be washed, fed, changed, and medicated four times a day. She had no concept of night or day, so would wake or sleep whenever the mood took her. When she woke up, she would call out for her husband or her daughter, both long since dead. Sarah would sit with her at these times trying to reassure her. When Mrs Harrington called during the day, Sarah would do the shopping and the washing and the housework while she could. Her piece work had gone by the board: there was not enough time to do that as well. She snatched her sleep when she could, rarely more than a few hours at a time. Robert had called down every weekend and his company boosted her spirits. He would insist that she catch up on her sleep while he watched over Lizzie. This was the most rest she would get for the entire week so she did take advantage of it. Robert had written to Barbara to let her know how ill Lizzie was and the almost daily letters from Barbara had also help lift her morale.

Five weeks after she had had her stroke, Lizzie Taylor passed away. It was a Sunday evening and she had been watching 'What's My Line?' on television, or at least, had had her head turned in that direction, when she gave a slight groan and slipped away. Sarah had not gone for the doctor straight away. She spent a few quiet moments saying her final goodbyes to the woman who had been both parent and grandparent to her. She closed Lizzie's eyes reverently, kissed her fragile cheek, combed her hair for the last time, and checked that everything was clean and tidy. Only then did she go to the front door and ask a passing neighbour if they would be good enough to ask Doctor Harrington to call. Respect for the dead included not leaving the body unattended.

She had phoned Barbara on the Monday morning at her place of work and sent Robert a telegram. There was no-one else she needed to tell. They both made arrangements to be with her as soon as they could, Robert arriving that evening, and Barbara the following morning. Throughout the days following Lizzie's demise, Sarah's friends supported her in every way they could. Robert made most of the funeral arrangements, while Barbara made the gallons of tea and mountains of sandwiches considered essential at such times.

Everyone in the village and for miles around attended the funeral. Even Sam and some of the factory workers came to pay their respects. Lizzie had been a popular and well-respected figure in the area. It was a lovely service and Sarah was touched by the many tributes and by the kind words of the mourners as they offered her their condolences. After the service there was more tea and sandwiches in the village hall. All went as well as could be expected and Sarah smiled and made small talk with those who had come to say farewell to Lizzie Taylor. She listened to the stories and the reminisces of the mourners with good grace and patience. Inside, however, she was screaming. She wanted it all to be over so that she could go back to her own home and crawl into bed. She was exhausted.

Eventually, however, it was all over. The last of the mourners drifted away, the last of the teacups were washed up, and the three friends made their way back to Sarah's home. Robert had thoughtfully arranged to have Lizzie's bed moved back upstairs and the furniture returned to its original position. Even so, the room looked strangely empty, almost like someone else's house. Her friends insisted that she went to bed for a while and Sarah did not raise much of a protest. When she awoke, some four hours later, and came down the stairs, Barbara went into the kitchen and returned with a bottle of wine and three glasses. 'I think we need this. I can't possibly face another cup of tea!' Sarah almost smiled. She felt awash with tea and sympathy. A good stiff drink would do her the world of good. Over a few glasses of wine they talked about the funeral and the mourners for a while before Robert started to shuffle in his seat a little and clear his throat. He looked over at Barbara who gave him an almost imperceptible nod.

'Sarah, Barbara and I have been talking.' Again he looked to Barbara for encouragement. 'We think that, now your gran's gone, there's nothing keeping you here.' Barbara interrupted: 'So I'd like it if you would come and live with me. Clare's getting married in a week's time, so she'll be moving out and I'd be glad of your company. And there's plenty of room in my flat for when Jean comes back.'

'We were thinking', Robert continued, 'That you should give it a few days to gather yourself together, catch up on your rest and get everything sorted, then come down to London. Once Clare's wedding is over, we can all go over to Belfast, confront this McAllister woman, and get Jean back. Then the two of you can move in with Barbara.'

'But what about your work?' Sarah asked, concerned that her friends would get in to trouble for her sake.

'Don't worry about me!' Robert reassured her. 'I'm my own boss now, and I've got a good foreman. Everything's in hand.'

'And I've told people in work that I've got scabies!' said Barbara with a devilish grin. 'They don't want me anywhere near them for at least a fortnight!'

Sarah's mind was slightly befuddled with the drink and with the events of the past weeks. She was not sure what the future would hold for her now, but, she thought, with friends like these, everything was bound to work out in the end.

Chapter Forty-three

Clare's wedding was a grand affair; her new husband a charming, attractive man, easy-going and as in love with Clare as she was with him. Clare looked beautiful in an off-the-shoulder, knee length white satin dress, nipped in at the waist and flounced out by a dozen net and satin petticoats. The church was full to overflowing with friends, relatives and well-wishers. A stunning bouquet adorned every pew as well as the altar, and there was a choir that sounded positively angelic. Sarah could not help contrasting this ceremony with the quiet solemn affair that had been her grandmother's funeral. Tears rolled unstoppably down her cheeks. She was crying from regret for what had happened and for what would never happen, and a hundred other emotions that she could not put a name to.

Robert handed her his handkerchief.

'I brought a spare one. I know you women. Always crying at weddings.'

Grateful for the cover, both literally and metaphorically, Sarah buried her face in the clean white cotton and once again thanked her lucky stars for having a friend like Robert.

As she left the church, looking radiantly happy, the new Mrs Blanchflower paused to pose for the photographer before tossing her bouquet in the air. Sarah watched as it spun round, losing a few petals on its journey, before being eagerly seized by one of the younger bridesmaids. There was much tittering and giggling and teasing of the bouquet catcher, all of it given and taken in good sport before the congregation headed towards the hotel in which the wedding reception was being held. Sarah and Robert had been seated side by side at the reception, which was a relief to Sarah, not only because she knew almost no-one else there but also because Robert understood how she felt. She confided in him that it seemed strange to be attending a wedding when her grandmother was barely cold in her grave; and putting a wedding before her search for Jean felt like a betrayal. Robert, as always, knew just the right thing to say.

'Your grandmother would certainly not want you to mope. She had a good innings. And from what I know of Lizzie, she would have enjoyed a good knees-up herself. She would have wanted you to be here for your friend's big day. And you know how much Barbara has been looking forward to it too. You wouldn't deprive her of that would you? Because she wouldn't have left you alone, you know. Besides,' he grinned mischievously, 'the sight of Barbara in baby blue – sure isn't that alone worth it?'

Sarah smiled. It was true that Barbara was notorious for dressing only in black, grey or navy, and was barely recognisable in the powder-blue knee length dress with matching bandeau hat that did her complexion no favours. Still, with her height and figure she carried it off wonderfully, leaving the other bridesmaids looking rather frumpy by comparison.

Robert continued, determined to win his argument. 'Another thing. Barbara would never have allowed you to go to Belfast without her. So, come on, cheer up and enjoy the party. Once we get Jean back, you'll not be able to go to many more parties for a while!'

Sarah allowed herself to be persuaded and did her best to have a good time for the sake of her friends. After a few glasses of wine, having a good time started to get a little easier and, when Robert demanded she get up and dance with him, she accepted with only the slightest pretence of reluctance.

She had never been able to jive very well but Robert did not seem to mind, laughing when she turned the wrong way in a spin or when she stepped on his toes as he pulled her towards him. She was slightly out of breath and flushed when the music changed. The first few notes of a slow number filtered into the air and several couples left the dance floor. Robert, however, pulled Sarah closer to him and held her firmly in position for a waltz. She tried to resist for just a fraction of a second. After all, they were not actually a couple and should not really be dancing this closely.

'Come on', coaxed Robert, 'you can't run off now. Not when they're playing our song.'

'We don't have a song' Sarah pointed out with the lilt of a laugh in her voice.

'Then this one will do. What do you think of it?'

Sarah thought it the most beautiful song she had ever heard.

'It's wonderful. What's it called?'

'"All I've got to do is dream" by the Everley Brothers.'

'And what do you dream of?' Sarah teased.

'This.' said Robert, holding her closer still.

It could have been the wine, or the exercise of the dance, or the excitement of the day, or it could have been the feeling of being held so close to Robert, that caused Sarah's flush to deepen.

The next morning, Barbara and Sarah were up early, despite the previous day's indulgences. While having breakfast they were interrupted by Robert pressing on the buzzer and demanding to be let in. Although they spent some time over coffee rehashing everything that had happened at

Clare's wedding, the friends were still early enough to pack a few items together and catch a tube to Euston Station in time to board the early afternoon train to Liverpool. Despite her misgivings, Sarah was in high spirits: she had really enjoyed the wedding and now she was finally going to see Jean again. Barbara and Robert, however, having consumed more alcohol than normal the previous day, managed to doze most of the way to Liverpool. While they slept, Sarah played out various scenarios in her mind. Most involved holding Jean in her arms and smothering her in kisses. The variations were whether or not she gave Mary Ann a good slap or just treated her with cold contempt.

When they arrived at the Liverpool station there was still plenty of time before they were due to board the ferry. A short discussion decided on them going for a meal. Sarah was so agitated she could barely eat. She kept talking about Jean: 'I wonder how many teeth she has now? I wonder if she's walking yet? Do you think her eyes will still be blue?'

Robert and Barbara indulged Sarah, letting her chatter on. They both thought it was nice to see her looking so positive.

They boarded the ferry in high spirits. As the ship drew closer and closer to Belfast, however, Sarah's mood started to change. 'What if we can't find her again? What if she doesn't recognise me? What if I can't get her back?'

Barbara was very firm with her. 'Look Sarah, Jean will be fine. You will get her back. Robert and I will see to that. In fact, I can't wait to give this Mary Ann a piece of my mind.'

'Sure you can spare it?' asked Robert, trying to lighten the mood. Barbara gave him a playful slap. 'Remind me: why did we bring him?'

The ship sailed slowly up Belfast Lough before docking at an infuriatingly slow pace. Another agonising wait for the gangway to unfold had Sarah's nerves in tatters. Eventually they disembarked and, together, the three friends walked towards the taxi rank. They climbed in and gave the driver the address of their destination. Once he had put their pieces of luggage in the boot, the taxi driver opened the passenger door again.

'Whiterock, you said? Where abouts in the Whiterock. It's a big estate now, ye know.'

Robert removed a slip of paper from his wallet and handed it to the driver, who stared at it intently for a moment before handing it back with a 'Rightoh! I think I know where that is.'

Levering himself behind the steering wheel, the driver set off on what the friends hoped would be the last stage of their journey.

In some ways, it was.

Chapter Forty-four

Danny McAllister was feeling good. He was back on dry land at last, admittedly not any land he had ever set foot on before, but land none the less. He had never realised that being trapped on a ship, no matter how big, would be like being stuck in a cage. Getting out of Belfast and putting the past behind him had been his priority and he had actually believed the advertisements; that by joining the navy he would see the world. Most of what he had actually seen was the ship's engine room, and by now he had seen as much as he ever wanted to of grey-painted pipes, panels and portholes. When he did go on deck, the heaving ocean had had a similar effect on his stomach. He had discovered, to his regret and rather belatedly, that he was a bad sailor. The only thing he enjoyed about the navy was the companionship of the other lads. In a way, it was rather like being on a building site, albeit one that moved continuously. Now, he and three of his shipboard buddies were about to hit the town after six weeks afloat. They were all in high good humour, looking forward to their furlough and a spell on the firm ground of Singapore.

A bar with flashing neon lights and the sound of Jerry Lee Lewis blaring out via speakers positioned near the door, drew them in like fish on a hook. Danny stood the first round, confident that it would be the first of many drinks consumed that night. He had barely placed the order when he felt an arm slip round his waist.

'Allo, Big Boy. You buy me drink, yes?'

Danny turned to see a pretty young local girl trying to mould herself around him. Confused, he looked to his friends. They were falling around laughing at him and Danny was sure they had set up this little scenario.

'Sorry love', he replied, 'I'm not drunk enough yet. Here,' Peeling her off him he steered her into the arms of his shipmate, Paul. 'He'll buy you lots of drinks. He's got lots of money. You go with him.'

Spotting an easier conquest, the girl sidled away from Danny and wrapped herself around Paul. Paul was only seventeen, probably a year or two older than the girl, and he was quite happy to have some female company for a change. Together, he and his 'companion' made their way to the back of the bar to the accompaniment of much jeers, teasing and ribald commentary from the others.

As he sipped his pint, it occurred to Danny that some things remained the same the world over. A group of lads; a few drinks; some female company and the 'craic would be mighty' as they said back home. His thoughts turned to home for a few moments as he wondered how Seamus and his wife were coping, whether things were getting any better for them. He had felt like a coward leaving them when they were going through so much but he had felt powerless and unable to be of any comfort or assistance to them. He hoped his mother would be able to do something to ease their pain. Funny, he mused, how we all depend on Mary Ann to keep us on the right track, even though we're grown men and women, we still turn to our mammy in times of need. His musings were interrupted by Manuel, the Spanish stoker.

'Ready for another one? How bout we try the local brew? It put hairs on the chest!'

Danny grinned. Forget about home. This was a night for getting drunk.

'Sure, Manny. Why not? Make it a double!'

Having downed a few of the most alcoholic brews the bar could offer, the shipmates were discussing the possibility of moving on to another bar – or 'seeing the sights' as they called it – when a ruckus occurred in the far end of the bar.

'Ye stole all me flipping money! I'll not stand for it! I want me money back!'

Recognising the sound of Paul's voice, despite its high pitched and agitated tone, the friend's barely glanced at each other before wading in to help.

'What's going on here?' demanded Stanley, a well-set-up, sturdy Welshman who worked alongside Danny in the engine room as an engineer.

'This bleedin bint! Stole all me money she did! One minute we're being all friendly like, the next, she's off with me wallet. And I want it back!' he cried, lunging at a very large, very imposing Chinese gentleman.

Drunk as they were, the shipmates knew a problem when they saw one. Or in this case, four. Three other equally large, equally impressive, Chinese gentlemen had stepped up behind the first.

'Come on, Paul' urged Danny, 'It's not worth it. Just put it down to experience.' He tried to drag the frenetic young man away from this potentially life-threatening situation, but Paul was having none of it.

'I'd a month's wages in that there wallet and she's not getting it!'

'Don't think she will be getting it anyroad.' muttered Stanley, more experienced in the way these things worked.

Paul managed to wriggled his way out of Danny's grip and torpedoed himself into the stomach of the leading Chinese bouncer. The man barely flinched. He lifted Paul by the throat and went to punch him in the face. Manny was first to react. Small but wiry, Manny knew how to handle himself in a fight. He launched himself at the big man's punching arm and, swinging from it, aimed a kick at his neither regions. It was enough to loosen his grip and Paul fell to the ground where he lay for a few minutes, totally stunned, while all hell broke loose around him. Among the screams from the other customers, the scraping of chairs and tables as they were hastily moved out of the way, and the grunts and yells of the protagonists, Danny swore softly under his breathe before joining in the fray.

Manny swung a chair over the head of one of the adversaries, while Stanley was laying into another with his fists. Danny ducked a haymaker of a punch and looked around for a handy weapon. A table leg had come adrift of its anchorage in the melee and Danny grabbed it. Standing up, he was just in time to thump it into the head of the man who had Stanley by the throat. By way of returning the favour, Stanley then threw an uppercut on the person about to do the same to Danny. Glancing round quickly, it seemed to Danny that the whole bar was in turmoil. Realising that this was a battle they could not win, he shouted to his companions to get out.

'Manny, grab Paul! Get him outside! Now!'

Manny, reluctantly it seemed, put down the chair he had been swinging about like a lasso, and grabbed Paul by the shoulders, dragging him to the door. Stanley and Danny stood shoulder to shoulder, trying to act as human shields to protect Paul and Manny. With the bar's staff slowly advancing towards them, they inched backwards to the door, trying to prevent any more bloodshed. Danny felt, more than saw, a figure to the right of him but before he could react the stinging in his right cheek told him he had been hurt. He swung round to deliver a low punch in the solar plexus only to stop short when he saw it was the young girl Paul had gone off with. She held the remains of a broken bottle in her hand and spat the words 'British pig-dog!' at him before lunging again. Danny was able to push her with enough force to topple her to the ground, where she fell in front of the advancing hoards, blocking their progress for just a moment. Danny had no time for pity or regret.

'Run!' he yelled, and together, Paul, Danny, Manny and Stanley scarpered as quickly as they could from the bar.

Several hundred yards later, confident that they were no longer being pursued, the shipmates stopped to recover their breath.

'God, that was a close one!' panted Stanley as he clutched his knees. Stanley was not built for running.

'But they've still got my money!' complained Paul.

'Never mind yer bleedin' money!' commanded Stanley through clenched teeth. 'You nearly got us all killed in there!'

'Look like Danny got most damage.' Manny was examining Danny's face in the glow of the street light.

'Look like you got cut bad.'

Danny touched the side of his face gingerly. It felt wet and sticky. When he glanced down, there seemed to be a lot of blood on his shirt. And now that he had stopped running long enough to take stock, he could feel the ache, and the shooting pains that suggested he should not move his facial muscles too much.

'I've been cut.' he said, stating the obvious.

'Let's get you back to the ship. Ship's doc will have you right as rain in no time.' Stanley patted Danny on the back.

'You put up a good fight, sonny,' he said approvingly. 'And as for you, Manny, I'm glad you were on our side!'

Manny grinned. 'You see how I knock two down with my chair? They not expecting that!'

'No, and I don't think yer man was expecting you to jump on his shoulders and bite his ear either!'

Despite his pain, Danny laughed.

And in the manner of a conquering army, they made their way back to the ship.

Chapter Forty-five

Sarah strained to stare out the taxi window as it approached the Whiterock estate. Every house was etched in her memory and she was curious to see which, of the many she had called on, had actually contained her daughter. When the taxi finally pulled up outside number eight, Sarah frowned. She had called on that house and, while it had appeared empty, no one on either side had admitted to knowing the McAllisters. It seemed people had been lying to her. Without waiting for the driver to open the door, Sarah shot out of the taxi and practically ran to the front door of number eight. Barbara followed her up the path, leaving Robert to settle with the driver, who, despite Robert's entreaties and promises of an extra large tip, refused to wait on them. 'I can spot trouble when I see it, and I see it now and I'm not waiting!' Robert was only halfway to the front door, therefore, when it was flung open by a half-dressed man demanding to know who in the name of Christ was banging so loudly so early in the morning.

A stunned silence was then followed by an incredulous query in unison of 'Danny?'

'Sarah?'

As they faced each other over the doorstep, Danny was first to regain his composure.

'What are you doing here? And who's that with you?' Danny had failed to recognise his erstwhile friends as he still remembered them as beatniks and rockers. It took a few seconds before he realised who they were.

'What on earth? My God, this is unbelievable! What on earth are you's all doing here?'

'We could ask you the same question!' said Robert, taking control. 'We thought you were in the navy!'

'I am. I mean, I was. I only got home yesterday. I've left now. But what am I doing? Come in! Come in!'

Danny ushered them into the house, still obviously puzzled by their presence. 'But what on earth brings you three here?'

'We've come to fetch Jean.' said Barbara, daring him to make anything of it.

'Who's Jean?' asked Danny.

Barbara, Robert and Sarah looked at each other, puzzled, before Sarah replied quietly: 'Jean's your daughter.'

'I have a daughter?' asked Danny with delight. 'I often wondered whether it was a boy or a girl.' His face changing to a frown, he added reproachfully, 'I wish you'd told me.'

The three friends were stunned. It took a moment before Sarah enquired; 'Didn't you get my letters?'

'You never wrote to me. And I wrote you lots of times. I wanted you to come and join me in Belfast, but you never answered me. And I wrote to you, Barbara. But neither of you wrote back. That's why I joined the navy: I thought you wanted nothing to do with me.'

'It was me mam, Danny' said a small voice behind them on the stairway. As one, they turned to face the speaker.

Anne Marie, clutching her dressing gown, slowly descended the stairs.

'She burnt all your letters, Danny. Yours, too, Sarah. And she made me promise not to tell anyone. And I'm sorry, but I didn't know what to do for the best.' Tears started to stream down her face.

'I'm sorry, Sarah! I'm really sorry! I didn't want to do it! I didn't even know I was doing it until it was too late! I'm sorry, I'm sorry!'

Anne Marie, wailing now, had slumped onto the bottom step, where Danny and Sarah knelt beside her, trying to make sense of what had just been said.

'It's okay, Anne Marie, it's okay. I know you wouldn't hurt Jean. It's okay.' Turning to Barbara, Sarah instructed her to fetch some water for Anne Marie, while Robert produced a handkerchief which he dangled in front of the crying girl. She snatched at it gratefully and, blowing her nose loudly, started to recover her composure. Danny, however, was slightly mystified. How did Anne Marie and Sarah know each other? How did Anne Marie know about Jean? Especially as he had been unaware of his daughter's existence. He could feel the scar on his cheek ache as screwed up his face trying to make sense of it all.

'OK. Look! I need a few answers here. None of this is making any sense to me. Let's go into the parlour and we'll all sit down and someone can explain to me exactly what's been happening around here.' Danny practically frogmarched his sister into the parlour and directed her, perhaps not as gently as he could have, into a chair. Everyone else followed. Amid the questions and counter questions, the puzzlement and bewilderment, the explanations and the clarifications, the series of apparent misunderstandings was made clear. As was Mary Ann's role in the proceeding.

It was Robert who grasped the nettle first: 'So where is Mary Ann right now? And more importantly, where's Jean?'

Anne Marie volunteered the information that her mother was up at the new church. 'She's on some committee or other. It's her turn to do the flowers, so she'll be there for a while and then she'll be at the nine o'clock mass. Father Hanson's moved here now and he only takes the nine o'clock so me mam always goes to his mass. She likes him', she finished simply.

'What time is it now?' asked Barbara.

'It's five to. It'll be over an hour before she's back.'

'Never mind about her coming back! I want to see her now! And I want my daughter now! Where is she? Is she with your mother?' Sarah demanded to know.

Anne Marie clenched her mouth shut and shook her head.

Danny grabbed his sister by the arms: 'Where is she, Anne Marie? Where's my daughter?'

Frightened by the strength of his grip, Anne Marie burst into tears again, crying out 'Ask me mam! Ask me mam!'

'Right! I'll ask me mam. I'll ask her right now!'

Without waiting to see if the others were following him, Danny strode to the door. It was only when he got outside that he realised he had no idea where the church was.

'Anne Marie!' he shouted. 'Where the hell's this bloody church?'

Anne Marie was forced to come out and point the way but Danny was not satisfied.

'You can lead the way. You'll have a fair idea of where me mam will be at this time. Come on!' he urged, driving the weeping girl in front of him.

'Danny! She not dressed!' cried Sarah.

'Doesn't matter, it can't be that far away.'

Lead by a mortified Anne Marie, the group trooped through several streets and up a steep incline to the newly built church on the top of the hill. By the time they reached it, the mass had already started. That, however, was no deterrent to Danny McAllister. Pushing Anne Marie aside, he strode down the aisle, looking left and right for his mother.

He found her eventually, in the second pew from the altar rails.

'There ye are, woman! Come out! You've got a lot of explaining to do!'

Mary Ann was startled to see her son. If she had not expected him to accompany her to mass, she certainly had no expectation of his behaving in such a manner in church.

'What do you think you're doing?' she hissed at him. 'Sit yerself down before everybody sees you making an show of yerself!'

'The only person making an show of me is you ma!' Danny did not moderate the level of his voice. He was furious and did not care who heard him. He was oblivious to the mutters growing around him as the rest of the congregation strained to discover what was happening.

'Out! Now! Or by God, I'll drag you out!'

As Mary Ann looked around, seeking some sort of explanation for her son's behaviour, her eyes fell on Sarah and her friends.

'You!' she cried.

'Yes, it's me', said Sarah. 'I'm come for my baby.'

A cruel, malicious smile spread slowly across Mary Ann's face. 'Well, you're too late. She's gone.'

'Gone? What do you mean, gone? Gone where?' asked Danny and Sarah, practically simultaneously.

'Where you'll not be able to find her.' sneered Mary Ann, looking pointedly at Sarah. Robert managed to hold Sarah back before she could scratch Mary Ann's eyes out. He was not able to stop Danny, however. Danny grabbed his mother by both her shoulders, pulling her up from the pew.

'Tell me! Tell me what's happened to my daughter!' he demanded. He had to shake her several times before she finally answered.

'Seamus has her!'

Danny dropped his hold on his mother as if he had been bitten. Turning round to a nearby pew, he sank down on to it, put his head in his hands and muttered, 'Oh fuck!'

Chapter Forty-six

Father Hanson had seen enough. Brushing aside an altar boy who was standing in his way, he descended from the altar.

'What is the meaning of this?' he bawled. 'I'll be having none of this ruckus in my church! What's going on? Mary Ann?'

He looked to her with a question in his eye. It was Sarah who answered, however.

'She lied to me! She told me Danny wanted nothing to do with me or our baby. She burnt all my letters to him and then, as if that wasn't bad enough, she pretended she was helping me when all the while she had planned to kidnap my daughter!'

The murmuring in the seats behind grew louder as this titbit of information was relayed down the length of the church.

Father Hanson looked from Mary Ann to Danny for confirmation.

'Is this true? Did you lie to me as well?' This last question was addressed to Mary Ann. 'You told me the child was unwanted, that it's mother wanted nothing to do with it. That's why you were bringing it back to give to Seamus and Mairead – so that they could give it a good home.'

The priest's voice resounded throughout the church. The congregation did not need to strain their ears to hear every word. He continued in the same vein: 'Am I to understand that you did indeed kidnap this woman's child? That you lied to your own son? And that you treated your own grandchild like a parcel of meat to be passed around as it suited you, woman?' He glared at Mary Ann, his face crimson with fury. There was a brief pause while everyone held their breath to hear what the priest would say next.

'That's it!' he bellowed. 'Time for confession. And a bloody good act of contrition, I'd say!'

A white-faced Mary Ann made to follow the priest, acutely conscience of the babble from the congregation behind her.

'Wait!' cried Sarah. 'I still don't know where Jean is.'

'Ask Danny.' suggested Mary Ann snidely.

Sarah turned to see Danny slumped in a pew. She was puzzled by his behaviour. He had not said a word since he first confronted his mother and his rage seemed to have subsided totally, leaving him lank and tired looking. She knelt beside him. 'Danny! Danny! What is it? What's wrong? Where's Jean?' He raised his head slowly. 'Of course: you wouldn't know anything about it.' He sighed again before taking her hand and, looking into her anxious eyes, tried to explain as succinctly as he could.

'My brother Seamus' wife, Mairead, was pregnant about the same time as you. Only she lost her baby in childbirth. And she's not able to have any more children. It almost broke my brother's heart. And I thought Mairead was going to follow her daughter into an early grave.' He cast a bitter look at Mary Ann. 'Now it appears my loving, caring, mother here, has stolen our baby to give to my brother.'

'But she can't do that!' cried Barbara who, to her credit, had refrained from verbal and physical violence thus far.

'Looks like she already has. The thing is, Sarah', Danny shook his head as he tried to articulate his thoughts. 'The thing is, I don't know if I could take another child away from them. It would break their hearts. If it was just up to me, I would gladly give them anything, including my daughter, if I thought it would help them. You have no idea how losing their daughter affected them.'

'I have every idea!' screamed Sarah, goaded beyond endurance. 'I've lost my daughter too!' She pointed at Mary Ann. 'That - that **woman** has stolen my daughter from me! How do you think I feel? A part of me has been torn away! Thanks to that evil witch of a mother of yours!'

'At least your bastard's still alive.' spat Mary Ann. 'I thought you'd be glad to get rid of it.'

Danny managed to hold Sarah back. Robert, however, was not so quick off the mark when it came to restraining Barbara. She stepped forward and fetched Mary Ann a heavy smack across the face. 'You horrible fucking bitch!' she cried. Barbara was less refined in her use of language than Sarah.

'Not in my Church, young woman!' interjected Father Hanson. 'Come with me, all of you. You, too, Anne Marie. I've a notion you had a part to play in this as well and I want to know all about it.' Turning to the altar again, he instructed Father O'Neill to continue the mass. 'And don't forget to pray for the souls of all sinners. We have enough of them here today.' he added grimly. He frogmarched the little band down the aisle. As she followed in the priest's wake, Mary Ann could hear the whispers, some of them none too quiet: 'And I thought she was a decent woman.' 'I always thought there was something funny about her.' She told me it was the debt collectors were after her! I'll never believe a word she says ever again.' 'The shame of it! Imagine stealing a child from its mother.' 'Hangings too good for the likes of her.' Even Sadie Flanaghan was shaking her head and tutting. To be disapproved of by her next door neighbour! Mary Ann had always considered herself superior to Sadie and to the rest of her neighbours, both in intellect and in moral conduct. Yet here she was, being ordered off to confession in front of everyone as if she were a naughty schoolgirl. It was insufferable. Keeping her eyes on the floor, Mary Ann hurried out of the church. Behind her the murmur of accusatory voices swelled like threatening thunder.

Once the group was outside, Sarah's patience came to an end.

'Can someone – anyone – ***please*** tell me where my daughter is?'

'Sarah, I'm so sorry. I don't know what to say.' Anne Marie was practically sobbing again.

'You can tell me where is Jean now!' Sarah was frantic with worry.

'She's with our Seamus, and they're heading for Australia. They decided to emigrate. Sailed just over a week ago.'

Sarah slumped slowly to the ground. Australia! It was the other side of the world. While she had been burying her grandmother, her daughter, too, was leaving her life forever. She could never afford to go Australia. Seamus and Mairead would probably never come back. She would never see Jean again. She let out an anguished yell. Robert knelt on the ground beside her and took her in his arms. 'Don't give up! We'll find her again one day. I promise you, darling, I'll work every day God sends as hard as I can so that we'll have enough money to go to Australia. We'll find her. No matter if it takes every penny we've got! Don't give up! And, listen, darling, I know it's not the same, but after we get married, we'll have our own kids.' Sarah stopped crying and looked up into Robert's kind brown eyes, brimming over with love and tenderness for her. She started to laugh. It was laughter bordering on the hysterical. *Here I am*, she thought, *I've buried my grandmother less than a week ago, I've just been informed that I'll never see my daughter again, and Robert has chosen this moment and this place to come out with the worst half-baked proposal I have ever heard. This has to be some sort of weird dream. A joke! It can't be real.*

The laughter was mutating into chesty sobs, bordering on wailing.

'She's hysterical' announced Barbara, 'and no wonder. Here, let me help.' Barbara took Sarah by the shoulders and shook her gently. 'Sarah! Sarah! Come on, look at me!' she commanded. 'You and I are going over to the Rectory and we'll have a little rest.'

As she and Father Hanson escorted a still sobbing Sarah away, Robert turned to Danny. 'Danny, I know we used to be friends but I'm telling you, while we're here, get rid of your mother, keep her out of my sight or so help me, I'll not be responsible for my actions, and you wouldn't want that.'

Danny nodded grimly. 'I need to have a word or two with her, but don't worry: she'll not get the chance to do any more harm to anyone. Least of all Sarah.' The last sentence was said softly, but no less intensely for that.

Mary Ann, however, was not waiting around. While the attention of everyone else had been focused on Sarah's collapse, she grabbed her daughter and made for home, berating Anne Marie all the way.

'What did you want to go and tell everybody all our business for? Didn't I tell you to say nothing to nobody? Wait 'til I get you home! I'll teach you to open yer mouth!'

Anne Marie was angry and indignant. Feeling, however, that they had provided the neighbours with enough entertainment for one morning, she held her tongue until they reached the house.

Then the worm turned.

'Mam, Sarah was right. You are a wicked, evil woman. You saw what losing a child did to Mairead and yet you deliberately set out to cause the same kind of pain to another woman – one who had done you no harm at all.'

'She almost tricked your brother into marrying her!'

'Well? Would that have been so wrong? I've seen it happen often enough round here. She wouldn't have been the first and she certainly wouldn't have been the last! And many a happy marriage has come of it. But you never gave her a chance, did you? As far as you were concerned, Sarah was an English protestant and that said it all. You let your bigotry get in the way of your son's happiness. You interfered in his life in the same way you interfere in everybody's life. Well, just for your information, you're not going to interfere in my life any more. I've had enough. I'm leaving.'

Mary Ann watched slack-jawed as her youngest daughter marched upstairs. Anne Marie was leaving her? But that wasn't right! Anne Marie was the child who was to look after her in her old age. She had always treated Anne Marie that little bit differently from the others. The others would leave and get married but Anne Marie was to be the comfort of her old age. Anne Marie could not leave her! Mary Ann stumbled to her seat by the fire side. She felt her whole world slipping away. She had been humiliated in front of Father Hanson and the entire congregation. Everyone within a three mile radius would know how she had lied and schemed. She would never be able to hold her head up in public again. Now her beloved daughter was leaving her. And that hurt hardest of all. To lose a daughter was an unbearable pain.

Chapter Forty-seven

One he had established that Sarah was being taken care of, Danny returned to his mother's house. He had intended to give her a piece of his mind and to ensure that he made his feelings towards her very clear. His intentions, however, were sidelined as he saw his youngest sister coming down the path, struggling with a suitcase.

'Anne Marie! What's happening?'

'Oh Danny. I'm leaving. I can't stay in the same house as that woman now that I know what she's really like – and what she's capable of.'

'Here', said Danny, taking the suitcase from her. 'Let me take that. Do you know where you're going to go?'

Anne Marie shrugged. 'Not yet. I was going to see Sarah first. Beg her forgiveness. Then, I don't know. Go to England somewhere. Mam'll not follow me there and I liked it when we did go over.' She blushed. 'Though, honest to God, Danny, if I knew what she had planned, I'd never have gone.'

Danny nodded. He knew what his mother was like and how hard it was for anyone to stand up to her. Even he had capitulated when he was ordered not to marry Sarah.

'Come on, our kid, let's go see Sarah.'

Anne Marie begged Sarah's forgiveness for her part in Jean's kidnap and Sarah, distressed as she was, still had the heart to see how miserable Anne Marie had been made by the whole affair. She also realised that it was Mary Ann who had dominated Anne Marie and forced her into playing her part. As Sarah hugged the young girl she reassured her. 'It's okay, I know it's not your fault and, you know, I really do think we can still be friends. Why don't you come and stay with me for a while, until you have time to decide what you really want to do? We can't have you going to England all by yourself. Trust me, it's not the big adventure you think it is!'

Anne Marie was only too happy to accept. She flung her arms around Sarah's neck and declared her the kindest, nicest, bestest, person she had ever met. Danny, too, was touched by Sarah's generous offer. He was fond of his youngest sister and, he realised with a start, he was still very fond of Sarah. He wondered again if, had his mother not interfered, would they have had a future together. Now he would never know.

One thing he did know for certain, however, was that there would be no going back for him. He too, would be moving on. Leaving Anne Marie to get to know Barbara and Robert, who were, as usual, doing all they could to make things better for everyone, he headed for his mother's house for what he hoped would be the last time. In an area like the Whiterock, news travels fast. As he approached number eight Whiterock Avenue, he noticed that the residents were also quick to voice their opinions. Scrawled across the door in red paint were the words: 'Kidnapping Scum', while under the window the writer had gone for 'Child Stealer' and 'Liar!'

Well, he though grimly, they're not telling a word of a lie. He pushed at the door which yielded easily under his hand.

'Mam?' he called. She didn't answer. He moved into the living room to find her seated in her usual chair by the fireside. She looked smaller, older and, for the first time, frail. He almost felt sorry for her. Almost, but not quite.

'Well, I hope you're proud of yourself.'

'Danny! Don't look at me like that! I only did what I thought was best!'

Danny looked at his mother as if seeing her for the first time. 'You know, I think you actually believe that. And I think that's probably the worst thing about this whole affair.' He shook his head and turned away. Within five minutes he had repacked all of his possessions and was leaving the house for the last time. He did not bother to say goodbye to his mother and did not, therefore, notice the silent tears that streamed down her cheeks.

The next day, when Sarah had recovered enough to travel, she, Danny, Anne Marie, Barbara and Robert, left for the Liverpool ferry together. After dumping their belongings in to their cabins, all five met up again for a drink in the lounge bar. There was not much conversation and what there was consisted mainly of the weather, the prospect of a smooth journey and the estimated arrival time. None of them wanted to bring up the fact that they were travelling back to England without baby Jean. Yet none of them wanted to be alone and an uncomfortable silence with company was better than the alternative. Eventually, Danny got up to go to the bar to order another round while Sarah and Anne Marie trotted off to the ladies. It was the first time that Danny had been alone with Sarah since he had left her at the bus station in London. It seemed like a lifetime ago. Danny seized his opportunity.

'Sarah', he began lamely, 'You don't know how sorry I am at the way things turned out. I can only beg you to forgive me. I treated you really badly. I acted like a right …, well. You know how I acted. But trust me, my mother had a hand in it too. If it wasn't for her, we could have been married by now. And Jean would still be with you.'

Sarah looked at Danny and shook her head. 'In a way, Danny, I think your mother did do me a favour. Marrying you would have been a mistake. I see that now. I only thought I was in love with you. In reality, you were the first person who was kind to me when I initially arrived in London.'

Danny tried to protest, to insist that they could have made it work. Sarah would not be persuaded. 'Danny, the only thing I regret, and the only thing I can't forgive, is that you mother took my daughter from me. And strange as it may sound, I think she actually thought she was doing the right thing by your brother. I suppose that's what it's like when you're a mother: you put your own family before anyone else. It's just a shame that she didn't think of Jean and me as family too.'

Before he could protest any further, Sarah continued. 'Robert has asked me to marry him and I've accepted. He's made me a promise that he will do everything in his power to get Jean back. And I believe him. Robert is a man that I can depend on. He's reliable and trustworthy and he loves me.' She smiled. 'And I love him. Really love him. This time I'm not just grateful for his kindness. I do want to spend the rest of my life with him.' As she looked towards the seat where Robert was showing Anne Marie how to balance beer mats, the expression on her face was enough to tell Danny everything he needed to know.

Danny sighed. Sarah deserved to be happy after all the misery he had caused her. He was amazed she could be so understanding and forgiving. What an idiot I've been, he thought, to throw away a treasure like her and now, when I've realised how stupid I've been, it's too late. With a nod to Sarah, Danny left the lounge bar and made his way upstairs. Once on deck, he walked to the ship's rail. Looking down on the churning waters, he brooded on his past and his future. He felt sick, and it was not all down to the swell of the sea. He could blame his mother all he liked, he mused, but when it came down to it, there was no-one to blame but himself. He had been weak and dishonest. He had lied to Sarah and to himself. He had taken the easy path, the line of least resistance. And it had lead him here. He saw his life stretching out in front of him, empty and full of regret. No wife, no child, no family, no friends, no job and no future. The navy had not been the exciting adventure he thought it would be and he had the scars to prove it. If he never sailed again, he would have no regrets on that score. He felt he had nothing to look forward to. Glancing down again, he wondered how cold the water would be. It would be a fitting end to a reluctant sailor. He put one foot on the bottom rail.

A tap on his elbow made him turn around.

'Sarah sent me to look for you. She's worried about you. God knows why. Anyway, she told me she has decided to take Robert up on his offer and is moving up to Scotland to stay with him and his mother. Anne Marie's going too. She wants to know if you fancy going with them. Robert needs good workers and, for some unfathomable reason, Sarah feels you shouldn't be on your own. That girl's a saint.' As Barbara finished talking, Danny looked at her in amazement.

'Don't look at me like that. If it was up to me you could sink or swim. But if she can forgive you after everything you've done to her, I suppose I can at least speak to you.' She gave him one of those looks that Danny had never been able to interpret. 'I suppose I'll be seeing you around then.'

Danny nodded, afraid to speak in case he said the wrong thing.

As he watched Barbara's retreating back, she saw her stop, turn, and putting one hand on her hip, look at him appraisingly before asking: 'Well? Are you coming, then?'

Danny sprang off the ship rails. In three steps, he caught up with her. Suddenly, it seemed like life might be worth living after all.

Epilogue

Many miles away, in a different stretch of water, Seamus and Mairead leaned on the rails of the ship taking them to their new life. Beside them, in her pram, sat their adopted daughter, playing with a rattle.

Mairead snuggled up to her husband. 'Are you worried we'll never see our families again?

Seamus shook his head. 'No. I've got everything I need right here.'

After a short silence , he spoke again. 'I suppose I'll miss me mam a bit. Sitting in her chair, bossing us around and setting the world to rights. She's proper tarragon, but her heart's in the right place.'

'To be truthful', admitted Mairead, 'I've always been slightly afraid of her.'

'Afraid of my mum? You must be joking. She's like a toothless dog – all bark and no bite. Soft as putty, she is underneath. Do anything for us kids, she would. I mean, if it wasn't for her, we wouldn't have Sinead.'

Mairead hugged her husband even closer. 'I am so grateful to her for that. I can't imagine life without Sinead now.'

Seamus kissed the top of his wife's head before turning to gaze out at the vast blue-green ocean. After musing for a while, he broke the contented silence.

'Mairead, you know the way this is a completely new start for us?' It was a rhetorical question so she simply replied with a 'Hmm?' as she let the blazing sun bathe her in warmth.

'Well I was thinking.' Seamus continued. 'What if we change our Christian names? You know that nobody outside Ireland can pronounce our names correctly anyway, so we may as well use the English versions.'

Mairead thought for a moment. 'You mean I'd be Margaret, like my mum? And the English for Seamus is James. That sounds awfully grand. I suppose I could call you Jimmy. And Sinead would be Jean.' She pondered the idea for a while. 'Hmm. I suppose that makes sense. New names for a new start in a new country.'

She rolled the names around in her head: James and Margaret McAllister. Jimmy and Maggie McAllister. Jim and Mags McAllister.

'Jimmy and Maggie sounds best.' she declared. 'So it's Jimmy, Maggie and Jean McAllister. One big happy family. I can't wait to start our new life. I have a feeling that everything will be wonderful, and that nothing bad will ever happen to us again.' She hugged her husband even tighter. 'I love you Jimmy McAllister!'

'And I love you, Maggie McAllister!'

As they kissed, baby Jean started to cry.

Printed in Great Britain
by Amazon